Lilah

Lilah

MAREK HALTER

Translated from the French by
Howard Curtis

BANTAM PRESS

LONDON · TORONTO · SYDNEY · AUCKLAND · JOHANNESBURG

TRANSWORLD PUBLISHERS
61–63 Uxbridge Road, London W5 5SA
a division of The Random House Group Ltd

RANDOM HOUSE AUSTRALIA (PTY) LTD
20 Alfred Street, Milsons Point, Sydney,
New South Wales 2061, Australia

RANDOM HOUSE NEW ZEALAND LTD
18 Poland Road, Glenfield, Auckland 10, New Zealand

RANDOM HOUSE SOUTH AFRICA (PTY) LTD
Isle of Houghton, Corner of Boundary Road & Carse O'Gowrie,
Houghton 2198, South Africa

Published 2006 by Bantam Press
a division of Transworld Publishers

A catalogue record for this book is available from the British Library.
ISBN 9780593052815 (from Jan 07)
ISBN 0593052811

Typeset in 13/16½pt Bembo by
Kestrel Data, Exeter, Devon.

Printed in Great Britain by
Clays Ltd, Bungay, Suffolk.

1 3 5 7 9 10 8 6 4 2

Papers used by Transworld Publishers are natural, recyclable products made from wood
grown in sustainable forests. The manufacturing processes conform to the
environmental regulations of the country of origin.

And God said, 'It is not good for the man to be alone.
I will make him a suitable helper.'

Genesis 2: 18

'If he deserves it, she is a helper; if not, she is against him.'

Midrash Rabbah, on Genesis 2: 18

The fewer dogmas there are, the fewer quarrels;
and the fewer quarrels, the fewer calamities:
if that is not true, then I am wrong.

Religion is established to make us happy
in this world and the next.
What do we need to be happy in the next world?
To be just.

To be happy in this world,
in so far as the poverty of our nature allows it,
what do we need?
To be lenient.

Voltaire, *Treatise on Tolerance*, Chapter XXI

Prologue

Antinoes is coming home.

My heart trembles.

My hand trembles. I hold the stylus tight between my fingers to make sure that the words the camphor ink is laying down on the papyrus are legible.

Antinoes, my beloved, is coming home!

Last night, a messenger in dusty tunic and sandals brought me a wax tablet. I immediately recognized my beloved's writing. A sleepless night followed. Tossing and turning, I pressed the tablet to my breast as if to stamp the words into my flesh.

Lilah, my sweet, my love, in three days and three nights I shall be with you again. Count the shadows of the sun. I am returning nobler and more victorious! And yet until I have you in my arms, until my lips are sated with the taste of your skin, I will have achieved nothing in two years of separation from you.

My heart is beating faster than it does before a battle.
Soon, by the will of your God of heaven and of the
mighty Ahura Mazda, god of the Persians, we shall at
last be man and wife.

All night long, my heart has been drinking in
Antinoes' words. If I close my eyes, they are still before
me. If I try to forget them, I hear my beloved's voice
whispering them in my ear.

That is my madness. And if I tremble, it is also with
fear.

This should be the hour of peace. The darkness is
receding. All is silent in the house. The handmaids have
not yet risen, the fires are not yet lit. The light of dawn is
as white as the milk that they say conceals poison at the
banquets given by the King of Kings.

Man and wife, that was our promise. Antinoes and
Lilah!

A children's promise – a lovers' promise!

I remember when we were like the fingers of one
hand. Antinoes, Ezra and Lilah. To see one was to see
the others. Two boys and a girl, always together. That
one was the son of a lord who attended the meals of the
Great King and the others the children of exiled Jews
mattered little.

The roofs of the upper town of Susa echoed to our
laughter. Whenever our mother called us, we heard a
single cry: 'Antinoes, Ezra, Lilah!'

Then my mother's voice fell silent. My father's too.

A deadly disease spread through Susa, through the

fields along the river Shaour as far as Babylon, striking rich and poor alike, not only in Persia, but also in Sion, Lydia and Media.

I remember the day when Ezra and I, drained of tears, stood before our mother and father, asleep in death.

We held hands with Antinoes – our grief was his too. We stood shoulder to shoulder. The three of us had become one, like some strange animal whose limbs had become inextricably entwined.

I remember the scorching summer's day when Antinoes led us into his magnificent home and presented us to his father. 'Father, this is my sister Lilah, and this is my brother Ezra. Whatever they eat, I eat. Whatever they dream, I dream. Father, let them come to our house as often as they wish. If you refuse, I will have no other roof over my head than that of their uncle Mordechai, who has taken them in now that they have neither father nor mother.'

Antinoes' father laughed until he could laugh no more. He called the handmaids and told them to bring fruit and cow's milk. When our stomachs were full, we hurled ourselves into the great pools of the house to cool ourselves down. Children are greedy for happiness.

Once more our days were carefree. 'My brother Antinoes!' Ezra would cry, and Antinoes would answer, 'My brother Ezra!' Together, they forged swords, bows and spears in Uncle Mordechai's workshop.

Oh, Yahweh, why must we stop being children?

I remember the day when the games ceased, and the laughter faltered at the touch of a caress.

Antinoes, Ezra and Lilah. Two men and a woman. A new expression in their eyes, an unaccustomed silence on their lips. The beauty of nights on the roofs of Susa, of embraces, the joy of bodies catching fire like over-heated lamp oil.

The three of us becoming one: that was over now. Now it was Lilah and Antinoes, Lilah and Ezra, Antinoes and Ezra. Lovers and siblings, jealousy and rage.

I remember it well, it churns in my memory, like the dark waters of the Shaour in the rainy season.

The handmaids have risen now. The fires are lit. Soon there will be shouts and laughter. It may be a fine day, alive with hope and promise.

As I write, my face is reflected in the silver mirror above the writing desk. Antinoes says it is a beautiful face, that my youth is the scent of springtime. Antinoes loves and desires me, and loves the words that speak of his love and his desire.

But all I see in the mirror is a furrowed brow and anxious eyes. Is this the face – this sad, preoccupied beauty – that will welcome my beloved on his return?

O Yahweh, hear the plea of Lilah, daughter of Serayah and Achazya, I who have no other god than the God of my father.

Antinoes is not a child of Israel, but he is faithful to his promise. He wants me for himself, as a husband must want his bride.

Ezra will say to me, 'Ah, so now you are abandoning me.'

Yahweh, is it not your will that our bodies should

Part One

Two Brothers
and a Sister

The Roofs of Susa

In his message, Antinoes had not specified the place where they would meet. There was no need.

As she approached the top of the tower, Lilah's heart beat faster. She stopped, closed her eyes, put her hand on her stomach, and tried to catch her breath.

It was not because of the dark, narrow staircase. She had found her way again easily enough. She had climbed these brick steps so often that it was no problem to find her footing. No, what made her breathless was the knowledge that Antinoes might already be up there, on the terrace, waiting for her.

In a moment, she would see his face, his gentle eyes, hear his voice, touch his skin.

Had he changed? A little? A lot?

She had often heard women complain that when their husbands returned from the wars, they were like strangers. Even when their bodies were intact, they themselves had become colder, more aloof.

But she had nothing to fear. Antinoes' message was eloquent enough: the man who had written those words had not changed in any way.

She moved the gold and silver fibula that held her veil to her beautiful tunic and adjusted her belt, inlaid with mother-of-pearl. Her bracelets jangled, and the sound echoed like bells against the blind wall of the tower.

Light-hearted and smiling, Lilah climbed the last flight of stairs. The door to the terrace stood open and the setting sun blinded her. She shaded her eyes with her hand.

No one was there.

She turned, looking round the little terrace.

No voice called her name.

No cry of impatience greeted her.

Disappointment pierced her heart.

Then she smiled with relief. She was behaving like a child.

Beneath the canopy that covered most of the terrace was a low table, surrounded by cushions and laden with fruit, cakes, and pitchers of water and beer. A large red ceramic vase held an enormous bunch of pale roses and lilac from the East, her favourite flowers.

Her disappointment faded away. No, Antinoes had not forgotten anything. Wars and battles had not changed him . . .

On their first night of love, he had covered their bed with rose petals from his father's garden. The summer heat had been stifling, but Antinoes had shivered with desire.

grow beyond childhood? That we should become men and women, each with his own breath, his own strength, the joy of his own senses? Is it not your will that the man's caress should delight the woman? Is it not your Law that a sister should find other eyes to love, another voice to hear and admire than her brother's? Is it not your teaching that a woman should choose her husband according to her heart, as did Sarah, Rachel and Zipporah, the wives of Abraham, Jacob and Moses?

Whichever I am faithful to, the other's pain will be just as strong.

Why must I cause pain when my brother and my lover have an equal place in my heart?

O Yahweh, God of heaven, God of my father, give me the strength to find the words to appease Ezra! Give him the strength to hear them.

That evening, that first night, seemed to Lilah both very close and very distant. So much had happened since . . .

Slowly eating grapes, translucent in the twilight, Lilah rested her elbows on the parapet. At this hour, when night was approaching like a caress, there was nothing more splendid than the view from this terrace.

A hundred cubits above the river Shaour rose the immense cliff walls of the Citadel. The royal courtyard, the Apadana, was lined with marble columns, carved in Egypt and transported by thousands of men and mules, which gleamed like bronze flames in the sun, and themselves were surrounded by marble terraces even more vast than the palace. Giant sculptures of bulls, lions and winged monsters guarded the Apadana, which was reached by flights of steps so broad and so high that they could have held the entire population of the city. Few, though, were entitled to climb them.

At the foot of the walls, enclosing the Citadel like a casket, were the palaces of the royal city, with their many gardens. In a last flash of brilliance, the rays of the setting sun, reflected in the lazy meandering of the Shaour, lit the gardens, then faded amid the dense cedars and eucalypts.

The royal city was encircled by a brick wall, pierced with small square windows and flanked by tall, crenellated towers, coloured red, orange and blue, which separated it from the busy streets of the upper town. These streets, squeezed between flat-roofed whitewashed houses, ran as straight as if they had been cut with a double-edged sword. They stretched far to the east, north and south: dark, crowded trenches, which Lilah could barely make out from here. She could still hear the hum of activity, though, and imagined a mass of people bustling about as the awnings on the stalls were lowered.

Antinoes' house and garden occupied a rectangular strip in the patricians' quarter, close to the royal palace. The garden was old and luxuriant. The elegant palms and cypresses that lined the path from the outer wall to the house were as high as the tower.

There was a sudden sound and Lilah froze. The shadows were already lengthening in the twilight. She looked at the door leading to the staircase.

All she had heard was a slight rustling. But she knew he was there.

'Antinoes?' she called.

A face emerged from the shadows, a face she had so often evoked in her daydreams: the broad, aquiline nose, the finely drawn nostrils, the well-defined lips, the arched eyebrows, the narrowed lids, the look in the eyes that made her tremble.

He spoke her name, very softly: 'Lilah.'

He wore the dress of a Persian warrior: a short, close-fitting, long-sleeved tunic, purple with large fawn circles, and equally close-fitting ankle-length trousers. The straps of his sandals were tied high up his calves. His belt was as wide as a hand, its gold buckle adorned with a lion's head. Three chains, of silver, gold and bronze, linked it to the bull's-head brooch on his right shoulder.

A felt ribbon embroidered with gold thread held his oiled and scented hair in place. A dazzling smile gleamed within his finely plaited beard.

He repeated her name, laughing now, almost shouting. 'Lilah! Lilah!'

Lilah began to laugh, too. He held out his hands to her, palms upraised. She moved forward slowly, a touch stiffly, and placed her palms on his. Antinoes' hands were hot. They closed over hers, and the mere touch was like an embrace. Antinoes' eyes sparkled in the setting sun.

'You're here,' she murmured, hardly aware that she had spoken.

He raised their entwined hands to his lips. He was still laughing, silently, as if he were out of breath. A caressing laugh, a laugh of pure joy, which enveloped them and carried them away.

They let go of each other's hands, the better to embrace. The laughter was swept away by their kisses. The kisses were swept away by their impatience.

For a long moment, the terrace around them seemed to contain the whole world. Susa had vanished. Time and troubles had evaporated. Only the deep, translucent sky of the dying twilight remained.

They undressed with all the clumsiness of long-separated lovers. Time, memory, impatience and fear faded away in their turn.

Once again, they were Antinoes and Lilah.

★ ★ ★

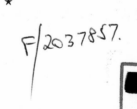

The silence of the star-studded night lay heavy on the city when, both out of breath, they untangled their limbs.

Here and there, torches glowed in the courtyards of the great houses. Naphtha flames, held in wide dishes, danced on the walls of the Citadel, as they did every night, forming a royal diadem that hung in the darkness.

Antinoes freed himself from Lilah's arms and stood up. He groped for a little applewood chest, which contained a flint and a wick. A moment later, a torch crackled into flame.

Now Lilah saw clearly the body she had held in the darkness. Antinoes' waist was slimmer, and there were two dimples low on his back above his buttocks. During the war against the Greeks, when the King of Kings' brother had kept him far from her, he had grown harder.

He turned as he slotted the torch between the bricks of the parapet, not far from the table still piled high with food, and she discovered the scar. 'Your thigh!'

Antinoes smiled with a touch of pride. 'A Lydian sword at Karkemish. It was only the seventh time I'd been in close combat, so I wasn't very experienced. He was on the ground. I should have been more careful.'

Lilah's fingers followed the twists and turns of the pale furrow in Antinoes' solid thigh.

He leaned down and seized her fingers, entwined them again with his own. 'It's nothing. It took only a moon for the wound to heal. Since then, I've only fought in a chariot. When you're in a chariot, the enemy

doesn't aim at the legs, but at the heart or the head. As you see, I still have both of those.'

Lilah fell back, and stared up at the sky. 'How many times,' she murmured, 'when the night and the stars arrived, I thought about that. Even though you were beneath those same stars, you were far away, and I imagined you dying. Or you were seriously wounded and you wanted to see me, but I had no way of knowing. A spear went through you, and then the wax tablet informing me of your death went through me too.'

Antinoes laughed. 'It would never have happened. The Greeks and Cyrus the Younger's mercenaries learned to fear me.' He knelt, keeping a slight distance between them, and looked at Lilah in silence, serious now. 'I know every inch of your face,' he whispered, closing his eyes. 'That was what I thought about. Your eyes, so black that I can see myself reflected in them even by daylight, your lashes, your long straight brows, as delicate as a wisp of smoke. Your high, stubborn fore-head, like a young bull's, your cheeks that blush both when you're angry and when I kiss them. I know every line of your mouth – I've drawn them a hundred times in the sand. The upper lip is longer and fuller than the other. A mouth so sweet, so alive, that I can always tell what you're thinking.'

His eyes still closed, he reached out his hand, trembling slightly. With his fingers, he traced the curve of a breast, glided over her belly, and stroked her hair, which hung loose down to her hips.

He opened his eyes. 'In the last two years, I've seen

many women,' he went on. 'The beauties of Cilicia or the northern Euphrates, the wives of the great warriors of Lydia . . . The more beautiful they were, the more they made me think of you; the more foolish or provocative, the more I dreamed of you. And whenever I came across one who could compare with you, I was angry at her for not being you.'

He caressed her gently, as if reinventing her body with his fingers, imprinting every curve, every inch of skin, on his palm.

'When I fought, you were with me. Arrows and swords could not touch me. The mere thought of your beauty protected me.'

Lilah gave a throaty laugh, leaned forward and embraced him, ready to kiss him again. She pressed her hard nipples against Antinoes' chest as if she wanted to be absorbed by him.

'I was never afraid when I fought,' he murmured, 'but every day, I was afraid you would forget me. Every day I dreamed you might forget Antinoes. The men of Susa, I told myself, would be mad not to see your beauty.'

'So, we both felt the same terror.' She bit the back of his neck, and he shivered.

'Don't laugh!' he cried. 'Now we're together for ever.'

For a brief moment Lilah froze at his words. But Antinoes' kisses wiped out the cold. Her belly was soon on fire again, as Antinoes'. member swelled against her thigh. She gripped his shoulders and pushed him down on to the cushions, her love's warrior and her lover's enchantress.

★   ★   ★

The moon was rising above the Zagros mountains when she whispered that it was time for her to return home.

'Stay the night!' Antinoes protested.

She smiled, and shook her head. 'No, not tonight. We're not yet man and wife, and I don't want my aunt Sarah to find my bedchamber empty in the morning.'

'Oh, come on! Your aunt Sarah knows perfectly well that you're here, and she's delighted.'

Lilah gave a little laugh and stroked her lover's eyelids, tracing his eyebrows with the tip of her index finger. 'Then I'm the one who wants to get back to my bedchamber by dawn, thinking about you, smelling your scent on my skin.'

'You'll smell it all the better if you remain here. Lilah, why must you go? We've only just been reunited.'

'Because I'm your lover,' Lilah whispered, kissing his brow. 'Your lover, but not your wife.'

She started to move away, but Antinoes sat up and gripped her wrist. 'When? When will you be my wife?'

She found it hard to meet his eyes. The darkness and the warm, flickering light of the torch made the shadows on his face seem harsher. She thought of how his face must look in battle.

'I'll go to see your uncle first thing tomorrow,' Antinoes insisted. 'We'll name the day. As far as I'm concerned, everything is ready. I've made offerings to Ahura Mazda and left a tablet with your name on it for the royal eunuchs. That's the law for high-ranking officers. As you know, the King and Queen may oppose

25

a marriage . . . between a Persian officer and someone who is not of our race.' He broke off with a grimace and shook his head. 'Lilah, what is it? Don't you want to be my wife?'

'I want nothing else,' she said with a smile.

'Then why delay?'

Lilah gathered her hair to cover her breasts, and searched for her tunic among the cushions. Antinoes waited for a reply, but when none came he stood up abruptly and walked to the parapet, barely illumined by the light of the torch. 'I came back to be your husband,' he said quietly. 'I shan't leave Susa again until that house down there is your home.' He pointed up at the diadem of the Citadel, shining unperturbed in the night. 'There, in a few days, I shall wear a helmet with red and white plumes and a leather breastplate with the insignia of the heroes of Artaxerxes. But without you, without your love, even a Greek child could vanquish me.'

He spoke without looking at her. Lilah put on her tunic. As she was about to hook the sides together, Antinoes came to her and seized her arms. 'It's Ezra, isn't it? It's Ezra who's holding you back.'

'I have to talk to him.'

'Hasn't he changed? Does he still hate me?'

Lilah did not reply. She freed herself from his grip and fastened her tunic.

'Does he know I've come back?' Antinoes asked.

'No. I'm going tomorrow.'

'To the lower town?'

Lilah nodded.

Antinoes grunted, and moved away from her. 'What a fool!'

'No, Antinoes, he's no fool. He does what he thinks is right. He studies and learns, and that's important.'

An ironic look on his face, Antinoes was about to reply, but Lilah raised her hand. 'Don't mock, that would be unfair. Soon after you left, an old man came to see him in the lower town. His name is Baruch ben Neriah. He used to live in Babylon. That's where he found out that our family possesses the scroll of the laws given by Yahweh to Moses. He's a gentle old man, and very learned. All his life he's studied from copied and incomplete papyri. He invited Ezra to join him in his studies. Since then, both of them have been immersed in the texts. Ezra is becoming a sage, Antinoes, a sage of our people, like those who led the children of Israel before the exile.'

'That's fine. Let him study! Let him become a sage! What do I care, provided he leaves you free to marry me?'

'Antinoes! You used to love Ezra as much as I did.'

'That was a long time ago.'

'Not too long ago to remember. You know as well as I do that Ezra is not cut out for everyday life. One day he will be a great man—'

'No. To be a great man, he'd have to stop being jealous. Jealousy lessens him, just as hatred weakens a warrior before a battle.'

Lilah fell silent, and tried to smile. She went up to him, stroked his naked torso, put her head on his shoulder, and held him tenderly. 'My one desire, my one joy, is to be the wife of Antinoes. Be patient a little longer.'

Antinoes buried his face in Lilah's hair. 'No! I've been patient long enough. I want you with me for the rest of our lives. I came back so that we could be together. And we will be. If Ezra can't accept that, we'll become man and wife in spite of him. All we need is your uncle Mordechai's approval.'

Lilah took away her arms. 'Antinoes . . .'

But Antinoes was not listening. He clasped her again to his naked body, indifferent to the growing coolness of the night. 'And if we can't be man and wife,' he went on, 'we'll be lovers for ever. If we have to leave Susa, we'll leave Susa, and I'll relinquish my chariot captain's breastplate and baldric. We'll go to Lydia, to Sardis. The sea is wonderful there, and I'll become a Greek hero . . .'

Lilah took his face in her hands and kissed his mouth to silence him. Passion inflamed them once more. 'I shall have no other husband but you, my beloved,' she said. 'Give me time to convince Ezra. I don't want our joy to be his sorrow.'

Bad News

The young slave pulled on the reins, the mules champed at their bits, snorting, and the chariot halted in the shade of a medlar tree.

Lilah stepped down, and signalled to Axatria to help her.

The handmaid took the huge basket from between the benches, and arranged the leather straps so that her mistress could hoist it on to her shoulder. 'It's too heavy.' She frowned. 'It's not for you to carry such a load.'

'It'll be all right,' Lilah replied, resting the basket on her back. 'No need to worry.'

'Of course I worry! I'm ashamed, too. Your tunic will be rags by the time you get to Ezra's house. God in heaven, what do you look like?'

Axatria tried to smooth the fabric, creased already by the straps, and adjusted the half-moon brooch that held Lilah's transparent shawl on her hair.

'Your hair will be out of place by the time you get to

your brother's house – and he loves to see you looking beautiful. And what would your aunt say if she could see you laden like a mule while your handmaid sits comfortably in the chariot?'

Lilah smiled. 'Ezra will be happy to see his sister even if she's a bit rumpled, and I won't tell Aunt Sarah, I promise.'

Axatria seemed neither amused nor appeased by this answer.

Giving a little shake to make sure that the straps rested against her hands, Lilah walked away from the chariot, along the street that cut through the last gardens in the upper town. She had not gone far when she tripped on the raised edge of a paving stone and stumbled. She had hardly had time to regain her balance than Axatria was gripping the basket. 'You see? It's too heavy. It'll be easier if the two of us carry it.'

'Let go.'

But Axatria would not yield, and tried to take the straps from her hands. Lilah was angry now and pushed her so forcefully that Axatria stumbled and almost knocked both of them over.

'Axatria! Leave me be!'

'Why should I let you do something so stupid?'

Axatria's naturally dark complexion had turned almost purple. She was not pretty, with a squat figure, heavy breasts and wide hips, even though she had never given birth. She had the flat face typical of the women of the Zagros mountains: a short nose, high cheekbones and thick, curly hair. But her dancing eyes, full lips, as frank

as they were sensual, and her eager, mocking expression
were not without charm. Now, though, her eyes blazed
with anger and her mouth was like that of a mother with
an unruly child.

'Axatria,' Lilah said, trying to sound calm, 'we've
agreed I'm to go alone. There's no point in arguing.'

'You agreed it with yourself,' Axatria replied sharply.
'It's just a whim.'

'It isn't a whim, and you know it.'

They were silent, glaring at each other. Lilah was the
first to look away. The young slave had been following
their quarrel as he stroked the cheek of one of the mules.

'Am I in your way?' Axatria asked, plaintively. 'Why
stop me seeing him, Lilah? You know perfectly well . . .
perfectly well . . .' Rage and distress prevented Axatria
from finishing her sentence. But there was no need. She
was right. Lilah 'knew perfectly well'.

Lilah was embarrassed by the tears that glistened in her
handmaid's eyes. 'It's stupid, quarrelling like this,' she
said, more harshly than she had intended. 'Wait for me
here. I shan't be long.'

Axatria straightened, eyes flashing. 'Very well, Mistress.
Since you've made up your mind, and I'm nothing but a
servant to you!' She turned away stiffly, lifted her tunic
and climbed into the chariot. Wisely, the young slave
lowered his eyes.

Lilah hesitated. What was the point of protesting?
There was only one thing she could say to mollify
Axatria, and she refused to say it.

She walked away with a heavy heart. It was a bad start

31

to an already delicate mission. Behind her, she heard Axatria lecturing the slave: 'Instead of eavesdropping, boy, turn this chariot in the right direction.'

Lilah had only to walk some sixty cubits before the paved road became an uneven dirt path that led to the labyrinth of the lower town. Prickly pear and acacia bushes, a few empty fields and ponds overrun by frogs were all that separated wealth from poverty.

Lilah's eyes were on the ground, her shoulder hurting from the pressure of the straps, as Axatria's words echoed in her mind. She had never seen her like that before.

Strong, intelligent and conscientious, Axatria had entered Lilah's service on the day she and Ezra had gone to Uncle Mordechai after their parents' death. Axatria had been twenty at the time, not much older than her young masters, a woman of insatiable energy. Within a few days she had fallen in love with Ezra.

At the time, he had possessed all the incandescent beauty of adolescence, which struck Axatria like a lightning bolt. Lilah was not surprised: she thought Ezra handsome – as handsome as Antinoes, who was much admired by the young Persian girls – but Ezra was wiser already.

Lilah had been amused by Axatria's feelings for him, but proud too, neither afraid nor jealous. Wasn't the tie that bound brother and sister an eternal one?

Axatria had been sensible enough never to display her feelings in words or gestures. However great her passion, she expressed herself entirely through the excellence of her service, the washing she did for Ezra, the meals she prepared for him. She was so discreet that he had not become aware of her love until the day Aunt Sarah had teased Axatria about it.

Axatria had been content with Ezra's gratitude, his occasional kindness towards her, gifts that were sufficient in themselves.

It was their love for Ezra, though, boundless but chaste, that had brought Lilah and Axatria together.

Then the terrible day had come when Ezra had left Uncle Mordechai's house and moved to the lower town. His uncle and aunt had tried and failed to stop him. Then Axatria had stood in his way, her face streaked with tears. 'Why? Why leave this house?'

Ezra had tried to push her away, but she had quite shamelessly collapsed at his feet and stopped him, clinging to him like a human millstone. Ezra had been forced to answer her. 'I am going to a place where the children of Israel have not forgotten the pain of exile. I am going to study what should never have been forgotten – all that my father Serayah, his father Azaryah, his father Hilqiyyah and all their fathers for twelve generations learned from their father Aaron, the brother of Moses.'

What was Axatria, a Persian from the Zagros mountains, to make of such words?

She was stunned into silence. Appearing to yield, she let go of Ezra. But as he stepped away, she clutched at his tunic. 'Take me with you, Ezra!' she begged, forgetting her dignity for the first and only time. 'I'm your handmaid, wherever you go.'

'Where I'm going, I have no need of handmaids.'

'Why?'

'Because it's impossible to study with a handmaid around.'

'You don't know what you're saying! Who'll cook your food, wash your clothes, keep your bedchamber clean?'

Ezra thrust her away from him. 'Be quiet! I'm leaving this house to be closer to the will of God, not to the will of a handmaid.'

For days, eaten away by shame and sorrow, Axatria had been unable to stop weeping.

She was not the only one. The house of Mordechai and Sarah echoed with tears and lamentations. For the first time, Lilah had seen her uncle brought low, incapable of work or even of feeding himself. Her aunt Sarah had closed her workshop for six days, as if in mourning. Axatria's tears had been swallowed up in the general sense of woe. She went about her daily tasks like a soul that had already passed into the other world. 'Why? Why?' she would mutter from dawn to dusk, in a stunned whisper.

Then one day Lilah had said, 'I know where Ezra has found refuge. Get ready, and we'll go and take him food and clothing.'

That had been the first time. Less than a moon later, they had again filled a basket and borrowed one of Uncle Mordechai's chariots, to which Mordechai had turned a blind eye.

Since then seasons had passed, rain, snow, stifling heat,

but neither exhaustion nor sickness had persuaded Lilah and Axatria to cease their visits to the lower city.

Hardly had the sun risen than Axatria would fill the basket set aside now for this purpose with pitchers of milk, loaves of bread, cheese, bags of almonds, barley and dates. The basket had become so bulky over time that it weighed more than a dead ass, forcing Lilah to tense her muscles beneath it.

Today she wanted to be alone with Ezra.

What she had to tell him would be difficult enough without Axatria's bustling presence.

Cries jolted Lilah out of her thoughts when she was half a *stadion* from the lower town. As if they had emerged from the earth, a group of about twenty boys, aged from four to eleven or twelve, wearing nothing but loincloths, appeared between the first tumbledown houses and came running barefoot on the hard pebble-strewn ground, yelling their heads off.

Two old men carrying tubs of tar on a hoist towards the upper town moved aside quickly to let them pass.

Raising as much dust as a herd of young goats, the children reached Lilah and came to a sudden standstill, their screams ceasing just as abruptly as their run. Smiling sweetly, they lined up in two perfect rows, the little ones gripping the rags of their elders.

'May the mighty Ahura Mazda and the God of Heaven be with you, Lilah!' they cried in unison.

'May the Everlasting bless you,' Lilah replied, earnestly.

Surprised that Axatria was absent, the children looked

from the basket to the chariot, which they could glimpse on the road to the upper town. Lilah smiled. 'Today, Axatria is waiting for you in the chariot. She has brought you honey bread.'

No sooner had she spoken than the children leaped into the air like a flock of sparrows.

Lilah adjusted the basket on her shoulder. The two old men bowed respectfully, then set off again with their burden. She responded to their greeting, and hurried on.

'Lilah!'

She heard the shout at the same time as the sound of running feet. 'Sogdiam!'

'Let me carry your basket.'

He was a well-built boy of thirteen or fourteen, but looked two or three years more. When he was not yet a year old, a fall from a brick wall on a stormy day had left him crippled. The bones of his legs had set haphazardly, but he had learned to use the misshapen limbs through an effort of will. Today, although his gait was grotesque and lopsided, he could run and walk for long distances without pain.

His fine features made people forget his misfortune, and his eyes burned with intelligence. Soon after Ezra had settled in the lower town, he had spotted Sogdiam among the orphaned children who ran around the streets. Before long, he had become Ezra's capable and devoted servant.

Lilah pointed to the piece of honey bread that Sogdiam was carrying. 'Eat that first.'

'No need,' Sogdiam said, as proud as a warrior. 'I can do both at the same time.'

Glad to relieve the pressure on her shoulder, Lilah passed him the basket. The boy strained his young muscles and slid the straps over his own shoulder. 'Axatria has filled it even more generously than usual today,' she said.

'It'll be all right,' Sogdiam groaned, gallantly.

Lilah smiled at him tenderly. He set off, arching his back proudly, to conceal the strain on his neck. They were being watched from the houses at the other end of the path, and Sogdiam would not have missed for anything in the world the opportunity of showing everyone that he was privileged to help Lilah, the only lady from the upper town who dared to enter the lower town.

'Axatria shouldn't have let you carry this,' he said severely, as he hurried along. 'At least she should have helped you.'

'I wouldn't let her,' Lilah said.

'Why? Because she is ill-tempered this morning? She was shouting at us just now.'

Lilah could not help smiling. 'It won't last,' she said.

'What's the matter?' Sogdiam threw her a questioning glance. 'Did the two of you have an argument?'

Lilah shook her head.

'It certainly looked like it,' Sogdiam insisted. 'There were tears in her eyes.'

'There are days like that, when you feel sad,' Lilah said, with a lump in her throat. Then she changed the subject. 'Tell me one thing. How do you know when we've arrived? Our chariot never comes near the lower town. You can't hear the wheels from here, and I don't see any of you in the fields. But no sooner do we get here than you all appear, shouting like Greeks.'

Sogdiam nodded proudly. 'It's me who knows, not the others.'

'You? How do you know?'

'Easy. It's your day,' Sogdiam said, as if stating the obvious.

'What are you talking about? I don't have a "day". I might have come yesterday or tomorrow.'

Sogdiam laughed. 'But you came today! You always come the day of your day.'

'But it's not just the day, it's the exact moment . . .'

'It's the same,' Sogdiam said. 'You always come at the same time of the day. Didn't you know that?'

'Well . . . perhaps not,' Lilah said, surprised.

'But I know. In the morning I get up and I know. Sometimes at night, when I go to bed, I say to myself, "Tomorrow, Lady Lilah will come." And you do. Ezra knows it, too. He's like me.'

'Are you sure?' Lilah asked, her voice betraying more emotion than she would have liked. 'Did he tell you?'

The boy chuckled. 'No need, Lilah. The day of your day, he washes himself thoroughly, rubs his teeth with lime to make them whiter, and asks me to comb his hair. In all the time you've been coming, haven't you noticed how handsome he is when you arrive?' Sogdiam was laughing so heartily that his limp became more pronounced.

Lilah laughed too to cover her emotion. 'It seems I have no eyes for anything, Sogdiam. Whenever I come here, I'm so busy making sure you have all you need, I just don't pay attention.'

Sogdiam admitted, with a pout, that this might be a valid reason.

They walked for a while in silence, along alleys and past meagre gardens. The houses of the lower town were mostly huts of cane and mud. Some, the *zorifes*, consisted merely of roofs of plaited palms supported by poles, with no walls. Women were busy over their frugal hearths, while their children tugged at their tunics.

Dirty as the streets were, and foul with stagnant water after the rains, Lilah had always refused to venture in with her chariot. The carved, cushioned benches, the axle heads inlaid with silver and brass were worth more in themselves than a hundred hovels in this wretched slum.

She and Sogdiam were being watched by inquisitive eyes. Everyone had known for a long time who this beautiful young woman was, and where she was going with the boy and the heavy basket. Men and women alike stared avidly at her splendid tunic, her elegant hair, her leather clogs with their curved tips. Even her walk was different from theirs: she moved forward with a light, lively step, hips swaying in a way that was reminiscent of dances, feasts, banquets, and amorous songs at twilight. In a word, beauty, and the rapture the world might be for others.

As often as they had marvelled at Lilah, the inhabitants

of the lower city never tired of the spectacle. For them, Lilah was a mirage, an image of something they would never know.

Most had never entered the upper town – if they tried, they were driven away brutally by the soldiers – let alone the Citadel. The most they could glimpse, above the roofs of the slums, beyond the gardens and the fine houses of the upper town, was the outer wall and colonnades of the Apadana. Against the morning sky, the Citadel seemed to touch the clouds, which was as it should be for the dwelling of the gods and the King of Kings.

Men and women alike had asked Sogdiam if the lady of the 'wise Jew', as Ezra was known here, lived in the Citadel. Sogdiam was so proud that they might think so that he answered yes. A woman as beautiful as Lilah could only live in the Citadel.

With relief, Sogdiam put down the basket outside the house.

'Ezra is probably still studying,' he whispered, pushing open the blue-painted gate cautiously so that it did not squeak.

The house was almost a palace compared to the hovels that surrounded it. The rough brick walls supported a roof of palm leaves covered with tarred earth, which afforded protection from both cold and extreme heat. Three little square rooms looked out on to the courtyard. Against the outer wall there was an arbour with a fragrant lemon tree.

'Wait,' Sogdiam whispered, as Lilah moved towards the study. 'I have to warn them!'

Lilah did not have time to retort that she had no intention of waiting: a clear voice spoke her name. 'Lilah!'

Sogdiam might have been right, Lilah thought. Now that it had been pointed out to her, she could see how well groomed Ezra was: the short glossy beard, the gleaming white teeth in a welcoming smile, the hair carefully parted and tied at the back of his neck with an ivory ring from the East that Lilah had given him. But his brightly coloured tunic, held in at the waist with a brown linen belt, did not conceal how thin he had become.

'Lilah, my sister . . .' He came forward, his arms open, then stopped dead. 'May I clasp you to me?' he asked.

Lilah gave a mocking laugh. Faithful to every line of Moses' laws, Ezra wanted to know if she was burdened by what he called 'the blood of womanhood'.

She went up to him and placed her fingers on his lips. He hesitated, torn between wanting to retreat and wanting to kiss her. Lilah laughed again, drew him to her and kissed his earlobe. 'Have no fear,' she whispered. 'I'm pure. Would I have come if I weren't? Don't you trust your sister?'

Ezra gave a small grunt of satisfaction. Lilah closed her eyes. She was happy to be with her beloved brother, and forgot for the moment the anxiety that had been tormenting her since the previous night. They held each other as if they had been apart, not for a few weeks, but for all eternity.

The same emotion overcame them each time they met. Brother and sister, born of the same flesh, sometimes so alike that they seemed to be of one body – but never of one mind.

Her lips pressed to Ezra's neck, Lilah opened her eyes. Sogdiam was watching them. Then he turned away and hurried into the house with the basket.

Ezra took a step back, but kept Lilah's hand in his.

'Sogdiam tells me you make yourself handsome whenever I come to visit,' she remarked in a serious tone, although there was still a touch of mockery in her eyes, 'but to me you seem thinner than ever. How is it possible? Axatria's baskets are full to bursting. Don't you eat?'

Ezra dismissed her questions with a wave of his hand. 'I'm perfectly well. It's Master Baruch you should worry about. We had some bad news, and since then he hasn't slept. This morning we haven't studied because he felt too weak.'

Lilah threw a worried glance at the room from which Ezra had emerged.

'Go in,' Ezra said, with a nod. 'He's waiting for you.'

Simply furnished though it was, the room gave an impression of warmth. The daylight came in through a wide opening in the west wall, and on either side of this window, which had a shutter of woven reed, were niches piled high with wax tablets. The north wall was covered with a rug, a gift from Aunt Sarah. It had taken a great deal of effort on Lilah's part to persuade Ezra to hang it, but in winter it had proved effective in protecting the room from the wind and cold that filtered through the poorly laid bricks.

In the middle of the room, a cedar chest, blackened by the oil lamps that had burned on it, served as a writing desk. Around it were a number of wide-necked jars filled with papyrus scrolls, and two stools. A leather bag hung from one of the ceiling beams, containing styli and sticks of dry ink.

A low bed stood against the wall opposite the window, consisting of a woollen mattress wrapped in linen, placed on leather trestles. An old man's head jutted out from the brown and green striped blanket, but his frail body barely showed beneath it.

Lilah knelt.

'Lilah is here, Master!' Ezra said loudly, behind her.

The blanket was pushed back more briskly than Lilah had expected. Two pale, deep-set eyes peered at her, bright eyes that contrasted sharply with the haggard face, the thousand lines on the brow and cheeks. Despite his great age, Master Baruch's hair was still dark. His curly beard, though, was as white as a lamb's fleece, and covered his chest. His withered lips were barely visible, but drew back to reveal a few stumps of teeth when he smiled. 'Lilah, my dove, may the Everlasting bless you.' The voice was weak and hoarse, but cheerful.

Master Baruch pushed back the blanket a little more. His hands seemed to be no more than bones held together by the shiny, pockmarked skin that still covered them. He squeezed Lilah's hands with the strength and gentleness that amazed her every time. She leaned down and kissed the old man's brow tenderly. 'Master Baruch, Ezra tells me you're ill.'

There was a strange creak and Master Baruch opened his mouth wide. Then he closed his eyes and his throat quivered. He was laughing. 'Ezra is young and very indulgent,' he murmured, once he had regained his breath. 'He's so certain the Everlasting is going to make me a "patriarch" he thinks I'm ill! The truth, my dove, is that I'm not ill at all.' He squeezed Lilah's hands. His eyes opened again to reveal his piercing, ironic gaze. 'It's simply my time to die, my dove. The Everlasting doesn't share Ezra's opinion! He doesn't want to make me a new Noah or Abraham. I shan't live three hundred years. Baruch ben Neriah I am, and Baruch ben Neriah I shall die. And soon!'

'The truth, Master,' Ezra said impatiently, 'is that you had a stomach ache all last night.'

'The stomach ache is nothing,' Master Baruch retorted, his voice firmer now. 'A stomach ache you're born with and you die with. I've had a stomach ache for almost a hundred years. The sad thing, the thing that's turning my blood to water and shortening my life, is knowing that I shall never see Jerusalem rise again from her shame. I shall die while the city chosen by Yahweh is still defenceless before her enemies. To know that the Ammonites and Ashdodites are dancing on the ruins of the Temple, that's my illness, my dove. That's the punishment inflicted on me by the Everlasting.'

Lilah frowned. 'Why do you say that, Master Baruch?

Those misfortunes are over. Nehemiah has long since rebuilt the Temple and Jerusalem is living according to the Law of Yahweh. That's what you told Ezra and me when you first came here.'

The old man raised his palms in protest, as if overcome by a wave of pain. 'Forget those innocent words, my child! Don't make my sin any worse than it is before the Everlasting.'

Lilah turned to Ezra, uncomprehending.

'Clearly you haven't heard the news,' Ezra said sombrely, 'and I'm not surprised. Nobody's likely to care about such things in Mordechai's house.'

With a shudder, Lilah remembered Antinoes' tablet. 'What news?' she asked.

'Nehemiah, son of Hakalya, died at least five years ago. And he failed.'

'Oh!' Her relief did not escape Ezra. She felt her cheeks turn red.

Master Baruch's voice rose, loud and clear. '"You will come back to me," Yahweh said to Moses. "You will obey my orders, and act according to them. And even if you are banished to the furthest borders under heaven, from there I will gather you and I will lead you to the place I have chosen for my Name to live." It was with these words in mind that Nehemiah, son of Hakalya, left Susa. That is what we must carry in our hearts.' He pointed at Lilah, his pale eyes neither smiling nor ironic now, but hard with anger. 'It is now fifty-four years since Nehemiah left for Jerusalem to re-establish the will of Yahweh. And all he has re-established is piles of bricks.'

'For four years Cyrus the Younger ruled over Judaea,' Ezra interrupted. 'We heard only rumours about Jerusalem and Nehemiah. The news that reached us was neither good nor bad. Merchants who came to Susa assured us that Cyrus had as much affection for the Jews as his father and grandfather. The Temple and the walls of the city were as splendid as they would be in a dream, they asserted. It was the gossip of caravan drivers drunk on palm wine. Music to the ears of an exiled Jew whose conscience might have been pricked otherwise.' He stretched out his arm, pointing to an invisible visitor in the courtyard. 'Some came here to bow down to Master Baruch, claiming to be pious. "Do you have news of Jerusalem?" we would ask. "Is Nehemiah still fighting the Philistines, and the people of Manasseh, Ammon and Gad?" "Oh, no!" they'd reply, confident as could be. "Nehemiah made the Law of Moses respected on the hills of Judaea and the banks of the Jordan. Jerusalem shines as it did in Solomon's day." How did they know? They'd had a letter, or heard it from a relative who was visiting. It was all hearsay.'

Ezra slapped his thigh, gave a harsh laugh, and fell silent. But his eyes blazed with fury, his face suddenly magnificent.

A thrill went through Lilah. At such moments no one, not even Antinoes, was as splendid as her brother.

Lilah had long been familiar with Ezra's anger. And when it came, she admired it as much as she dreaded it. His throat was as delicate as a woman's, but when he was angry his voice would grow sombre and curiously resonant. It made the air tremble and everyone's heart beat faster. His whole body appeared to grow heavier, and he would move about, shaking his limbs, as if they could not contain the strength of his muscles. Lilah was not surprised now to see him turn abruptly, walk to the window, then to the door, and come back at last to the bed. He clapped his hands, as if to frighten off a pack of stray dogs.

'Now we know the truth. In the month of Nissan, Artaxerxes waged battle on his brother Cyrus beneath the walls of Babylon. Cyrus was killed, and the lies and rumours died with him. Today the truth has crossed the desert. And the truth is that the Temple of the children of Israel has no doors, no roof − and if it has, no one guards them. No one knows the Law. Apparently trading goes on there, and money-changing. The walls of Jerusalem may have been rebuilt, but they're still wide open. The Philistines, the Ammonites, the Moabites, all the enemies of the children of Israel, come and go as they please. The Law given to Moses by Yahweh no longer holds sway, any more than it did on the day Nebuchadnezzar conquered Judaea, any more than it did during the sixty years when our fathers trampled the dust of exile, or during the hundred and fifty years that have passed since the decree of Cyrus the Great that returned Jerusalem to the children of Israel. The truth is that we might almost be back in the time when the Hebrews who had left Egypt danced before the Golden Calf at the foot of Mount Sinai. That is the news,

Sister. Nehemiah was ambitious and headstrong, but he failed.'

Ezra sat down on a stool and slapped his thigh again.

'How can you be certain?' Lilah could not help asking.

Her brother stared at her in surprise. Lilah smiled at him gently. She had not tried to oppose him, but had simply said what she was thinking. She was so accustomed to the fire of Ezra's speeches that she no longer fell under their spell, as she had when they were younger. But now Ezra's anger had turned against her, as the desert wind abruptly changes direction. That, too, was something to which she was accustomed. She placed a hand on her brother's knee. 'You may be worrying needlessly,' she said tenderly. 'If the rumours from Jerusalem after the battle of Kounaya were false, why should these new ones be true?'

Ezra pushed away her hand, but before he could say a word, Master Baruch spoke: 'That's a good question, my daughter. If a bird flies in one direction, why shouldn't it fly in another?'

Rigid with anger, lips quivering, Ezra looked the two of them up and down.

Master Baruch pointed to one of the jars with a bony finger. 'Show her the letter.'

Ezra pulled a papyrus from among the twenty or so in the jar and threw it to Lilah. 'It's from Yaqquv, the guardian of the gates of the Temple. He was appointed to the post by Nehemiah himself before he died. The letter was written in Jerusalem two springs ago. It did not reach the Levites of Babylon until after the death of

Cyrus the Younger. One of them brought it to Master Baruch, because it was addressed to him. Everything I told you is there, written by Yaqquv, who saw it with his own eyes.'

Even though it was rolled round a cedarwood stalk, the papyrus strip was worn, yellowed and torn: it looked as if it had been handled by hundreds of people. The ink was ochre in colour, different from that used in Susa. The writing was not Persian or Chaldean. Lilah recognized the tall, joined-up signs of the Hebrews, which Master Baruch was teaching Ezra. She could barely decipher them.

As if guessing her thoughts, Ezra took another papyrus from the jar. This one was shorter and newly written. 'I translated the important points into the language of Babylon, made more than forty copies and distributed them to the exiled families in the upper town. I was hoping to open their eyes to the wounds of Jerusalem. You might have had one in your hands. But perhaps it was madness to hope I could touch our uncle's heart, or even cross his threshold.'

Lilah lowered her eyes. He was right: this bad news had not entered Uncle Mordechai's house. She turned to the old man. 'I'm ashamed, Master Baruch. Ezra's right. As you know, our uncle's house is closed to anything that comes from his nephew. But our uncle will come to regret it, I'm sure.'

Master Baruch glanced at Ezra and sighed. 'We're all ashamed, you, Ezra and I. All of us. Nehemiah was so confident when he set off. "I confess the sins of the children of Israel. We have sinned against you, Yahweh. I am in sin, my father's house is in sin." That's what he said as he left the Citadel. And we can say the same thing now. Time has passed, but nothing good has come of it.'

He grimaced and fell silent. His fingers again sought Lilah's hand. Ezra respected his silence, and the three were quiet for a moment. There was nothing to add. The words already spoken were enough of a burden.

Then Lilah heard noises from the adjoining room, which was used as a kitchen. Sogdiam must be putting away the provisions.

As rapidly as he had flown into a rage, Ezra regained his composure. Calmly, he replaced the papyri in the jar, then sat down again beside Lilah. She did not need to turn to know that he was looking at her, and did not doubt his affection for her, but she kept her head down and her eyes on Master Baruch's hand squeezing hers.

She had come here to tell Ezra that Antinoes had returned and she wanted to marry him. But how could she do that now? How, after all she had heard, could she say, 'I, too, have news. Antinoes has returned from the wars to marry me. I spent the night with him. I love him. I can still feel his caresses on my hips. He wants to make me a great lady, one of those who enter the Citadel and bow down before the King of Kings'?

Suddenly Master Baruch's voice rose, drawing her from her thoughts. 'Ezra has the anger of youth, and that's good,' he said, with a half-wicked, half-serious smile. 'All I have is the remorse of age. I was not much older than the two of you when Nehemiah left Susa for Jerusalem with the consent of his King of Kings. At the time I was living in Babylon, among the exiles. I spent my days studying the teachings of Moses. A man named Azaryah came to me. "Baruch," he said, "Nehemiah is forming a caravan for Jerusalem. He's going to rebuild the walls and the Temple. He needs hands and minds he can trust. He thought of you because it's said you know a great deal about the Law that Moses received on Mount Sinai." I gazed at this Azaryah with the look your brother sometimes has. Blazing dark eyes . . . although mine have always been light blue.'

Master Baruch stopped. His throat quivered with a grating laugh – whatever the gravity of a situation, he could always find amusement in men's trials and tribulations, especially his own.

'I thought about it for a while, then answered seriously, "I'm studying, and can't interrupt my studies."

'"Come on," he insisted, "you can study in Jerusalem. Is there a better place to study?"

'I refused again. "Going to Jerusalem will mean interrupting my studies, and I can't do it." He lost his temper. He was breathing like an ox, this Azaryah, he was as red as a beetroot. "Is that your answer to Nehemiah, Baruch ben Neriah?" he asked. "That you'd rather study than rebuild the Temple of Yahweh?" "Yes, that's exactly what you're going to tell him," I replied, very proud of myself. "Baruch ben Neriah obeys a higher will. When you're studying the Law of Yahweh, you don't interrupt it, even to rebuild the walls and Temple of Jerusalem.'''

Master Baruch was laughing, but the tears that welled in his eyes were not tears of joy. 'Oh, Nehemiah, poor Nehemiah! May the Everlasting bless him for all time!' he exclaimed, beating his chest with his fists.

Lilah risked a glance at Ezra, who was listening impassively, head tilted. She waited a moment, then got up with a determined air. 'I'm going to make herb tea with honey,' she said to Master Baruch. 'I've brought some fresh herbs. And I'll bake some biscuits that you can dip in a little milk. It'll do you good and calm your stomach.'

She went out before Master Baruch could protest. But his laughter pursued her. She had to admit, however reluctantly, that Ezra was a good pupil and had learned a lot from Master Baruch – all except one thing. He had not learned how to laugh and joke. That was a true gift, especially when your eyes burned with the tears you were holding back.

The kitchen was only six feet wide and twelve feet long, but it was simply and efficiently laid out. A long flat stone, worn smooth by daily use, protruded from the far wall, with a furrow cut into it to drain away the water through gaps in the bricks. Sogdiam was cleaning onion shoots and turnip roots. He had already put away the sacks of vegetables and dried fruits in big cane baskets with lids, which were lined up on the side. Under a board of palm-tree wood, which was used as a table for kneading, cutting or crushing, there were other baskets, without lids, containing a few cucumbers and two small, white-veined melons.

Bunches of mint, sage, peppers, aniseed, cardamom and oregano hung from the ceiling beside pieces of mutton and dried fish, which swayed in the heat from the brick oven. Two feet high and shaped like a water tank, the oven stood in the middle of the room. Inside it, right at the bottom, a thick layer of embers glowed between big stones, on which stood a pitcher of boiling water. A cleverly angled opening in the roof let out the smoke without allowing rainwater into the room.

No sooner had Lilah entered than she asked if the dough for the biscuits was ready. Sogdiam threw her a look, wiped his wet hands on his tunic, then lifted a cloth from the kneading board. Five round balls rested on it.

Lilah pressed one with a finger. The dough sank, soft but firm, and resumed its shape when she released the pressure.

'I made them early this morning,' Sogdiam said, resuming his task. 'We had some flour left over from last week.'

'So now we just have to bake them, if the oven is hot enough.'

Sogdiam thought of replying that he had kept up the fire since dawn for that very purpose. All Lilah had to do was place her hand against the bricks to discover that he had spoken the truth when he claimed to know the day on which she would come. Now he judged it wiser to keep silent.

What was the point? Lilah never noticed his efforts. With the back of his wrist, he rubbed his eyes, which were smarting more from the injustice than the heat of the oven.

Unafraid to soil her beautiful tunic, Lilah picked up one of the balls of dough, flattened it between her palms and then, with a gentle, regular movement, rolled it between her hands until it was a thin, soft disc. She leaned against the oven and, with the skill of habit, bent double, plunged her face into the heat and stuck the disc to the inner wall. It sizzled. She stepped back, straightened, pushed a lock of hair off her brow, then seized another ball of dough. 'While I'm making the biscuits, Sogdiam,' she said, 'heat a pitcher of water with mint leaves and the green part of the onions I brought. Make sure you cut them very small first. And pour a jug of milk for Master Baruch.'

Sogdiam obeyed without a word.

For a while they busied themselves in silence. The space was so narrow that they constantly brushed against each other, almost colliding as Sogdiam placed the herbs in the pitcher of hot water at the bottom of the oven.

No sooner had Lilah, her cheeks and brow reddened by the fire, stuck the last disc of dough into the oven than she wiped her hands, lifted the lids off the baskets, and made a face. She was surprised to find nothing there but the bags Axatria had prepared that morning.

She stood up abruptly, knocking Sogdiam's arm as he was pouring goat's milk from a big gourd into a double-handled pitcher. The gourd fell from his hands, the pitcher overturned and milk spattered the vegetables and the wall beside the draining table. Sogdiam caught the pot before it rolled off the table to smash on the floor, then let out a torrent of oaths in the dialect of the lower town.

'I'm sorry, Sogdiam,' Lilah cried. 'It's my fault.'

'Yes, it is!' Sogdiam exploded, pushing the cork back into the gourd with his fist. 'You said it − it's your fault! Ever since you came into this kitchen you've been treating me as if I wasn't here. Your eyes are open, but you don't see me any more than if I were a spirit from the underworld.'

'Sogdiam!'

'Sogdiam, do this! Sogdiam, do that! Sogdiam got up at dawn to make everything ready. Sogdiam isn't lying when he says he waits for you. All you have to do is put the biscuits in the oven. Everything has been cleaned and put away. You can lift every lid in this room! You don't have Axatria to help you today, so I'm helping you instead. But if Sogdiam wants you to say thank you, he's got a long wait.'

'So, now Sogdiam is also losing his temper, is he?' Lilah took him by the shoulders, drew him to her and pressed her lips to his brow. 'Forgive me, Sogdiam,' she whispered. 'It's a bad day. Ezra's angry, Axatria's angry, you're angry and I . . .' Sobs rose in her throat. She hugged Sogdiam tighter, not so much to comfort him as to reassure herself. 'Of course I see you, my Sogdiam. Of course I thank you.' She kissed his eyelids. Sogdiam did not reply, and dared not put his arm round her waist. He stood stiffly, breathing in gasps and shaking all over.

Lilah pushed him away gently. There was still so much mistrust in his eyes, she was reminded of a wild animal that could never be truly tamed. 'Smile.'

His lips stretched into a grimace that was not a smile but betrayed the depth of the affection he felt for her and his hunger for love.

Lilah took his chin and forced him to look at her. 'You'll never be my husband, Sogdiam,' she said quietly, 'because I'm too old for you. But I'll often regret that. And I know that we'll always be friends.'

They remained like that until Sogdiam, with a gleam in his eyes now, seemed convinced that Lilah was not joking. Then he freed himself. 'It's all right,' he said. 'There isn't much spilt milk. I'll wipe it up.'

With a knot in her stomach, and surprised at the strength of her own feelings, Lilah watched him go about his work, cleaning and putting away the flat stone, the containers and the utensils. He was a serious and loyal young man, braver and more determined than most boys of his age in the upper town.

'I wasn't inspecting your work, Sogdiam,' she said. 'I'm well aware you do far more than Ezra asks of you. I was just surprised by how empty the baskets are. Ezra eats nothing, and Master Baruch has the appetite of a bird, yet there's almost nothing left of the barley and the dried vegetables that Axatria and I brought you last time. There must have been at least four or five *minas* of each.

I find it hard to believe you ate the rest. And there's no reason to throw it away.'

Sogdiam did not reply immediately. 'We don't throw it,' he admitted at last. 'We give it away.'

'You give it away?'

'It was Ezra's idea.'

'What do you mean?'

Once again, Sogdiam took his time replying. He looked into the oven, where the biscuits were darkening. For some time now, the room had been filled with the sweet smell of barley, but neither had noticed.

'Your biscuits are turning brown,' he said.

'Lord Almighty!' Hurriedly Lilah seized a long wooden spatula and a thick serge cloth. She bent down to the oven, screwing up her eyes against the heat, skilfully prised the biscuits loose with the spatula, without breaking them, and collected them in the cloth. She stood up again, breathing hard, face bathed in sweat. 'One moment more and they'd have burned.'

'The herb tea must be ready, too,' Sogdiam said, and he took the pitcher out of the oven.

Lilah placed the steaming golden biscuits on a platter of woven palms, then added a few dates and the pot of milk. She looked at Sogdiam, who was filtering the tea into a large bowl. 'What do you mean, you give away the food?'

Sogdiam looked at her reproachfully. As reluctantly as if he were about to betray a secret, he pointed his chin at the courtyard. 'Three or four moons ago, a woman from the *zorifes* came here. She was moaning so loudly you could have heard her in the upper town. We gave her a little barley.' He stopped, and smiled. 'Wait.' He bent over the oven and took a small earthenware dish with a lid from beneath the ashes. 'A surprise for Master Baruch,' he announced, lifting the lid with a cloth and waiting for Lilah's reaction.

In a wreath of steam, a mouth-watering aroma reached her nostrils. 'Mmm, it smells wonderful.'

'Turnips, dates and chopped fish mashed together with cardamom, basil and curdled milk. A dish I invented.'

'But Master Baruch has a bad stomach and says he won't eat anything!'

'Oh, he has a bad stomach until he gets this under his nose! You'll see, as soon as he smells it, he'll shake with pleasure.' Sogdiam shook, too, but with laughter.

Lilah laughed with him. 'I didn't know you were so fond of cooking.'

'I try this and that. I mix things, and taste them. If I like what I taste, I suggest it to Ezra and Master Baruch. They don't eat much, but they taste. They aren't hard to please. Sometimes, they really like it. Especially Master Baruch, to be honest. He always used to ask for barley gruel, because of his teeth – or, rather, his lack of them. And I was fed up with always smelling the same smell here in the kitchen . . .'

Lilah had dipped a wooden spoon in the dish. The delicacy of the flavour surprised her. 'It's good.'

Sogdiam glowed with pride.

'But you didn't use everything in the baskets, making this kind of food,' Lilah went on. 'So tell me – the woman who came here, what was she complaining about?'

'You won't let go, will you?' Sogdiam sighed. '"No more flour," she was bawling, "no more flour, nothing more to eat!" She said she had three boys and no more food left to give them.'

'What happened then?'

'She made such a commotion that Ezra had to leave his study. "Sogdiam, why do you let the courtyard get so noisy?" he asked. I explained to him. "Why doesn't her husband give her enough to feed her children?" was his reply. How was I supposed to know? I asked the woman. She told me she didn't have a husband. Ezra was angry. "She has three sons and no husband?" I reminded him that my mother had also had a son and no husband. "That's why you took me in," I said. Ezra gave me one of his black looks – like a moonless night, I always say. Master Baruch was laughing into his beard but, as usual, didn't say anything. The woman was still weeping in the middle of the courtyard, moaning loud enough to set your teeth on edge. Ezra came to a decision. "Give her what she wants," he said, "as long as she stops wailing. I need to study in peace." And there you are.'

'What do you mean, there you are? Did you give her all your reserves?'

'No. Just enough for four days.'

Lilah shook her head, too surprised to react. 'How long ago was this?'

'The month of Kislev.'

'And you've been giving her grain since then? Is that why your baskets are always so empty?'

Sogdiam lowered his eyes, trying to conceal a wicked little smile. 'Her and others.'

'Others?'

'The woman came back four days later. Not alone, but with six other women. Younger than her, also from the *zorifes*. They weren't weeping, but they told me they were all in the same situation, with one or two children and no husband. The summer and autumn were very dry, and the harvests were poor, so they couldn't glean. They were starving. You could see it, I swear.'

'And you gave them food, just like the first woman?'

'I asked Ezra first. He gave me another of his moonless-night looks. Then he asked if we had enough. I told him we did. "So give it, I don't want them to cry – but be sure to share it fairly. They don't all have the same number of children."'

Lilah was silent for a moment. 'Is that what he said?' she asked, in a low voice.

'Yes.' Sogdiam was staring at her anxiously now, biting his lip. 'Do you think I did wrong? They're women like my mother and—'

'Oh, Sogdiam,' Lilah said, smiling to stop herself crying. 'Of course you did what you had to do.'

As Sogdiam had predicted, Master Baruch forgot the pain in his stomach and his desire for herb tea when he smelt the dish the boy had prepared. For a moment, he allowed himself to be overcome by the aroma of the food. 'Delicious,' he murmured, a rapturous look on his face, while Lilah made sure he was comfortable. 'Exquisite!'

Sogdiam had helped Lilah to bring in the bowls and place them on the writing chest. His eyes shone with pride. 'I was thinking of you as I cooked it, Master. And your teeth,' he added, with a bow.

'May the Everlasting bless you, my boy, wild as you are.'

'Wild now, Master,' Sogdiam said, serious again, 'but one day you may make a good Jew of me.'

Master Baruch roared with laughter. 'It takes more than a dish of turnips and fish to become a child of Israel! But perhaps the Everlasting will make an exception for you.'

Sogdiam laughed and went out, dancing despite his limp.

'I didn't know Sogdiam took such good care of you,' Lilah observed, as she wrapped a blanket round Master Baruch's frail shoulders.

'For a barbarian,' Master Baruch chuckled, 'the boy certainly has many qualities. Perhaps the Everlasting has already made an exception for him.'

Ezra had pushed his stool under the window, and sat there with a scroll across his knees. He had not looked up during this exchange.

'Master Baruch, can't you persuade Ezra that he, too, must eat from time to time? The news from Jerusalem won't be any better if he dies of hunger.'

'You're right, my dove. You're absolutely right. His

studies won't be any better either, I might add. An empty stomach does nothing for the eyes or the ears.'

'I eat my fill!' Ezra protested, without looking up.

'Increase your fill, then,' Lilah said, annoyed.

Apparently indifferent to the quarrel that was brewing, Master Baruch closed his eyes as Lilah filled his bowl. But after he had eaten a mouthful, he murmured, in that voice of his that was always obeyed, although it seemed never to give an order, 'Such is the irony of the Everlasting. We're gloomy and sick because we received bad news from Jerusalem. Sogdiam does the cooking, and the shadow of Jerusalem no longer pains our stomachs, only our hearts and minds. Is that why Nehemiah failed? Or because the people of Jerusalem no longer have the hearts or the minds to suffer what they've become? Lilah is right, my boy. Do honour to our Sogdiam and share my meal.'

Reluctantly, Ezra resolved to try. After swallowing a few spoonfuls, he seemed to find the food pleasant, and emptied the bowl rapidly.

Lilah looked at him and smiled. Ezra was like that. Severe, obstinate, tormented by the desire to do the right thing, the correct thing. And sometimes too impatient, too impulsive and unyielding, unconcerned about the realities of life, as if the years of childhood were still with him. But perhaps that was only the result of his faith: according to Master Baruch, he was becoming wiser than any sage, purer than any zealot.

Ezra became aware that his sister's eyes were on him. He looked up at her and gave the smile that had delighted her for more than twenty years, the smile that spoke of the indestructible love that linked brother and sister, uniting them in the same tenderness, like two sounds in harmony on the same lyre, sweeping away all doubt and discord.

Today, though, Lilah remained deaf to its call. With a pang, she looked at Ezra's beloved face and thought of her beloved Antinoes. God of heaven! How could she speak the words she had been repeating to herself all night? How could she say to Ezra the phrases she had written on the papyrus scroll now hidden under her bed?

She closed her eyes, and the prayer she had uttered during the night again filled her mind. *O Yahweh, God of heaven, God of my father,* she implored, *give me the strength to find the words to convince Ezra! Give him the strength to hear them.*

Ezra misunderstood her silence and her closed eyes. 'Lilah, my sister, don't be sad. I'm eating – and you were right to insist. It's very good. Who could have predicted that Sogdiam would become such a cook? He was like a dog when he came here, all skin and bone.'

Recovering her composure, Lilah smiled at him affectionately. 'He told me about the women you give food to.'

'Oh yes, we had to.' Ezra drank his cup of milk in little sips. 'It's of no importance.'

'What do you mean, it's of no importance? Of course it's important! Those women are in need. Who can help them, here in the lower city, if not Master Baruch and you?'

Ezra threw a glance at Master Baruch over his cup. The old man was wiping the bottom of his bowl with a piece of biscuit, which he then swallowed before looking up with an ironic glint in his eyes.

'In future,' Lilah went on, 'I'll bring more so that you don't have to go without yourselves.'

Master Baruch chuckled. 'Lilah, my dove, it isn't Ezra who helps the poor women, let alone me. It is written in the scroll of the Law given to Moses. "Do not gather the gleanings of your harvest, but leave them for the poor man and the migrant!" Do we glean the grain and bring it here? Lilah, without you the women who came into this courtyard would now be hearing their children scream with hunger. And we, the sages of Zion, would have nothing in our bellies but the bitterness of bad news and remorse.'

Blushing, Lilah rose hurriedly to clear the table. She was about to leave the room when Ezra asked, as if he had only just become aware of it, 'Didn't Axatria come with you today?'

'She's waiting for me at the gate to the upper town.'

Ezra laughed in surprise. 'Why? Is she afraid to see me?'

'Oh, no, all she thinks about is seeing you . . . I asked her to let me come alone today.'

'Why?'

Lilah hesitated. Master Baruch had let his head roll back against the cushions supporting him and seemed to have dozed off. 'Antinoes is back,' she said, in a low voice.

Ezra's expression did not change, and he said nothing. Had he heard?

'I saw him yesterday. He fought Cyrus the Younger's Greeks and was awarded the breastplate of the heroes of the King of Kings.' Lilah fell silent. Her own words seemed to her out of place and offensive. She had wanted to say, 'I love him. I want him for my husband. He wants it too, more than anything. I love to be in his arms. And I also love you, with all the love in a sister's heart.' But the words that had emerged from her mouth had been cold, fearful and colourless.

And Ezra's face remained stony, as before.

For a moment, they were both silent and motionless.

'Is that why you stopped Axatria coming with you, so that you could tell me this?'

'No,' Lilah breathed, hoping that Master Baruch was not about to wake up. 'That wasn't why. It was so that you and I could talk. Antinoes hasn't changed his mind – he hasn't changed at all. Neither have I . . .'

Ezra rose abruptly and went to sit on his stool.

'You loved Antinoes, Ezra. We—'

'Be quiet!' Ezra cut in. 'I was a mere child, then an ignorant young man. As ignorant as it's possible to be in our uncle's family. As ignorant as the children of Israel have become in exile. But not any more.'

'Ezra, I know that as well as anyone, and I'm proud of what you are, of what you've become. I would never—'

'A Persian warrior comes back to the royal city of Susa,' Ezra interrupted. 'What of it? It may be news to you, my sister, but not to me.'

Lilah put her hands together to stop them shaking, but she held her brother's gaze. 'Don't be so unyielding! Have you forgotten that you used to call Antinoes "Brother"? Have you forgotten that he held your hand when you wept for our father and mother, that when you kissed me, you kissed him too?'

Ezra gave a curious smile, a beautiful, profound smile, which did nothing to soften his expression. 'I haven't forgotten anything, Lilah. I'm working every day with Master Baruch so that we don't forget anything of what we are – we, the people who have a Covenant with the Everlasting. I never forget anything that doesn't deserve to be forgotten. I haven't forgotten that you're my beloved sister, and that without you there would never be any life in this hovel, any beauty, any tenderness. I haven't forgotten who we are. I haven't forgotten that nothing, not even your Persian warrior, can tarnish the eternal love of Lilah for Ezra.'

Master Baruch had woken, and was watching Lilah intently. She stood up and walked to the door, intending to leave without a word. But she could not help it: she turned and said, with a knot in her stomach, 'Nothing that comes from my Persian warrior can tarnish me, Ezra. It is he who gives me life and beauty and tenderness.'

A Day for Anger

Mordechai's wife Sarah always supervised the women workers. She would go from one loom to the next, inspecting their work: the regularity of the stitches, the arrangement of the colours, the tension of the weft, the texture of a line, the quality of a knot. Today, though, she found it hard to concentrate. She was constantly drifting out into the empty courtyard where the autumn sun cast long shadows that vanished from time to time with a passing cloud. There her mouth, so perfectly shaped for the sweet things in life, would grimace in irritation, a frown would crease her brow, and her face would set hard as she went back into the workshop.

It was a long, vast gallery, with a series of arches along it that allowed the daylight to penetrate all the way to the whitewashed wall at the far end, where seven weavers sat side by side.

Reels of thread were piled round the looms along with shuttles, empty and full, reglets for keeping the lines taut, and pails filled with bone or wood needles. Bronze blades of different sizes, used for measurement, were laid out carefully on low trestles. At one end of the workshop, behind two large shuttles on pedals, some fifty baskets contained an assortment of woollen threads of every colour in creation. At the other end, the finished rugs hung from wooden racks.

A few of the workers walked to and fro, carrying baskets of shuttles. The weavers, though, sat at the looms. The frames hung from bronze rings sealed into the wall at a man's height, and the looms rested on little trestle tables, beneath which there was space for the women's legs. Some sat on cushions, bending their legs with their calves under their buttocks. Others chose to put a pile of scrap wool between their buttocks and the rough brick floor.

Their hands moved with speed and precision, sliding, separating, pulling, counting. Weights that looked like tiny wheels were attached to the vertical threads. Every time the shuttles passed, the women would be hit in the stomach, or on the thighs or chest. The clank of the shuttles and the banging of the reglets could be heard out in the courtyard. Sometimes the noise was so loud that it was like the sound of some fabulous, insatiable animal chewing.

Not one of the workers glanced up or turned away from her loom. They sensed Sarah's approach, as if they had eyes in the backs of their heads, and their hands seemed to fly even faster and more skilfully between the threads.

It was nearly fifteen years since Sarah had opened her

workshop, at Mordechai's suggestion. Today she knew every speck of dust in it. She could tell from the sound of the shuttles, the reglets and needles, if the work was good or not.

Sarah watched the women's progress closely. Each day she would appear unheralded, sometimes in the morning, sometimes in the afternoon. The sweetness of her appearance, the placid roundness of her body and her face, matched one part of her character. She lost her temper only when the same worker repeated the same mistake. Often, she would caress a woman's shoulder, neck or cheek, especially if she was a young girl, new to the workshop and intimidated by it: they were encouraged by a little kindness to forget the pain in their fingers and back.

Very occasionally, she would praise someone, but compliments were useful only for their rarity value: nothing was worse than a skilled worker who became too proud of herself. That was a sad waste, like those wonderful peaches from the Zagros mountains that came to the upper town in the month of Elul, ripe peaches that had to be eaten immediately because they were already on the point of becoming rotten.

Sarah did not want older women as weavers. However experienced they were, they were often ill-tempered. And as it was for the mind, so it was for the body: for flexibility, nothing equalled youth.

The girls she chose had to be willing to learn. She liked to employ a few clever ones too. But they all had to know how to do as they were told.

A workshop of high repute such as Sarah's could not be run without strong leadership. For all her smiles, Sarah's tongue could be sharp, her eyes pitiless. And although the merchants who supplied her with wool or tools were often seduced by her curves, they soon learned to be on their guard when the time came for payment.

Many of the carpets and rugs Sarah produced embellished the seats of the chariots her husband built. But she could also make carpets and rugs in the styles of Judaea, Media, Parsumash, Lydia and Susa. There was hardly a noble family in the Citadel, or in Babylon or Ecbatana, that did not own something made in the workshop of Sarah, wife of Mordechai and daughter of Reka.

After a good dinner, washed down with palm beer, Sarah liked to say with a laugh, covering her mouth with her chubby fingers, that she had at least one thing in common with the King of Kings: her workshop also reigned over all the regions of Greater Persia. She hoped the Everlasting would forgive her this vanity.

Today, though, her thoughts were elsewhere.

Her niece Lilah had still not returned from the lower town.

She did not need to keep her eyes on the courtyard to know that. She would have heard the noise of the chariot wheels on the flagstones.

She forced her mind back to the work, and turned to a tall, thin young woman who was following her respect-fully a few paces behind. 'Helamsis, have you counted how many carpets we've finished today?' she asked.

'Five, Mistress. They're on the trestle.' Helamsis pointed to the far end of the workshop.

Sarah began to walk in that direction. 'Have you checked that they're the right size?' she asked.

Helamsis' answer was lost in the clatter of the shuttles and reglets. Sarah did not ask her to repeat it. When her mistress was in this kind of mood, it was better to obey her quietly and agree with her as often as possible. Even if Helamsis swore on the wrath of Ahura Mazda that every piece was of exactly the right length and width, Sarah would still go and check for herself.

That was what she now set about doing. Then, when she was satisfied, she put the shuttles back on the trestle with a sigh. There was nothing to criticize: they were perfect. She was about to ask Helamsis to take them to Mordechai's workshop on the other side of the courtyard when she heard the long-awaited rumbling.

'Ah!' Helamsis, who knew what had caused her mistress's impatience, sighed with relief. 'Here's Lilah's chariot.'

'What a way to behave!' Sarah exclaimed. As she had reached out to help Lilah from the chariot, Axatria had bumped into her. 'Can't you apologize, my girl?' Sarah roared.

The reproach had no effect. Axatria strode across the outer courtyard, dragging the empty basket behind her, and disappeared between the columns that led to the second courtyard, where the living quarters and the kitchens were.

'What's the matter with her?' Sarah asked Lilah, unable to get over what had happened.

'Oh, today's the day for anger,' Lilah replied, jumping nimbly from the chariot. 'Everyone's angry, Axatria, Ezra, even Sogdiam.'

'Angry? Why? Because of *him*?'

Lilah could not help smiling. *Him* could only be Antinoes. She just had time to adjust her shawl on her shoulders before her aunt took her by the elbow. 'Come, let's not stay here. I've had some sage and rose tea brought to my bedchamber.'

What Sarah called her bedchamber consisted, in fact, of two spacious rooms. One was a true bedchamber, while the other, furnished with low tables, chests and a large number of cushions, was used as a sitting room. From it, there was a view not only of the second courtyard but also of the gardens surrounding the house, a tranquil and delightful sight. Between the cypresses and the eucalyptus trees, the imposing walls and columns of the Citadel could be seen. Sarah was very proud of the room, and loved to receive her women friends there, as well as the wives of important customers.

'So, tell me, tell me everything!' she said, avid for news, as she lay down on the cushions. 'What did he say?'

Lilah knew that her aunt's gaiety would soon vanish. But she avoided replying directly to her impatient questions. 'Ezra and Master Baruch have had bad news from Jersusalem,' she said, as if that was what she had been asked. 'The sage Nehemiah died without accomplishing his mission. The Temple may have been rebuilt, though Ezra has his doubts. But it is desecrated by all kinds of bad practices, and the city itself is lawless again, with no protection for the Jews.'

Sarah stopped pouring the tea into silver goblets, and frowned. 'I knew that. Mordechai told me about it a few days ago. It's sad, I know,' she said, putting down the pot of tea, 'but, well . . .'

'Ezra was furious. He thinks we exiles have been deceived. We've let ourselves be too easily taken advantage of. The Law of Yahweh isn't respected, and the children of Israel are in danger.'

Sarah gave a sigh of irritation. 'Ezra is always furious. He thinks we're guilty of everything.'

'No, Aunt. He thinks only that we give too little attention to what's happening in Jerusalem—'

Sarah waved her hands as if to dispel smoke. 'Lilah, Lilah, my child! Leave these things to Ezra and Mordechai. They're not women's concerns. What I want to know is what Ezra said about your marriage to Antinoes.'

Avoiding her eyes, Lilah looked up at a flock of swallows circling above the garden. Was she also about to lose her temper?

She had been dreading this moment since she had left the lower town. She could guess in advance every one of the words that would be spoken: words of reproach she had heard so often, and which never had the slightest effect on her. If Ezra was frequently unfair to his uncle and aunt, they were no less unfair to him, obstinately refusing to judge his behaviour with a modicum of good faith. Couldn't they at least respect his choices and admire his courage?

If only they would make an effort to understand him a little instead of constantly reproaching him! Today was definitely a day for anger.

Lilah tried to calm herself with a mouthful of the scalding herb tea, which her aunt loved: sharp yet sweet, it seemed to have been conceived in her image.

Sarah was leaning towards her. 'I know you were with Antinoes last night,' she murmured, her face creased with curiosity. 'I heard you come home.' She chuckled. 'I'd have liked to see you then, so that you could tell me everything, but Mordechai had decided to sleep with me, and that's not something that happens often!'

The questions came thick and fast, and Lilah replied as briefly as she could. Yes, Antinoes loved her as passionately as ever. Yes, he had become a hero of the King of Kings. Yes, he wanted her as his wife. Yes, yes . . .

'And Ezra?'

Lilah bit her lips, then, seeing her aunt's large eyes shining with impatience, she smiled. 'Ezra is like Antinoes,' she replied. 'He hasn't changed either.'

'Hasn't changed? You mean . . .'

'You know what I mean, Aunt.'

There was no tenderness in Sarah's face now. 'You mean he won't hear of your marriage, is that it?'

'He's devoted to his studies, and nothing else interests him,' Lilah replied patiently.

'All I know is, he's mad and he'll cause you a lot of

unhappiness.' Sarah's voice was as harsh now as it was when she discovered a defect in a carpet.

Lilah was on the point of standing up and leaving the room. She, too, would have liked to speak her mind, to say loud and clear that she was no longer a child, that all this was no one's business but her own, and that she'd prefer to be left in peace. But that would not have been the truth. Whether she liked it or not, her marriage to Antinoes was everyone's business.

'I didn't tell him about the marriage,' she forced herself to reply calmly. 'There was no point.'

'No point? No point in telling him about your marriage? What are you talking about?'

'There's no rush, Aunt Sarah. Give Ezra a little time. He knows Antinoes is back. He'll think about it.'

'Think about it!' Sarah cried. 'We know what he's going to think about it!'

Lilah said nothing.

'And what about you?' Sarah went on, frowning. 'You want this marriage, don't you? You and Antinoes love each other – you're promised to each other . . .'

'What we've promised each other is no one's business but ours, Aunt!' Without intending to, Lilah had spoken curtly and had slammed her glass down on the tray.

Sarah gave a muffled moan and turned towards the garden. She was weeping. She had a very particular way of weeping: soundlessly, almost without tears. A violent shudder rippled through her.

'Aunt Sarah!'

'Don't you want to get married?'

'That's not what I said.'

Her aunt looked at her for a moment in astonishment, then shook her head. 'I don't understand you! I haven't understood your brother for years, but now you . . .'

'Ezra is doing what he thinks is right,' Lilah said, remembering that she had used the same words in trying to calm Antinoes.

'Oh really? What does that mean – right? Doing all he can to hurt his uncle and aunt?'

'Aunt Sarah, Ezra isn't a child, and hasn't been a child for a long time. Uncle Mordechai and you know what he's doing in the lower town and why. You should be proud and recognize his greatness.'

'His greatness?' Sarah cried. 'In the lower town? As if that wasn't enough to make us ashamed! He could just as easily pursue his studies here – even with that old sage of his, who turned up out of nowhere, like a beggar. There's no better man than Mordechai. Even after all this time, he would still welcome Ezra with open arms. But, oh, no!'

'Aunt Sarah, there are laws for the Hebrews,' Lilah said, passionately now, and rose from the cushions. 'Laws for all of us, at every moment of our lives. Laws that come from the God of heaven. In our exile we've forgotten them. They're written on Moses' scroll, which has been passed from father to son in our family for generations. Now the scroll of the Law has come to Ezra. He wants to study it. Not only to study it – he wants to obey its teachings. Isn't that his right? Perhaps even his duty! Shouldn't we admire him for it as we're taught to admire the ancients, the patriarchs, the prophets?'

'What modesty! Is Ezra the equal of the ancients, the patriarchs and the prophets now?' For a moment, they glared at each other. Then Sarah shrugged. 'You sound more and more like him,' she said, disappointment in her voice.

'I don't sound like him. But I understand why he says what he does.'

'You're lucky, then.' Sarah rubbed her brow and eyes, as if trying to extract an image from them. 'The three of you were in the house, in the garden,' she sighed, 'always squabbling, but always adoring each other. My brother Ezra here, my brother Antinoes there! I can still hear you.'

'Ezra is not the same as he was, Aunt Sarah,' Lilah replied, severely.

'Oh, I've noticed that! And you're not the same, either.' Sarah's voice broke, and her neck and chin quivered. 'Antinoes is a chariot captain!' she sobbed. 'He fights beside the great Tribazes. He can enter the Apadana whenever he likes and be invited to share a meal with the King of Kings . . .'

Lilah knew exactly what her aunt was feeling. Sarah had always loved Antinoes like a son – but she also loved the fact that his family was noble, and his name renowned. She was proud to be able to tell her customers that Antinoes, son of Artobasanez, the late satrap of Margiana, would soon be her niece's husband and Mordechai's heir.

Lilah moved away from the table and the cushions. Immediately her aunt stood up and rushed to her. 'Lilah! Forgive me, my dear. I know how difficult this is for you. You love Ezra and . . . we all love him.'

Lilah let Sarah take her hands.

Her aunt sighed, and mustered a little smile. 'Perhaps you're right. You've always got on with him well. Perhaps it's better not to speak to him about Antinoes for the moment. His mood can be so changeable. In a few days . . .'

It sounded like a false hope, and Lilah turned away, embarrassed. But her aunt held her back, her face serious again, her voice low and firm. 'It's better not to say anything to your uncle either, my dear, until Ezra's made up his mind. Mordechai so much wants you to be happy. This marriage is really important to him – to all of us. And to the workshops. Do you understand?'

The Queen's Friends

How could she sleep?

Antinoes' voice said, 'We are together for ever. Without your love, even a Greek child could vanquish me.'

Ezra's voice said, 'Do not soil the walls of this room with his name.'

Aunt Sarah's voice said, 'This marriage is really important to all of us.'

Lilah flung off the blanket, which had got tangled between her legs. A bad dream had woken her, and she had tried in vain to go back to sleep. The darkness of her bedchamber seemed to weigh on her, the air as stifling as if someone had been burning sticks of cedar.

She groped for her shawl and put it on over her night tunic. Then she pushed back the shutter noiselessly and stepped out, barefoot, on to the narrow terrace that ran alongside the women's rooms, its crenellated wall overlooking the inner courtyard.

She took a deep breath, and the constriction eased in her throat.

Veiled by clouds, the sky was heavy and opaque, moonless and starless. The west wind blew in from the desert. Soon it would die down, and the *zarhmat*, bringing the autumn rains and winter ice from the north, would chase it away.

The diadem of the Apadana shone above the sleeping city, as it did every night. Lilah could not help thinking again of Antinoes.

Her eyes searched for the tower that had witnessed their lovemaking. It was hidden in darkness, but she saw it anyway, just as she still felt Antinoes' breath on her skin, the thrill of his caresses.

She placed her hands on the wall, searching for the support she wanted from her lover's shoulders and solid chest. For that was what Antinoes represented for her: not only the heat of desire but a peace and a calm that no one else could give her – certainly not Ezra.

Regret overwhelmed her now. Aunt Sarah had been right. She had lacked courage when she had seen Ezra. At the first sign of his anger against Antinoes, she had fallen silent. She had broken her promise.

What would she say to her lover when they met again? 'Be patient. Be patient a while longer . . .'

'I've been patient for so long already,' he would reply.

Was he asleep at the moment, or awake, like her, his mind in turmoil? Was he up there on the tower, trying to glimpse her through the darkness?

She smiled at her own childishness.

'Lilah . . .'

The whisper made her jump. She turned, heart pounding.

She could see nothing but the blackness of night.

'Don't be afraid, Lilah. It's only me.'

She recognized Axatria's voice. A shadowy figure took shape beside her. 'Axatria, what are you doing here?'

'I didn't mean to frighten you.'

'Why aren't you asleep?'

Axatria gave a tender little laugh and took her hand. 'For the same reason as you.' She lifted their joined hands and pressed them to her cheek, which Lilah realized was damp with tears.

'Why are you crying?'

'I've been telling myself I was silly and that I ought to ask your forgiveness.'

'What have I to forgive you?'

'My foolishness. My ill-temper. Our quarrel this morning. I thought of joining you in your bedchamber because I knew you wouldn't be sleeping, but . . .'

Lilah embraced her. 'I forgive you, Axatria. Of course I forgive you.'

Axatria pushed her away gently, sighed, and wiped her tears with a corner of her tunic. 'I'm afraid.'

'Of what?'

'If you quarrel with Ezra, what's to become of me?'

'Axatria . . .'

'Lilah, Antinoes came back to marry you, and because of that, you're going to quarrel with Ezra.'

Lilah looked out at the darkness and said nothing.

'Ezra will never agree to your becoming Antinoes' wife, and if you marry him without his blessing, he'll never see you again. You won't be his sister any more.'

'How can you be so sure? Did he tell you that?'

'There's no need. You know very well that's how it'll be.'

Far away in the royal city, dogs barked. The sound of a horn or a flute rose in the darkness. Then the wind carried away the echo. In some houses the night was a celebration . . .

'Ezra can't live without you,' Axatria sighed, 'but he'd rather not see you than share you with Antinoes.'

Lilah knew Axatria was right: she had put into words exactly what Lilah dreaded. 'Antinoes can't live without me either,' she replied in a low voice. 'He tells me I protect him in battle.'

Axatria nodded. 'I believe him.'

Axatria squeezed Lilah's hand until it hurt. They were so close, Lilah could feel Axatria's body shaking with sobs, even though Axatria was trying to control them as best she could.

'You'll have to choose Antinoes. You're too beautiful and proud to remain in your brother's shadow. But if Ezra won't see you, he won't want to see me either.'

Lilah braced herself not to yield to Axatria's contagious emotion. 'Nothing has been decided.'

'I'll lose the little Ezra gives me,' Axatria continued, as if she hadn't heard. 'I'll lose everything. But who could blame him? He's doing what he thinks is right – that's all he thinks about, doing what is right. He studies to be a just man, listens to Master Baruch. Everything he says and does is in a spirit of justice. He even believes he's right to be jealous of Antinoes. In the law he studies, a Persian cannot marry a daughter of the land of Judaea.'

'Nothing has been decided,' Lilah repeated, more firmly. 'We must trust in the Everlasting.'

'You can! He's your God. But what about me? Shall I make offerings to Ahura Mazda, Anahita or Mithras? I love to hear Ezra talk about the God of heaven. But I'm not Jewish. I have no god and no country. I'm just a handmaid from the Zagros mountains who loves her master − even if he hardly looks at her, which your aunt finds so amusing . . .'

'Axatria!' Lilah took the handmaid's face in her hands to silence her. 'Axatria, nothing has been said or done. You, too, must be patient.'

The sun was already high when a loud knocking was heard at the gate of Mordechai's house. Two servants ran to it, grumbling, ready to turn away an impatient customer.

No sooner had they raised the beam that kept the gate shut than it was thrust open from the outside, and a dozen soldiers rushed into the courtyard. They carried spears and wore felt helmets with red plumes, leather breastplates and baldrics decorated with black tassels that held straight daggers. In the workshop, Sarah gave a cry of terror.

The weavers broke off from their work and crowded behind their mistress. The soldiers lined up in double file.

A chariot came through the gate and stopped in front of them in the middle of the courtyard.

Mordechai had heard the noise from his own workshop and came running from the opposite side, wide-eyed with admiration for the elegance of the horses, the high body of the chariot, its serpentine golden handrail, and the lining of the interior with its blue and yellow geometric pattern. The spokes of the wheels were carved in the shape of leaves and the hubs lined with silver. It was an expensive piece of work, and not from his workshop. The customer had strange tastes, but clearly also the means to indulge them. Mordechai walked forward to welcome the visitors but, before he could even bow, he froze.

The gold carving on the front of the chariot was instantly recognizable: the head of a winged man resting on a sun wheel and surrounded on both sides by winged lions.

The emblem of the King of Kings.

God of heaven!

The man standing behind the driver noticed his astonishment. He made a gesture, and two soldiers moved aside to let Mordechai pass.

'Come closer,' the man said curtly. He had the round body and soft cheeks of a eunuch. He wore a plaited and oiled shoulder-length wig, and was neither tall nor fat, with a surprisingly withered face, and a small mouth framed, like his eyes, by deep lines. His splendid ochre tunic was itself full of folds and pleats.

Mordechai hesitated. Sarah was coming towards him,

her face as white as a sheet. The women had retreated
into the workshop, clinging to one another.

The eunuch grunted with impatience and waved his
hand again. Mordechai walked up to the chariot with as
much dignity as he could muster. When he stopped
again, the eunuch was looking him up and down as if he
were not sure which species of animal he was dealing
with.

'Are you Mordechai the Jew, son of Azaryah, son of
Hilqiyyah, Mordechai the chariot-maker?'

It was less a question than an assertion.

Mordechai was normally an imposing figure: tall, with
a narrow, angular face, lively eyes and coal-black eyebrows. There was hardly any situation he was unable to
face. But now there was a noticeable quiver of fear in
his voice as he replied, 'Yes, I am Mordechai, son of
Azaryah.'

Should he bow? Treat him as if he were a lord of the
Citadel?

The soldiers around the chariot waited impassively,
and the driver was as still as a statue. Out of the corner of
his eye, Mordechai noticed more soldiers at the entrance
to the house beside a wagon drawn by two mules.

The eunuch gave a half-smile, which seemed to trans-
form his face into a pool of water shivering in the wind.
'My name is Cohapanikes. I am the third cupbearer to
the Great Queen, mother of the King of Kings, first
master of the world. I have come for your niece Lilah,
daughter of Serayah.'

Behind her husband, Sarah let out a cry. Other cries

could be heard from the workshop. Mordechai's mouth fell open. He was gasping for breath.

The eunuch seemed pleased with the effect of his words. He raised his arm, which was as smooth and pale as his face, and brandished a cane of Egyptian ebony with an ivory and coral tip. 'It is the Queen's wish! Obey!'

Mordechai found it hard to take this in. 'The Queen wants Lilah?' he said in astonishment.

'Are you deaf? It is an order from Queen Parysatis. Your niece Lilah must follow where I lead.' He laughed again. 'Don't make that face. The Queen is doing you a great honour, chariot-maker. Come on! Hurry up! The Queen is waiting, and the Queen does not like to be kept waiting.'

Sitting in the wagon, Lilah needed the whole journey across the city to recover her composure.

It had been Axatria and Aunt Sarah who had come running and told her, with much rolling of eyes, about the incredible thing that was happening.

'But why?' Lilah had asked. 'What does she want with me?'

There had been a gleam of pride in Sarah's eyes, chasing away the terror they had held a short while earlier. 'She must have heard of your beauty,' she had suggested. 'Perhaps she wants you in her service.'

The idea had seemed so preposterous to Lilah that she had stood rooted to the spot.

Panic had seized the household. Axatria had tried to dress Lilah appropriately, but Sarah had pushed her away:

nothing was suitable – nothing was beautiful enough – and they did not even have time to rearrange her hair.

'It's because of Antinoes,' Lilah had said at last.

Axatria and Sarah had looked at each other, all pride and excitement gone from their faces. Axatria had grimaced and shrugged her shoulders. 'That may be so, but *he* won't tell you that,' she had muttered, gesturing to the outer courtyard where the Queen's eunuch could be heard shouting.

The third cupbearer had brusquely refused the wine Uncle Mordechai had offered him while he waited, then had stormed and threatened until Lilah was ready to come out.

At last he had fallen silent. He had screwed up his eyes, and looked her up and down with the same arrogant expression he had previously used for Mordechai. At last, a smile of satisfaction had creased his flabby face. It was not a reassuring smile.

When Lilah had sat down on the bench in the wagon, Uncle Mordechai had looked at her out of his pale face, begging her with his eyes to be careful. Sarah had lifted a trembling hand, tears already down to her chin. Axatria and the handmaids and workers who had gathered by the gate stared at her as if they would never see her again.

The third cupbearer had given the order to depart. The wagon had set off, and Lilah had closed her eyes, trying not to think of what might await her.

★　　★　　★

Their procession attracted attention as it passed through the streets. Two soldiers ran in front of the third cup-bearer's chariot, and the wagon followed, surrounded by the other soldiers.

They had turned on to the royal road, which was so wide that twenty horse-drawn chariots could have passed along it side by side. It started at the southern ramparts of the upper town, crossed into the royal city through a gate surmounted by two huge towers, and ended at the foot of the Citadel. It was straight, lined with trees and rosebushes, and the middle was paved with pink and white marble tiles, as perfect as a woven carpet. Only royal chariots and soldiers during processions, on feast days or when the King of Kings was on the move, were allowed to use it.

A horn blared as they approached the towers of blue-glazed bricks decorated with hundreds of winged lions. Without slowing, they passed through the wall into the royal city. As they did so, Lilah glimpsed rows of guards stationed in front of the two huge leaves of the gate with their bronze carvings.

The cloudy grey light returned as they came out on the other side. The soldiers running by the sides of the chariot and the wagon stopped, and were replaced by four horsemen in long tunics who took up position beside the chariot.

The royal way continued, as straight as ever, lined now with coloured walls – ochre, yellow and blue – surmounted by square, crenellated towers. No one walked here, and there were no signs of everyday life.

Lilah soon lost her bearings. The walls were so high that they even concealed the cliffs of the Citadel.

The procession veered right abruptly, turning from the royal road into a narrower street with lower walls, and Lilah gave a start. The flights of steps and gigantic walls of the Citadel rose before them, barely half a *stadion* away, closer than she had ever seen them.

She pulled her shawl across her chest. She felt a knot in her throat. Her astonishment and curiosity turned to fear. There were more gates, arches and courtyards. At last, they entered a huge garden. From here, Lilah could see the ceramic friezes and the multitude of characters decorating the steps leading up to the Citadel.

To her surprise, their escort turned left, away from the Citadel walls, and they entered a copse of pines, palms and cedars. The east bank of the Shaour appeared between the tree-trunks. The wheels of the vehicles and the hooves of the horses again echoed on flagstones. In front of them rose a huge palace, built on a terrace at a lower level than the river. The windowless outside wall of white bricks stretched as far as the river's east bank. It had only one gate, coloured scarlet, which opened as the party approached, leaving them just enough time to pass before it closed again with a muffled sound.

The horsemen, the chariot and the wagon came to a halt in a long, narrow courtyard, lined with cowsheds and water tanks. Beyond a porch and a metal gate, Lilah made out a series of smaller courtyards, arches, colonnades and patios. Servants approached, all dressed in green and purple striped tunics. Their smooth cheeks and short hair indicated that they were eunuchs.

The third cupbearer got down from his chariot. 'Take her to the cleansing room,' he ordered, without looking at Lilah. 'She needs to be ready as soon as the Queen has finished her meal.'

Lilah could not help recalling the rumours that circulated about Queen Parysatis, stories that, once heard, could not easily be forgotten, of the kind that people whispered to each other, fearing the very words they were speaking.

The Queen was surrounded by a host of servants – handmaids and eunuchs – over whom she held the power of life and death, which she exercised according to whim. Some had to apply her ointments and scents to themselves before she used them, others had to taste her food and drink. She feared poison, although she was an expert in the use of poisonous plants. Sometimes she had a eunuch's tongue cut out if he had accepted a less than perfect dish, or a maid's hands were cut off for not rejecting an ointment the Queen found less than smooth.

Parysatis, it was said, had only two loves: her sons and the power she enjoyed as a queen and the mother of the King of Kings. It was whispered that her pleasures were as refined as they were cruel, her whims infinite, her desires unusual and never sated. The lords of the Apadana would break out in a cold sweat whenever they had to share her meal. Two of the wives of her eldest son, Artaxerxes the Second, had died because they had opposed her. And Lilah had heard Antinoes express surprise that the most powerful generals were more afraid of the Queen's hatred than they were of the massed armies of the Greeks.

And now Parysatis had brought her here from Mordechai's house. A young Jewish woman from the upper town – little more than an insect in the Queen's eyes.

But an insect whom Antinoes, son of Artobasanez, the late satrap of Margiana, wanted to marry . . .

Did Parysatis wish merely to satisfy her curiosity?

The voice of a eunuch drew Lilah out of her reflections. He presented her with a basket of bracelets and necklaces.

'Take these jewels and put them on. You will soon be taken to our queen.'

Rather than obey, Lilah looked out through the wide window. A low sky, swollen with clouds, hung over the plains and hills to the west of the Shaour. It was not easy to tell what time of day it was. Lilah felt as though she had been in the palace for a long time, but that might have been the result of waiting and the long process of washing and dressing to which she had been subjected.

How pointless it had been for Aunt Sarah and Axatria to fuss over her clothes and hair before she left Mordechai's house! Saying little, treating her with neither formality nor familiarity, a number of handmaids and young eunuchs had led her to a small room where her clothes had been removed before she could protest.

The handmaids had pushed her, naked, into a narrow pool, into which the eunuchs had then poured the warm, scented contents of two big jars. To her shame, they had washed her as if she stank like a girl from the lower town. Then they had taken her into an adjoining room, where laurel and eucalyptus leaves burned in braziers. They had dried her, and scented her with a thick, oily golden cream. She had had to wait for her skin to absorb it.

Shocked as she was to be stripped, prodded and smeared in such an unrestrained way, Lilah had soon realized that the handmaids and eunuchs performed their tasks with unmistakable coldness.

She could not even look them in the eyes. Their expressions remained distant and indifferent. As they worked, they spoke no more than was strictly necessary. They seemed to be thinking about nothing and seeing nothing. In their hands, Lilah was not a person, merely a duty to be fulfilled.

At first Lilah was ill at ease and fearful, but she had exploded with anger when they brought her a white linen tunic so thin as to be transparent. It left her right breast and most of her back bare, and ended mid-thigh. Her cheeks scarlet with shame, she had demanded to put on the tunic in which she had arrived. Her fury had raised barely a smile from the handmaids.

'No woman appears before the Queen in her own clothes unless she is the wife of a lord of the Apadana. That is the law. Queen Parysatis has ordered you to wear this tunic, and you must obey. Have no fear. You will be given back your clothes and jewels when it has been decided that you may go home.'

Then they had given her a shawl to cover what her tunic revealed, and had made her wait – for so long that she had had plenty of time to think of the moment when she would be displayed to Parysatis in this shameful attire.

Now the eunuch was pressing her to put on the bracelets of silver and ivory. 'Do not look at the Queen before you bow,' he advised her. 'And do not speak except to answer the questions you will be asked.'

The handmaids led her into a small square courtyard that was like a well. A eunuch in guard's uniform stood at the entrance to each of the several corridors that led off it. Four of the eunuchs came and took up position around Lilah. Together, they plunged back into the vast labyrinth of the palace.

In the dark corridor Lilah had the curious impression that they were walking in a circle. Suddenly she was blinded by the white light of day. A few more steps, and they were on the threshold of a strange room. The high ceiling was supported by thin cedar columns covered with brass, and between the capitals of these columns brightly coloured ropes were stretched. From the ropes there hung, parallel to each other across the room, a dozen immense transparent lilac veils.

Although each veil was very thin, together they obscured the far end of the room from view. They swayed gently in the breeze, iridescent and shimmering in the daylight.

Lilah was aware of the sound of voices, and a few tenuous notes played on a harp. Then there was a bang, and the eunuchs stepped aside to let her pass. One of them took hold of her shawl and, without a word, ordered her to walk towards the veils.

Holding her arms tight across her half-naked chest, Lilah stopped before the first veil, uncertain what to do. With the tip of his spear, the guard lifted it and signalled her to continue.

She had to go through the remaining veils herself. They brushed against her, enveloped her, blinded her. Soon, she no longer knew in which direction she was moving.

Again, she was startled by a bang and stopped, as if she had been caught doing something wrong. At that moment a voice rang out imperiously: 'What is the name of the one who approaches?'

Stunned, Lilah murmured her name, and the voice repeated the question.

'Lilah,' she said again, as loudly as she could. 'Lilah, daughter of Serayah.'

'Come two veils closer.'

She obeyed, looking up at the beams on the ceiling to orient herself. Few veils separated her now from the rest of the room, and she made out a colonnade leading to a garden.

'Why have you come here, Lilah?' the voice asked.

She could not reply. A shiver of fear went down her spine, insidious and clinging. Her hands were shaking. She closed her eyes to regain her composure and not let emotion overcome her. The strangeness of this situation was only there to impress her, to make her imagination run riot, to show her how weak she was. The veils were only veils, not monsters or wild beasts. Lilah rose to her full height and opened her eyes. 'I have been summoned by the Queen,' she declared.

'Come closer.'

Heart pounding, Lilah lifted the veil in front of her. Only two remained ahead. She made out a dais between the columns, with a few figures on it. In the middle a long bed stood beneath a canopy.

The notes of the harp were now distinct. Lilah caught a glimpse of the musician – a woman – beside one of the columns. Armed guards stood at the edges of the room, the grey daylight reflected in their metal breastplates.

'Come closer, girl, come closer,' a woman's voice, different from the one Lilah had previously heard, ordered.

Lilah realized that the Queen had spoken.

Breathless now, she lifted the last veils. Still trying to hide her exposed breast with her free hand, she moved forward a few steps. The floor here was of marble. The cool air from the garden made her shiver. She remembered the eunuch's injunction and bowed briefly, bending one knee. She held her right hand in front of her, palm upwards, and raised it to her lips as she rose.

A deep laugh came from the bed. 'Well, well. Come closer.'

Supported by pillows, Parysatis was half lying on the

bed, which was covered with a green and purple silk rug. She was surprisingly small, her body almost hidden beneath a kind of cape embroidered with gold threads and precious stones. A silver band with strips of coloured silk attached to it held her hair in place. Her face was like that of a prematurely aged child. Her skin, as clear and fine as highly polished ceramic, was furrowed with deep lines on the brow, cheeks and neck. She was smiling, but her large sky-blue eyes, flecked with gold, were fixed and expressionless.

In a clatter of bracelets, her hand appeared, as white as milk. She waved her ringed fingers impatiently. 'Come closer! Let me see you in the light.'

Lilah obeyed. Two very young handmaids were kneeling on the bed, staring at her impassively. Beside it, on a wide stool, the third cupbearer sat, smiling the same ironic, self-satisfied smile he had worn when he had first seen Lilah in Uncle Mordechai's house. Behind him, other handmaids and a few eunuchs, all very young, knelt on the dais, waiting. One of the eunuchs held on his knees the cedar planks whose banging had punctuated Lilah's progress through the veils.

'Come on, show yourself!' Parysatis cried.

Lilah hesitated. She could not be any closer to the Queen's bed. What more did she want?

'Turn her,' the third cupbearer commanded.

The two young handmaids glided to the foot of the bed and each seized one of Lilah's wrists. Holding her arms apart, they began to spin her round like a top.

★　　★　　★

Now Lilah understood why she had been forced to wear this tunic that left her half-naked. The handmaids continued to turn her round. She closed her eyes, as dizzy with shame and anger as with the spinning. She had no need to see the Queen's eyes, or the cupbearer's. It seemed to her as though every inch of her skin was being flayed to satisfy their curiosity.

'Well, Cohapanikes, what do you think?'

'She's beautiful, my queen. A beautiful girl, that much is obvious.'

Parysatis nodded. They watched Lilah as she whirled, the short tunic lifting to reveal her thighs. Then, with a click of her fingers, the Queen ordered the handmaids to let go of Lilah's arms.

Lilah had to make an effort to keep her balance. Mustering all the courage she could, she raised her eyes and looked at the Queen.

The fine network of lines around Parysatis' eyes creased. The blue eyes narrowed, cold and calm, as impassive as the eyes of a snake waiting to strike. 'Beautiful, but full of pride, that's obvious, too,' she observed, without raising her voice.

'You have to admit Antinoes has good taste,' the eunuch said, amused. 'They say also that Jewish women are prudes in lovemaking, but not without skill.'

'Quiet, Cupbearer!' Parysatis cried. 'Keep your tongue for my wine!'

Cohapanikes' smile froze. The notes of the harp vibrated like a threat. For a few moments longer, Parysatis continued to stare at Lilah. Suddenly she pushed back

the cape and reached out her hands. The young handmaids rushed to support her as she got out of bed.

Standing, Parysatis was not much taller than the girls
serving her. Her thin tunic, visible now through the
open cape, revealed a body that was younger and firmer
than Lilah had imagined, which made the marks of age
on her face seem all the stranger. Parysatis became aware
of her surprise and looked at her mockingly. 'You
thought me older than I am, didn't you, girl? Typical of
the young! They see lines on a woman's neck and think
she's old.'

'My queen—'

Parysatis silenced her with a gesture. 'Be quiet. If you
aren't, you'll lie. And you must never lie to me.'

Her face relaxed. She came closer still, lifted her ringed
hand, and touched Lilah's bare arm lightly. Her fingers
were soft and warm. She moved them from Lilah's
shoulder to the back of her neck. Lilah gave a start, and
had to make an effort not to retreat. The Queen's fingers
glided over Lilah's chest, pressing as if she were searching
for the bones beneath the skin. It was not so much a
caress as an inspection. Lilah felt as though she were
being examined like an animal.

'You have beautiful skin,' the Queen said. 'How old
are you?'

'Twenty-one.'

'And you have no children yet?'

'No, my queen.'

Parysatis chuckled, and her mouth opened to reveal
small teeth, many of them as black as coal. She turned to

the third cupbearer, who had joined her and seemed huge beside her.

'Do you hear that, Cohapanikes? Twenty-one! Not much younger than this palace! She should have been married long since. When I was your age, girl, the great Darius sought the gold of his throne between my thighs every night and I had already given birth to the King of Kings who is your master today.'

She gave a high-pitched laugh that shook her chest. In a gesture that seemed surprisingly friendly, she took Lilah's hand. 'Follow me.'

She drew Lilah between the columns. The handmaids, the eunuchs, the cupbearer, the musician and the guards followed at a distance of a few cubits.

'Your father and mother are dead,' Parysatis said.

'Yes, my queen.'

Still holding Lilah's hand, Parysatis descended the steps leading to the garden. Lilah had the impression that she could tell lies from truth merely by the touch of her hand.

'And you have known Antinoes a long time,' the Queen said.

It was not a question. Parysatis was simply demonstrating the strength of her curiosity, as well as her royal power. But there was no longer any room for doubt in Lilah's mind: Antinoes was indeed the reason for this strange encounter . . .

'I've known him since we were children, my queen,' she replied.

Without slowing down, Parysatis chuckled again.

'Since you were children! And you have no child your-self? You're surely not a virgin?'

'My queen . . .' Lilah hesitated, her voice muffled by shame.

Parysatis waved their joined hands brusquely. 'Don't lie, I told you! And don't be a prude! Of course you're not a virgin. Parysatis can tell if a girl is a virgin as soon as she looks at her.'

For a while, they advanced in silence. Lilah made an effort to conceal her fear and her humiliation at being almost naked in front of everyone.

Letting go of Lilah's hand as abruptly as she had seized it, Parysatis turned into a path lined with bamboo. The garden, enclosed by the outer walls of the palace, was extremely dense in the middle, the undergrowth tangled. As they passed, thick clouds of butterflies flew up from the clusters of amaranth and buddleia and whirled above their heads.

Adapting her pace to the Queen's, Lilah wondered what mad questions Parysatis would ask next. Would she get out of this palace alive? What should she answer and not answer? What did the Queen want? Was Antinoes in danger?

The path sloped gently towards the centre of the copse. A strong smell, pungent and feral, came from the undergrowth. It grew stronger and more unpleasant as they advanced. It was a smell such as Lilah had never known, but it did not seem to trouble Parysatis.

The undergrowth thinned, and a clearing appeared. Here, the bamboo trunks were merely a low hedge bordering a pit a dozen cubits deep and with sides as sheer as if they had been cut with an axe. At the bottom, Lilah was surprised to see thick bushes, ponds, stunted trees with torn trunks, and the ground furrowed with well-trodden paths of soft earth.

Not much more than twelve or so feet from the path along which Parysatis was advancing, a platform of logs jutted out. Black carrion birds were sitting on it and as the two women approached, they flew off, screeching, on heavy wings.

'Come closer, Lilah,' Parysatis ordered, without turning. 'Let me introduce you to my friends.'

As if in response to her command, a roar split the air. It was answered by another, then another. Down in the pit, the bushes moved. Lilah glimpsed flashes of fur, and cried out. Simultaneously, two lions with waving manes leaped on to the platform, and stood there, mouths open to reveal shiny yellow fangs. With their huge paws, they stamped on the logs as if they were about to launch themselves into the air. Lilah was unable to hold back another cry, certain they were about to leap at her.

But it did not happen.

One of them tipped back its head and raised its muzzle towards the sky. Its flowing mane spread over its breast like a corolla of fire. It gave another terrible, ear-splitting roar, while the other, whipping its tail, growled and turned in a circle.

Lilah was petrified. Her teeth chattered and her bare skin was covered with gooseflesh. The lion roared again, not as loudly this time – perhaps it was becoming bored.

Its mouth opened threateningly and its ink-black pupils fixed on the newcomers, whose smell excited it, but it lay down. Behind it, with the humility of a lesser male, the other lion followed suit.

For a moment, silence fell. The birds had stopped flying above the copse. Lilah could sense Parysatis' eyes on her, the humiliating smile, the greed and cruelty.

So the rumours were true: Parysatis' greatest pleasure was to have people at her mercy, to observe their fear.

Lilah's pride sustained her: she struggled to dismiss the terror that would have stopped her fleeing a moment earlier. She rose to her full height, held her shoulders back and clenched her jaws, aware of the hate growing in her heart.

'Until now,' Parysatis said, 'my lions have never jumped as far as this path. Have no fear, Lilah. Come closer.'

Lilah lowered her arms and obeyed without hesitation. Behind her, the handmaids, the eunuchs, the third cup-bearer and the guards stood a fair distance away and showed no desire to move any closer unless Parysatis ordered it.

'Forgive me for crying out, my queen,' Lilah said, 'it took me by surprise. I've never seen a lion before. They're beautiful.'

The Queen half closed her eyes and laughed. 'Don't act proud, Lilah. I know you're afraid. Everyone is afraid of Parysatis. Haven't you heard that in the upper town? I'm sure you have. I know people tell tales about me. And they're right to fear me, because it's true: I'm cruel and pitiless. These creatures you see before you are my friends. My only friends. They rid me of anyone I find troublesome. That's what it means to be a queen, the wife of one King of Kings, the mother of another. Even my sons may one day put poison in my bread. But they're the only ones who have nothing to fear from my friends.'

She laughed, walked up to Lilah, and again took one of her hands in what appeared to be a gentle, affectionate gesture, but was in fact quite terrifying: it drew Lilah so close to the bamboo at the edge of the pit that she could feel it rubbing against her bare legs.

'You're beautiful, but that's neither here nor there. My palace is full of beautiful handmaids, and up there, in the Citadel, my son has hundreds of concubines, each more beautiful than the next. Beauty bores me, Lilah. They think I envy it, but they're wrong: it bores me. You have a little courage and a lot of pride. Perhaps some intelligence, too. That's a lot of qualities for a girl. That fool Cohapanikes is right: your Antinoes has made a good choice, which is a point in his favour. It's braver and more difficult for a man to choose an intelligent woman than a beautiful one.'

For a moment, she was lost in thought. Below, the bushes moved. A black panther with a magnificent coat appeared on one of the paths and raised its golden eyes towards her indifferently.

It occurred to Lilah that the Queen had only to move her hand to throw her headlong into the pit. She had no doubt that Parysatis, small as she was, was strong enough to do it.

'You've known Antinoes since you were children, but do you know the man you take between your thighs when he comes back from the wars?'

Lilah shuddered. She had barely heard the question. Down in the pit, more animals had appeared in the bushes. Four impatient she-lions took up position beneath the platform and growled.

'A warrior is like a young lion,' Parysatis continued, without waiting for a reply. 'He kills, he tears the flesh, he thirsts for blood. He rapes, he forgets. He's not meant for a young girl like you. But Antinoes is a good boy. His father was useful to me once. He behaved well. I may be cruel, but I'm not disloyal. Your Antinoes is like his father, honest and upright. There are not many people in this palace you could say that about. He's fought for my son Artaxerxes, but hasn't raised his hand against Cyrus the Younger.' Parysatis grinned. 'Did you know that my friends have rid me of all those who raised their hands against Cyrus the Younger at the battle of Kounaya? What a banquet that was!'

She laughed, and held out her hand, still joined to Lilah's, towards the two lions, which seemed now to be dozing on the platform. 'Look at them! They've eaten their fill!' She laughed again. 'You're Jewish, Lilah. What will you do if the King of Kings names Antinoes satrap of Bactria? Will you follow him to Meshed, Bactria or Kabul? Will your God follow you that far? To a place where you won't have your uncle or your brother with you, or any of your people?'

'I shall follow him,' Lilah replied unhesitatingly. 'Long

ago we made a promise to each other. I shall keep mine as he will keep his.'

Parysatis gave Lilah a sideways glance and let go of her hand. She seemed pleased with herself, as if she had enjoyed a good piece of entertainment.

'I like you, Lilah. You're innocent, but I like you. What I don't like is the thought of your becoming Antinoes' wife. I don't know what I'm going to do with you.'

The Sage of the Lower Town

Through the beaten earth of the kitchen, then rising through his feet into his crippled legs, Sogdiam felt a heavy vibration. He listened carefully, and heard a rumble of a kind that was too rare in the lower town not to attract attention. He went out into the courtyard. A chariot and horses: he was sure of it. Hooves and chariot wheels were making the ground shake. He heard people shouting, children yelling, still quite far away. He saw dust rising above the wall of the house and the surrounding roofs. As incredible as it might seem, someone was venturing into the streets of the lower town with a chariot and horses!

The dust came nearer. He had a premonition that whoever it was would be on their way here, to Ezra's house.

Through the open door of the study, he glimpsed Master Baruch hunched on a stool, flourishing a papyrus scroll in his hands as he talked. On the other stool, staring at the wall in front of him as if it were the most fascinating of landscapes, Ezra was listening. From time to time, he bowed his head. Sogdiam had seen them like this so many times that, for him, it was the most normal, most reassuring sight in the world.

He limped rapidly across the courtyard and opened the gate that led to the street. Some of the neighbours, drawn like him by the noise, were already there.

Sogdiam thought of Lilah. Could it be her chariot? But it wasn't 'her day'.

This might be a special occasion, though.

No, it was impossible! Lilah would never come in a chariot, as special as her visit might be. She would be too embarrassed to flaunt such luxury in a slum like this.

He frowned. If it wasn't Lilah, who was it? A noble of the Citadel? Or guards, soldiers: the kind of people who never brought anything good with them when they came into the lower town.

Suddenly, at the end of the street, men and women stood aside. Some climbed on to the walls, others jumped into the gardens. Two black horses appeared, their coats as shiny as silk, their manes woven with tassels of red wool, drawing a light chariot with iron-clad wheels, its body strengthened by a strip of brass. The handrail at the side was lined with leather sheaths and pouches – room enough for spears, arrows and a long-bladed sword.

The kind of chariot Sogdiam had never seen before. A war chariot!

Too stunned to move aside, Sogdiam stared open-mouthed as the chariot and horses came straight towards

him. The officer who held the reins was wearing a
pointed felt helmet decorated with woven ribbons and
a long cape of blue wool flecked with yellow. Behind
the chariot was an escort of about ten soldiers carrying
spears. Children yelled with excitement.

Nimbly, Sogdiam leaped to the gate to allow the chariot
to pass into the courtyard. But as the horses, nostrils
quivering, passed – so close to him that he could feel their
breath on his cheek – the warrior brought the chariot to
a halt with a mere flick of his wrist on the reins.

The soldiers ran to take their places against the wall of
the house on either side of the gate. The children
stopped yelling. The warrior got down from the chariot.
A plain sheath containing a broad knife with a steel hilt
lay against his thigh. The gold brooches holding his cape
were decorated with the heads of bulls and lions. He was
smiling through his beard – and the smile was for
Sogdiam: the officer was staring straight at him.

Brave and proud though he was, Sogdiam retreated
into the courtyard. The officer followed him through the
gate and held out his hand. Then everyone in the street,
neighbours and children, heard these incredible words:
'Don't be afraid, Sogdiam. I'm your friend.'

Sogdiam blushed and threw an anxious glance towards
the study. Master Baruch and Ezra had noticed nothing.

Leaving the soldiers, the chariot and the crowd of
onlookers in the street, the warrior closed the gate
behind him. He took off his helmet, and his oiled hair
fell to his shoulders. Sogdiam turned hot, then cold. He
knew who the officer was.

The man Ezra hated. The man Lilah loved.

He swayed slightly as anger, envy, vexation and pleasure danced a sarabande in his heart. The warrior frowned, but there was nothing threatening in his expression, quite the contrary. He uttered the words Sogdiam had been waiting for: 'I'm Antinoes and I've come to see Ezra.'

'Ezra is studying,' Sogdiam replied, sounding, he thought, weak and foolish. 'He's with Master Baruch. He can't be disturbed.'

Antinoes looked at him in surprise, then turned towards the study and saw that Sogdiam was telling the truth. He nodded, pulled the end of his cape on to his shoulder, and made as if to walk towards the house. Sogdiam, unafraid, considered barring his way, but his legs refused to move. Antinoes also came to a halt.

By now Ezra had stopped studying, and was staring out at the warrior with his dark eyes. Beside him, Master Baruch was silent. Antinoes raised a hand in greeting. In response, Ezra turned his back. He unrolled a scroll on the table and said something to Master Baruch. The old man nodded, and the two of them resumed their murmuring.

'You see?' Sogdiam said, with all the confidence he could muster. 'They haven't finished. You'll have to leave.'

As if he had not heard, Antinoes continued to gaze into the study. Then, to Sogdiam's surprise, he burst out laughing: a good-humoured laugh, without a trace of irony. 'That's all right. I'll wait. Bring me a cup of water, will you?'

Relieved, Sogdiam hurried to the kitchen. When he came out again, Antinoes was standing in the middle of the courtyard, as if keeping guard on the wall of a citadel. His cape fluttered in the sharp north wind. The stormy light filtering through the low, dark clouds glinted on his knife as well as in his eyes. He showed no impatience, and made a friendly gesture to Sogdiam when the boy handed him the cup.

To Sogdiam, the thought of Lilah snuggling in this man's arms was as painful as a burn. It was one good reason to hate him. Ezra was another. Yet Sogdiam could not help blushing with pleasure when Antinoes gave him back the cup and said in a soft voice, 'Lilah loves you a lot, young Sogdiam. She told me so. She said you were very brave and not at all like other boys.'

Sogdiam bowed his head and wondered how to reply, but had no time to speak: Antinoes was walking towards the study. When he reached the doorway, he bowed politely. 'Forgive me, Master Baruch, if I interrupt your teaching. I have come to talk to my brother Ezra. I haven't seen him for a long time.'

There was a strange silence. Master Baruch looked up at Antinoes, eyes glittering with curiosity: he did not seem the least bit offended. Ezra, though, stood up, pushing back his stool noisily. He walked up to Antinoes, coming so close to him that Sogdiam thought they would either embrace or fight. But his face was cold and his voice made the boy lower his eyes. 'You're

111

disturbing me in my studies, stranger. I don't think that's very polite.'

'Ezra!'

'You come here dressed and armed as if for war, flaunting your gold to the people of this town who are dressed in rags, and you claim that I'm your brother, which is a lie. You can leave the way you came. We have nothing to say to each other.'

Antinoes clutched his cape. Sogdiam sensed the shudder of anger that went through him, yet when he spoke, his voice remained low and calm. 'You know as well as I do how one of Artaxerxes' officers has to move around. He travels by chariot and is always escorted. It doesn't matter if he's in the Citadel or the lower town, for him there's only one law and one kingdom. And you're wrong. I have something to say to you, something you need to hear. I came back to Susa to make Lilah my wife. I'm sure you know that already. But I've come here to ask you, as someone who was once my brother, not to condemn Lilah if she makes that choice.'

There was a silence so heavy that Sogdiam felt it weighing on his shoulders. He was embarrassed that he was still in the courtyard, hearing this conversation, but it was too late, now, to hide in the kitchen.

His face more closed than a blind wall, Ezra hesitated. Sogdiam feared he would throw Antinoes out into the street.

'My sister is free to choose her husband,' he said, his voice as chilly as the north wind.

Antinoes raised an eyebrow. 'You won't oppose her decision, then?' he asked.

Ezra smiled, which did nothing to soften his expression. He turned to Master Baruch, as if calling on him as a witness, but the old man was bent over a papyrus, clearly indicating that he wanted no part in this quarrel.

'My sister is free to make her own decisions,' Ezra said. 'But there are laws for us, the children of Israel and the people of the Covenant. They are not the same as your laws, son of Persia, just as our God is not the same as your gods.'

'What do you mean, Ezra?'

'"Do not give your children to Molek," the Law of Moses commands. "Do not profane the name of your God. A woman who goes with an unclean man is herself unclean." And if a woman is unclean, her brother can no longer go near her. He can no longer be her brother. Lilah will choose.'

'Oh, I understand!' Antinoes laughed bitterly, anger getting the better of him. 'If Lilah becomes my wife, you'll never see her again.'

'It's not my decision. I'm obeying the Law and the Word that Yahweh taught Moses. The Law says that the women of Israel must find husbands among the men of Israel. And you are not of our people. That's all.'

'You have a short memory, Ezra. There was a time when you put your arm round my neck and made me swear we'd never be separated. A time when you said, "Lilah is the heart and the blood that unites us."'

Ezra's mouth half opened. His brow and cheeks had

turned scarlet. Sogdiam saw him clench his fists until the knuckles turned white, and thought he was about to hit Antinoes. Then everything relaxed suddenly. Ezra's chest swelled and he gave a small, harsh laugh. 'Yes, there was a time when I wasn't yet Ezra. But that's over. And you're wrong. I have a long memory, much longer than you could ever imagine. It goes back to the first days of the people of Israel. To the day when Yahweh called to Abraham on the mountain of Harran.'

'You talk about your God, Ezra, but all I hear is your jealousy!' Antinoes retorted. 'You know I've always respected your God. You know that even if Lilah is with me, she will always be with you.'

'I think you should leave now.'

'Ezra!' Antinoes roared, raising his hand. 'Don't force Lilah to choose between us. Don't make her unhappy!'

Ezra did not reply. He turned, went back into the study and closed the door – which Sogdiam had never seen him do before.

Antinoes stood there for a moment. At last he turned, his eyes blank. In the street, the horses were snorting with impatience. The soldiers could be heard scolding the children, and the children laughing in reply.

Antinoes turned abruptly, his face pale. He walked away like a blind man. As he reached Sogdiam, he raised his hand. Sogdiam jumped when Antinoes laid his hot palm on his neck and stroked it lightly. Then, without a word, he left the courtyard, climbed into his chariot and set off at a trot, forcing the soldiers and the children to run.

⋆   ⋆   ⋆

The workshop was fragrant with the fine powder of cedar- and plane wood, juniper and oak. The aroma of peas and roast pork mingled with the smell of almond gum and freshly tanned leather.

To Mordechai, it was like music, a deep, haunting song against which the noise of saws, planes, gimlets, chisels and mallets stood out. The large, well-ventilated workshop, cluttered with shafts, hobbles, benches, towers of ropes and newly mounted wheels, was more than just a pleasant place to work: it was a world in which he was king. A world of infinite possibilities in which every kind of chariot needed in the Susa region could be made – chariots with two or three seats, drawn by mules, horses, sometimes asses and oxen, war chariots and travelling chariots, chariots for royal parades or for everyday transport.

Today, however, perhaps for the first time in his life, Mordechai was unable to savour the pleasure.

He came and went without seeing the workers or the work in progress. He had lost interest in it. He stood at the side of the street, ears pricked, trying to detect the sound of a chariot. Not one of his own, or a customer's, but the chariot of the Queen's third cup-bearer, which had carried Lilah off to Parysatis' palace that very morning.

With a heavy heart, he had been awaiting her return for hours. It was almost dusk, and there was still no sign of her. The keen north wind made the light hazy. It would soon rain. And still Lilah had not returned.

Mordechai knew that on the other side of the courtyard, bustling among her weavers, Sarah was worried
too. She had pestered him for news a hundred times. He
had none. How could he have had any? The hundred
and first time, Mordechai had ordered the door leading
from her workshop to the courtyard to be barred.

But it had brought him no peace.

He continued listening for the rumble of a chariot.
The street was a busy one, and many chariots came and
went. But Mordechai had a sharp ear: he would
recognize the third cupbearer's chariot anywhere. No
other chariot made the same sound, because none was so
heavy or had such big wheels.

Perhaps he was wrong . . . He heard a commotion in
the street, soldiers shouting orders to the crowd to step
aside, the points of spears moving above onlookers'
heads. But the sound this chariot made was different —
too light. He saw two magnificent black half-breed
horses, an officer with a felt helmet standing in the
chariot. A war chariot . . . Despite himself, he looked
behind the escort, hoping to see the little mule-drawn
wagon that had carried Lilah off. There was nothing.

But the Persian officer was driving his horses straight
towards the workshop. Mordechai's heart leaped, and he
let out a cry. 'God of heaven! Antinoes!'

Anxious though he was, Mordechai welcomed Antinoes
warmly. He was proud that the lively, curious boy who,
a few years earlier, had run between his feet in the
workshop and called him Uncle Mordechai, just like

Ezra, was now a Persian warrior. Moved, Antinoes opened his arms wide. Both overcame their embarrassment in an embrace that filled them with nostalgia.

Mordechai laughed. 'I'm not really used to embracing one of Artaxerxes' officers in full dress uniform!'

'Under the uniform, I'm still me!' Antinoes protested, taking off his helmet and cape. 'I haven't changed all that much and I'd still like to call you Uncle Mordechai.'

Mordechai felt tears welling in his eyes. With sheer delight, Antinoes breathed in the smells of the workshop. Here, too, nothing had changed. 'During the last campaign,' he said, passing his hand over the smooth surface of a shaft, 'I saw many beautiful places. You can't imagine how vast and wonderful the world is. But I always missed this workshop.'

Eyes shining with emotion, Mordechai could not resist showing him a few new inventions, from which his latest work had benefited.

Meanwhile, rain had started to fall in great drops on the dusty street. Soon, it was pouring down on the city. Lightning flashes streaked the sky. Mordechai hustled his workers to put the fragile pieces of wood in a safe place. Antinoes parked his chariot inside the workshop. The soldiers in his escort took refuge in a neighbouring inn, where they were served bowls of fermented milk and bread stuffed with lamb's offal and herbs.

In the blink of an eye, the crowd vanished as if by magic, and the street was deserted. Mordechai glanced at it anxiously. 'I hope this rain doesn't last long . . .'

Antinoes looked at him in surprise. Mordechai forced

a smile and drew him to the other side of the workshop.
'I've been forgetting my duty to a guest. Come into the
house and quench your thirst.'

'I ought to say hello to Aunt Sarah first . . . and Lilah,
if that's all right with you.'

'Later,' Mordechai said. 'For now, we have to talk.'

They sat down on long cushions in the dining room.
As the handmaids bustled about them, Mordechai
declared in a sombre tone, 'Lilah is not at home.'

Antinoes put down his cup of palm beer and looked
him straight in the eyes.

Mordechai sighed as if a stone were weighing on his
chest. 'One of the Queen's cupbearers came to fetch
her.'

'Parysatis? Lilah is with Parysatis?'

'Since this morning.'

'May Ahura Mazda protect her!'

'And our God Yahweh! Yes, my boy.'

They were silent for a moment. The rain was still
falling as heavily as ever on the flagstones in the courtyard, filling the air with the smell of wet dust.

'I was hoping she'd be back before nightfall,'
Mordechai resumed, 'but with this rain, the cupbearer
won't want to get wet bringing her back. I'm getting
worried. She's been too long in Parysatis' hands. What if
the rumours about her are true?'

'I should have guessed,' Antinoes said, without
answering Mordechai's agonized question. 'In a few days'
time, I'll receive the arms of Artaxerxes' heroes. I'll be
given a new command. That was what attracted Parysatis'

attention to me, especially as I also deposited the tablets announcing my marriage to Lilah.'

'But what does she want with you? Why summon Lilah?'

'Parysatis likes nothing better than to interfere in the marriages and careers of the officers loyal to her elder son. That way, she can keep an eye on everything our King of Kings does.'

'Lord almighty!'

'It works. She's so powerful now that Artaxerxes himself fears her. They say her lions ate some of our king's favourite generals because they'd fought Cyrus the Younger, sword to sword.'

'But Cyrus led an uprising against Artaxerxes!' Mordechai said indignantly. 'He was marching on Babylon and Susa in an attempt to usurp his brother's place!'

'Cyrus was Parysatis' favourite son. That's all that matters. Artaxerxes didn't even dare oppose his mother. But now Parysatis can't hatch any more plots against him so she has to be content with manipulating the lives of his officers.'

'Do you think—' Mordechai's voice broke, and he passed a hand wearily over his face. Then he asked, more firmly, 'Do you think we need fear for Lilah?'

Antinoes paused for a moment. 'We can fear anything from a mad queen with a lot of power. Perhaps she only wants to see her and persuade her not to marry me. Or perhaps she wants her as a handmaid. Who knows?'

'You have friends in the Citadel. They could—'

Antinoes interrupted him with a gesture. 'Tonight, I'll be refused entry to the White Palace. If I insist, I'll upset Parysatis. But if Lilah isn't back by tomorrow, I'll go to the Queen, whatever the cost.'

'God of heaven!' Mordechai muttered. 'We were so happy that you'd come back and were going to marry Lilah. Now I don't even dare talk to Sarah for fear she'll start moaning!'

The rain had eased, but daylight was fading rapidly. Neither Mordechai nor Antinoes had asked for a lamp. The sky was perfectly suited to their mood.

'And to think I quarrelled with Ezra!' Antinoes suddenly groaned.

'Oh?' Mordechai said, lifting his eyebrows. 'How is the sage of the lower town?'

'I thought it would be a good idea to talk to him about Lilah and me,' Antinoes said. He shrugged his shoulders and looked out again at the wet, shadowy courtyard. He jumped when he thought he heard the rumble of a chariot, but it was only a noise from the workshop.

'Don't say anything, Antinoes,' Mordechai said, exchanging the anxiety that had been tormenting him for his usual anger against Ezra. 'Don't say anything! I can guess what happened. Our sage Ezra treated you as if he didn't know you. He threw back at you a few phrases from those scrolls he reads all day long and told you that you couldn't make Lilah your wife because the Everlasting was against it.'

Antinoes could not help smiling bitterly. 'Yes,' he said. 'He's threatening never to see Lilah again if she marries me.'

Mordechai raised his eyes to the streaming sky. 'Oh, Ezra!' he moaned. 'I loved that boy like a son. You were there, Antinoes, you know I'm not lying. I still love him. He's the finest, most intelligent young man the Everlasting has ever given life to. But I admit it: sometimes Sarah has to hold me back, I get such a strong desire to run to the lower town and teach him a good lesson. May Yahweh forgive me!'

He moaned again, sweeping the air with his powerful arms, and his long face, usually so full of life, seemed to drain of all energy, as if washed by the rain. 'Ezra isn't Parysatis,' he said. 'If we have to celebrate the marriage without Ezra, we'll celebrate it without Ezra. Lilah will have to be content with my approval. Provided—'

He broke off and leaped to his feet. Axatria was crossing the waterlogged courtyard, waving a lamp. The sound of the rain covered her cries until she was near.

'Lilah is back, Master Mordechai! Lilah is back!'

She stopped when she saw Antinoes. She caught her breath, and a radiant smile lit her rain-drenched face. 'She's here, she's fine. The cupbearer brought her back in his gilded chariot. He was soaking wet and shivering, and nowhere near as proud as he was this morning.'

Night had fallen and the lamps had been lit in the long communal room by the time Lilah, in a weary voice, finished telling the story of her encounter with Parysatis.

She sat bolt upright, despite the exhaustion in her face, which was accentuated by the shadows cast by the lamps. But only Antinoes noticed the grave, hard gleam in her eyes.

Overjoyed that she was back, Mordechai and Sarah plied her with questions. Sarah and Axatria wanted to hear again how she had been bathed and scented, and how she had passed through the veils in the reception room, while Mordechai was anxious to understand clearly what the Queen had told her.

Lilah replied calmly, carefully avoiding describing the tunic she had been forced to wear, as well as some of the things Parysatis had said at the edge of the lion pit.

Antinoes watched her in silence, reining in his desire to take her in his arms, caress her and reassure them both as he breathed in her scent. Lilah's composure, the curious assurance she showed after such a day, intimidated him, he had to admit, made her seem slightly strange to him, for the very first time since they had become Antinoes and Lilah.

'So Parysatis didn't forbid anything, didn't demand anything?' he asked at last, concealing his surprise.

'No,' Lilah replied, looking him straight in the eyes, and smiling tenderly at him, with even a touch of amusement. 'The Queen has a high opinion of Antinoes, hero of the King of Kings. She intends to make him a lord of the Citadel.'

'May Ahura Mazda protect me!' Antinoes cried. 'That's an admirer I could do without!'

'Why?' Sarah asked. 'You should be pleased.' She

turned a casket upside-down in front of them. The necklaces and bracelets that Lilah had worn in the palace fell on to the table with a jingling noise. 'Look! Gold, silver, even lapis-lazuli! Would the Queen have offered these jewels to Lilah if she had something bad in mind?'

Antinoes whistled through his teeth. 'Less than a year ago, Parysatis gave the wife of one of her nephews some rings. One for each finger. Then she commanded her eunuchs to cut off the poor woman's hands and feed them, with the rings on, to her lions. She was screaming with pain, so Parysatis made her drink a potion that burned her throat to a cinder. That way, she was able to watch her die slowly, as her blood drained away, without being disturbed by her screams.'

'God of heaven!'

A shiver passed through them all, which had nothing to do with the coolness of the storm. They did not dare look at each other, let alone at Lilah.

Lilah laid a hand on Antinoes' thigh. 'Come now,' she said, with a soft, warm laugh. 'Don't frighten us any more than you have to. We all know what the Queen is like. But she didn't cut anything off me and her lions seemed to have eaten their fill. She was curious to see a young Jewish woman. There's nothing extraordinary about that.'

Antinoes met her eyes and nodded, a trifle hesitantly.

'A young Jewish woman who'll soon be the wife of a great Persian,' Mordechai said. 'In my opinion, we mustn't delay your wedding any longer. Antinoes already went to see Ezra. Too bad for Ezra!'

Lilah stiffened, and her mouth set in a hard line. She took her hand off Antinoes' thigh.

'I thought it was my duty to speak to him,' Antinoes said softly.

'And you can imagine how it turned out.' Mordechai sighed. 'He treated Antinoes like a stranger. The shame of it!'

Antinoes smiled to tone down Mordechai's criticism. 'Ezra is famous in the lower town. The children showed me the way to his house. Everyone was impressed with the chariot and the escort.'

'But of course!' Lilah said coldly. 'A war chariot with an escort, an armed officer! I'm sure it was most impress-ive.'

'Lilah!' Sarah protested.

'It was pointless to set Ezra against you any more than he already is,' Lilah went on, to Antinoes.

'Lilah,' Mordechai cut in impatiently, 'it doesn't really matter what Ezra thinks. You don't need his blessing to marry Antinoes. You have mine, and that's all that matters.'

'Oh, yes!' Lilah said. 'That's all that matters. It's the law, and Ezra can't complain about that.'

'The important thing is to hurry up before the Queen changes her mind. Ezra will come round.'

Neither Lilah nor Antinoes seemed to be listening to Sarah and Mordechai. They were looking at each other. Antinoes would have liked to explain why he had needed to see Ezra, and that he had taken care to avoid an ugly confrontation. But Lilah's face silenced him. Her beauty was unchanged, despite the strain that showed in her taut cheeks and temples, and in her pursed lips. But a curious flame burned in her eyes. It had been there ever since her return from the Queen's palace. An icy flame, calm and intense at the same time, which she had never had before.

Then she closed her eyes. Antinoes had the impression that Lilah was retreating from him. That, too, was a new sensation.

While Mordechai was still speaking, Lilah stood up. Antinoes immediately did likewise, without daring to touch her.

'No, Uncle,' Lilah said calmly. 'I know you're thinking only of my good, but things can't happen like that. Parysatis doesn't really care whether I marry Antinoes or not. Whatever we do she can undo with a word. As for Ezra . . .'

She turned to Antinoes and placed her hand on his chest, as if leaning on him for support. He took her wrist and held it.

'Antinoes has known since the first day we loved each other,' Lilah said, 'that we need Ezra's blessing before we can marry.'

'Lilah!' Sarah cried, standing up.

Mordechai seized Sarah's shoulders and clasped her to him.

'What I'm saying is true, Aunt Sarah. What would our marriage be like if I could never see Ezra again?'

Again there was silence.

Without a word, without even attempting to touch

her, Antinoes walked away from Lilah. A few moments later, he rode off in his chariot. The rain had only just stopped, and the soldiers of the escort, bellies heavy with beer, had to wade through the muddy streets.

It was several more days before everyone breathed more easily. So many significant events had taken place in such a short time that everyday life had faltered.

The wedding of Lilah and Antinoes had not been forgotten, but no one spoke of it. At Mordechai's vigorous urging, Sarah – in an unaccustomed effort – managed to hold her tongue and even to avoid meaningful glances.

Meanwhile, as the autumn sun returned to the transparent sky over Susa, the thought of the Queen was on everyone's mind, as threatening as a cloud of ash. It would wake Mordechai at night, and during the day he would often stop in his work, thinking that he could hear the third cupbearer's chariot.

As for Lilah, she would wake with Parysatis' smile before her eyes. In her dreams, the Queen's ambiguous caresses became reality again. She saw herself standing naked on the platform above the lion pit. And the lions all had the Queen's face, that strange face like an aged child's.

Her anger with Antinoes, for stupidly strutting about the lower town in his warrior's uniform, had faded. She was sorely tempted to run to him and melt in his arms, to find again the peace and trust she had once known. Who else could she tell about the resolution she had made during her humiliating visit to Parysatis?

She resisted the temptation. Deep inside her, a decision was being born, a decision which went beyond love, but which she would eventually share with her beloved just as she had shared the breath of desire.

But it was not yet time.

In any case, Antinoes was quite busy. Every day he had to go to the Citadel. Like all officers of his rank, he had to appear in the great royal courtyard of the Apadana, while the King of Kings was taking his meal, either alone or with a few of his concubines.

Then, if he so wished, Artaxerxes would summon some of his officers to keep him company behind a screen. He would question his generals and heroes about their battles and the customs of the countries they had passed through or conquered.

A quarter of a moon passed in this way. Then finally, one morning, Axatria prepared the basket of provisions to take to the lower town.

When Lilah saw her, she smiled in approval.

It was 'the day of her day', as Sogdiam called it. She was ready to see Ezra and, at last, to say to him the words she had uttered a hundred times in the silence of the night.

Lilah and Axatria each carried one strap of the basket. As usual, the children walked with them, shouting. This time they were close to the house before Sogdiam came to meet them. Eyes bright with annoyance as well as excitement, he explained without pausing for breath that he had known Lilah would come today and that he

127

hadn't forgotten her. 'But just as I was leaving the house, Ezra wanted me to make some herb tea and bake a few little loaves. He and Master Baruch have a visitor. Someone important!' He took hold of the leather strap of the basket, which Lilah was holding in order to take some of the weight off Axatria. 'Someone important, and someone he hasn't quarrelled with,' he added, stealing a glance at Lilah.

'Antinoes should never have come in a chariot.'

'Yes, he should!' Sogdiam protested. 'Everyone was pleased to see such a fine chariot in our streets. It doesn't happen often.' Sogdiam paused for a moment, lost in thought. 'He's handsome, too,' he said, his voice throbbing with admiration. 'And kind, for a Persian. Ezra lost his temper, but Antinoes was calm – as if the enemy were firing arrows at him on a battlefield and every one of them missed.'

Lilah blushed, and looked away.

Axatria had the presence of mind to change the subject. 'What makes you say the visitor is important?' she asked.

'Because he is,' Sogdiam said. 'Ezra and Master Baruch stopped studying as soon as he entered the courtyard, and Master Baruch stood up to greet him. Zachariah, his name is, Zachariah, son of Pareosh. They ordered me to bring him food and drink. It's obvious he's important, Axatria.'

As they crossed the courtyard towards the kitchen, Lilah and Axatria glanced at the study, the door of which was open as usual. Master Baruch, Ezra and the visitor were sitting on stools, conversing animatedly.

Lilah had no idea who the man was, but she immediately identified him as one of those Jews from Susa or Babylon who, unlike her Uncle Mordechai, still dressed in the manner of the old days before the exile. He wore a long tunic with dark blue and grey stripes and a cylindrical hat. His hair was short and thick, and his beard long and sparse, neither trimmed nor shaped in the style the Persians preferred. He seemed taller than Ezra and at least forty years old. His mouth was small, his eyes mobile, his voice insistent. He underlined his words with his chubby hands, as if he were writing them in the air.

Axatria and Lilah were careful to empty the basket quietly in the kitchen. They could hear the voices in the study, but the walls muffled them, so that only the occasional word reached them. Soon Lilah's curiosity got the better of her. She placed a finger on her lips to silence Axatria and Sogdiam, slipped out of the kitchen and slid along the corridor with her shoulder against the wall until she was close to the study door.

'Ezra, what I say, I think,' the stranger was saying. 'Everyone in my family thinks it, too. I have a hundred and fifty sons and nephews. Your letter planted an arrow in our hearts. We knew nothing of the disaster. We were happy with the work Nehemiah was doing in Jerusalem—'

'You were happy because you were here, living a life of luxury!' Master Baruch interrupted him, sarcastically. 'You weren't with Nehemiah. You didn't care what was happening in Jerusalem, where happiness still has no place! You forgot about the wrath of the Everlasting, who chased us from the land of Judaea for being deaf to His word.'

'You're right, Master Baruch. You're only too right!'

'Of course I'm right, Zachariah! The things I reproach in you, I reproach in myself a hundredfold. We are here, under the protection of the King of the Persians, while the Everlasting waits for us there.'

'That is the way things are,' Ezra interrupted, in a firm, calm voice. 'Some of the children of Israel are here, and some are there. In other words, they are nowhere. They have been a people, from father to son, but they are no longer a nation living on the land to which Yahweh led Abraham.'

'So why did Nehemiah fail?' Zachariah cried. 'He left at the will of the King of Kings. He left with gold and soldiers. He left with the hand of Yahweh upon him!'

'Are you so sure?' Ezra asked.

'What do you mean?'

'If Yahweh's hand had been upon him, he would not have failed.' Master Baruch sighed. 'Since when has the will of Yahweh not been done? Do you think, Zachariah, my friend, that the walls of Jerusalem and the Temple would not have been rebuilt if Yahweh had wanted it?'

'That's where the error lies,' Ezra said, in the same even tone. 'Nehemiah went to rebuild the walls, but Yahweh did not support him. Why? Because it is not only the walls of Jerusalem that need to be rebuilt, Zachariah.'

'I know,' Zachariah said. 'The Temple too and—'

'It was hearts and minds that broke down the walls of the Temple,' Ezra asserted. 'It was hearts and minds that allowed Babylon to reduce the land of Judaea to dust. It is hearts and minds that must be rebuilt before we can put the stones back on the walls.'

There was a silence.

'You're right, Ezra,' Zachariah said, in a low voice. 'As the proverb says, "The fathers eat sour grapes and the sons' teeth are set on edge."'

Ezra's laugh was almost a cry. 'No, Zachariah! You're wrong. You and your people and all the exiles who go around moaning about the past. You're letting your ignorance guide you. Have you forgotten Ezekiel's words in Babylon? "All lives belong to Yahweh! The father's life belongs to Him, as does the son's life, for Yahweh is just. He does not condemn the son for the sin of the father. On the contrary, if the son is without sin, He makes him fruitful. He who lives in the Law of Yahweh lives without fear. The blood of the father does not fall on the son, the sin of the father does not flow in the son's veins." That is the justice that Yahweh taught Moses, Zachariah. And the reason that Yahweh has not allowed Jerusalem to rise again is because we are not living according to His decrees. None of us, Zachariah. Not you, me, your people, the exiled Jews, or those living in Jerusalem who claim to be children of Israel.'

Lilah heard what sounded like a moan. The three men

131

remained silent for a long moment. Lilah was about to move away from the wall and show herself at the door when Zachariah spoke again. 'You speak the truth, Ezra,' he said, his voice filled with emotion. That's why my people and I turn to you. That's why I've come to you to say, "Lead us, and we will follow."'

Ezra grunted. 'It isn't to me you should turn, but to the Word of Yahweh. That is what will lead you. You don't need me for that.'

'Oh, yes, we do! No one knows the scrolls of Moses better than you – Master Baruch says so himself. Question us, Ezra! You will hear only stammering. If you explain one thing to me, I understand something else. You must have realized that by now.'

'Do as I do. Do as Master Baruch does. Take the scrolls, read and learn. That's all you can do.'

'How can the ignorant man learn what he doesn't know, if you won't guide his heart and spirit?' Zachariah objected. 'How can he turn to the words of the Almighty if you and Master Baruch don't make their meaning clear through your studies?'

'Zachariah!' Master Baruch chuckled mockingly. 'Your words flatter me, but I don't advise anyone to undertake such a long journey with me as their light. As you can see, I'm nothing now but a lamp without oil.' Then he laughed, and shouted, 'Lilah, my dove, when have you ever feared to disturb us? Stop hiding behind the door and come in.'

★   ★   ★

Lilah's entrance put Ezra and his visitor in an awkward position. Zachariah hardly dared look at her, but Master Baruch greeted her so effusively and with such good humour that it was impossible for them to maintain their serious tone.

Zachariah soon left. They promised him that he would be welcome as often as he liked.

After the outer gate had closed behind him, Master Baruch gave a half severe, half mocking sigh. 'You heard for yourself, my dove, that Zachariah has a bad conscience. It's clear he doesn't know much, and it's also clear that he'd be more useful in Jerusalem than stuck here moaning. There are dozens like him, and they all admire your brother. But although admiration may be sweet to the ears, it doesn't lead to knowledge, let alone to courage.'

Lilah turned to Ezra, certain he was going to reply. But he said nothing, merely looked at her. Perhaps he had not even heard Master Baruch's provocative remarks. She knew that look so well that there was no need for words. She read fear in his eyes, questions . . . and expectation. 'Are you going to talk to me about Antinoes?' the eyes whispered. 'Have you come here, my beloved sister, to tell me what I don't wish to hear?'

With a loud sigh, Master Baruch sat down on the bed.

Lilah smiled. 'Why mock their admiration, Master Baruch?' she said softly. 'Perhaps it's merely the truth.'

'What do you mean?' Ezra asked, with a frown.

'That it's time for you to be what everyone expects you to be.'

Ezra smiled disdainfully. 'Oh, people expect something of me, do they? I only care about what Yahweh expects of me. And I answer Him by staying here and completing my studies, reading His Word until it's as natural to me as breathing.'

'Do you think that's always the right answer?'

'Lilah! Are you trying to teach me wisdom?'

Master Baruch had half sat up, and was moving his hands above his snowy white beard. 'Let her speak, my boy, let her speak!'

'Zachariah says to you, "We need you. Explain it all to us. Lead us." Why refuse?'

Ezra laughed nervously. 'And where should I lead them?'

'To Jerusalem.'

Ezra leaped to his feet. 'You're mad!'

'Do you think so? Do wisdom and courage mean anything if we don't continue the work Nehemiah began? As Master Baruch says, "What's the point of moaning if it doesn't lead to action?"'

Ezra glanced at Master Baruch. The old man had stopped laughing. His eyes were bright and alert, although his breathing was almost inaudible. Sogdiam and Axatria appeared in the doorway, carrying platters. Ezra did not take the slightest notice of them. 'As I told Zachariah, the reason Nehemiah failed is because Yahweh judged it wasn't yet time to rebuild Jerusalem.'

'An easy excuse for someone who lacks the courage to confront his destiny.'

Ezra blushed to the roots of his hair. Lilah went to him

and seized his hands. She felt a tremor go through his body. 'Didn't Moses, Aaron and all the people of Israel discover that the hand of God was upon them when they confronted Pharaoh?' she asked softly. 'Isn't that what you taught me, Ezra?'

Master Baruch chuckled. 'That's good, my girl, that's good!'

'Moses often asked Yahweh, "Why me?"' Ezra said harshly.

'And the Everlasting replied, "Because I have decided it,"' Master Baruch flung back at him.

Ezra shook his head and took away his hands from Lilah's. The blush remained on his cheeks, but now his black eyes shone not with anger but with another emotion. 'Come on,' he said, after a moment's reflection, 'you're forgetting that Nehemiah was able to leave Susa and lead the exiles to Judaea because the King of Kings had decided it was in his own interest for him to do so.'

'Yahweh planted a sensible policy in Cyrus the Great's mind,' Master Baruch said.

'Yes, Master. But I don't hear anything like that coming from the Citadel now.'

'What if it did come?' Lilah said. 'What if Artaxerxes summoned you and said, "Go, Ezra. Lead your people to Jerusalem. Rebuild the walls of your Temple."'

'Lilah, you're mad.'

'Answer me, Ezra. If he asked, would you accept?'

Ezra stared at her.

Master Baruch's eyes were two slits, the pupils barely visible. His beard shook.

Ezra began to laugh, a sharp, nervous laugh. 'Come on, Lilah! You know it's not possible. Look at me. Look at this room – look at our surroundings! Why would the King of Kings spare me so much as a glance?'

'Because Yahweh wants it.'

Ezra's face clouded, and he raised his hand. 'Lilah, don't talk like that. It's not—'

'Let her have her say, my boy,' Master Baruch interrupted, without smiling.

'I've been thinking about it for days now, Ezra. And now I know I'm right. I know it as Zachariah and all the people who call you "the sage of the lower town" know it. Do you think they admire you because you spend your days poring over papyrus scrolls? Or because you've become as wise as, if not wiser than, Master Baruch?'

She glanced at the old man, who encouraged her with a nod.

'No. What they admire, Ezra, is the stubbornness that made you come here and stay here. And we need that stubbornness in order to hope, to stop being a people scattered like crumbs in the dust of Artaxerxes' kingdoms.'

Axatria and Sogdiam were listening in the doorway. Ezra made a move to chase them away, then changed his mind. He smiled, and stroked Lilah's cheek. 'I love your words, my sister. They prove your affection for me. But what you're saying is false. The exiles don't expect anything like that. If they did, they would have crossed the desert with Nehemiah, and Yahweh would have stretched His hand over them. No, they're perfectly happy here, just like our uncle Mordechai, I can assure you.'

'Because no one has stood up and shown them where their duty lies,' Lilah insisted. 'Because no one has taken the first step into the desert. Because no one has gone to the King of Kings and said, "Let me go to Jerusalem and rebuild the Temple of the God of heaven."'

Ezra laughed. He clasped Lilah to him joyfully. Axatria, Sogdiam and Master Baruch had not seen him so happy for a long time.

'Lilah! We aren't children any more. We're too old to play with dreams. But when you say such things, I realize how much you love me—'

'No, Ezra!' Lilah pushed him away with a gesture as firm as her voice. 'Don't treat me like a child. I'm not blinded by my love for you. I know who you are. Now it's up to you to find out how much your words and your courage are really worth.'

Ezra's joy had already vanished. Now he looked helpless and confused. 'I have no desire to be what you describe,' he breathed. 'I'm studying with Master Baruch. My studies can't be interrupted, even to rebuild the walls of Jerusalem.'

'Ah, now he's saying what I said to Nehemiah!' Master Baruch cried in a shrill voice. 'Oh, yes, that's precisely the kind of stupid remark I expected of you, my boy.'

'But isn't it what you taught me?'

'Oh, yes, I said it, I said it!' Master Baruch's small, frail body shook with laughter. He winked at Lilah. 'And now I say this. Studying has no end, but the master of studies does.'

There was a strange silence.

Lilah walked to the door and out into the courtyard.

'Lilah, you cannot say what the will of God is!' Ezra cried behind her. 'That would be blasphemy.'

Lilah turned and nodded, smiling. 'That isn't my intention. But if Artaxerxes commands you to appear before him, remember how Moses urged Aaron to appear before Pharaoh.'

For a long time, as the chariot took them back to the upper town, they were silent, lost in thought. But at last Axatria spoke. 'Once again you saw Ezra and you didn't mention your marriage. Your uncle and aunt will be worried.'

'Ezra knows everything he needs to know about my marriage,' Lilah replied.

'But he still doesn't want it.'

'That doesn't matter.'

Axatria opened her eyes wide in surprise. 'Don't you want to get married any more?'

'Did I say that? I made a promise. I will marry, Axatria. Afterwards.'

'Afterwards?'

Lilah did not reply.

Axatria was silent for the length of one street, her eyes fixed on the head of the young slave driving their chariot. 'Do you really believe what you told Ezra?' she said at last. 'That the King of Kings will summon him to the palace?'

'Yes.'

'But Ezra's right – it's impossible! How could the King of Kings know who he is and that he—' She broke off, and looked intently at Lilah. 'Oh!' she gasped. 'Parysatis didn't send for you just to give you a few jewels, did she?'

Lilah smiled, but said nothing.

The Promise

The bath-house was long and narrow. The walls and ceiling formed a vault of glazed bricks, decorated with sea monsters, men who were half fish and birds that no man had ever seen with his eyes. Wreaths of fragrant vapour muffled the lapping of the water, the whispers and laughter.

The eunuchs had led Antinoes up to a canvas screen at one end, which blocked the view of the long pool that filled almost the entire space. Servants were boiling eucalyptus, benzoin oil and amber resin, which they then poured into the water. The air was so heavy and fragrant that it was a while before Antinoes could breathe freely.

His baldric had been removed, as had his weapons and even his sandals: potential assassins had been known to hide their blades in them. He sat down on a low bed, and a swarm of handmaids brought him brass trays laden with brightly coloured drinks and little cakes powdered with almond and dripping with cardamom-scented honey.

He was already starting to sweat. He had prepared himself to be patient, and had determined that he would not let fear undermine him. Yet when the voice rose from behind the screen, he jumped as if swords had suddenly been unsheathed around him.

'Antinoes! Handsome Antinoes! Discreet Antinoes! It seems the only way I could persuade you to greet me was to send for you, even though you've been back in Susa for many days.'

'My queen . . .' Antinoes stammered, unsettled as much by the ironic sensuality in Parysatis' voice as by the reproach itself. 'My queen,' he went on, trying to make his voice sound firmer, 'how could I have dared to appear before you without your summons?'

There was a raucous laugh on the other side of the screen. 'How indeed? How could you have dared?' Parysatis laughed again. Antinoes relaxed: it had been the right answer.

He heard the sounds of water, but no more words for a long time. Antinoes did not dare to eat or drink. The bed where they had put him was soft and welcoming, but he sat upright and stiff, as motionless as the eunuchs and handmaids around him.

'It would seem you are not lacking in courage, young Antinoes,' Parysatis said suddenly. 'Our King of Kings has set his eyes on you and I had to do likewise.' Her voice came from further away now, and echoed against the vault. 'Karkemish, Gordion, Sardis, Arbeles and

Opis . . . Can you hear how much I love you? I know the names of all your battles by heart. Does this Jewish woman of yours, this Lilah, know as much as I?'

At Lilah's name, Antinoes felt the bite of fear. Even during the battles Parysatis had mentioned, he had rarely felt it with such intensity.

'Well, Antinoes?' Parysatis said impatiently. 'Must I wait for your answer?'

'No, my queen. I was simply thinking that you are right. Lilah does not know the names of my battles.'

'Modest Antinoes!' Parysatis chuckled.

Again there were sounds of water, and women's laughter. Antinoes heard the Queen giving orders, demanding clothes and drink. Her voice came closer. He could hear the rustling of cloth. She must be standing quite close to him behind the screen.

'So you want to marry her?'

'Yes, my queen.'

'She tells me you made her a promise.'

'Yes, my queen. We were children, but we haven't changed.'

'How can that be? You, the son of my beloved Artobasanez! Your father let you run around with that Jewish girl?'

'He loved her like a daughter, and I like a sister.'

Parysatis laughed. 'Don't lie, soldier. You don't love her like a sister. Is it true that Jewish women are quite inventive when they make love? That's what I've heard.'

'I don't know, my queen. I've never known any other woman.'

'Oh, Antinoes!' Her laughter echoed. 'Antinoes! No Greek woman, no Assyrian woman, not even a girl from the mountains?'

Antinoes sensed that the eunuchs who were watching him were smiling. He did not move a muscle of his face, sure that whatever expression it showed – whether of fear, composure or anger – would be reported to Parysatis and would be circulating throughout the Citadel by evening.

'No, my queen,' he admitted.

'So,' Parysatis whispered, 'you love her.'

Antinoes heard a sound like the cooing of a pigeon, then realized that Parysatis was laughing again.

'A hero of the King of Kings in love with a Jewish woman! That's a rare occurrence in these parts! But you're not a child any more, Antinoes. Childhood promises are doomed to die with childhood.'

There was nothing he could say to that, so he said nothing.

'It's true, then,' Parysatis said, amused. 'You *are* brave. You don't dare say, "Yes, my queen."'

Again, he said nothing.

'Do you know that if you marry this Jewish woman, you'll become the son of a chariot-maker?'

'Yes, my queen.'

'Come now, don't be stupid! Don't answer, "Yes, my queen." Say, "No, my queen, it's impossible. I, a future satrap, cannot marry a Jewish woman." If you can't live without her, make her your concubine. A hero of the King of Kings, a future satrap, can have as many concubines as he wishes.'

'My queen, you speak the truth. I love Lilah. She is my lover, and the woman I have promised to marry.'

'Oh, how foolish you are.' There was no laughter in Parysatis' voice now: it was cold and hard.

Proud as he was, Antinoes could not stop his breathing becoming faster and more irregular. He could not stop sweat pouring down his brow – and not only because of the stifling air.

'What have you to say to me, Antinoes?'

He closed his eyes. 'My queen, I obey my king in everything. I have deposited the tablet announcing my marriage, as an officer must.'

On the other side of the screen, there was a long silence. Then a loud handclap. The eunuchs rushed forward and, in the twinkling of an eye, moved aside one of the canvas panels.

Stunned, Antinoes now saw the pool of warm, transparent water, in which half a dozen young girls were swimming. And close to him, on a bed, a pale-faced eunuch massaging Parysatis' small, oiled body.

She was lying on her stomach, naked, her eyes closed. Pressed against the bed, her face seemed more strangely crumpled and aged than ever. Antinoes bowed low and remained in that position.

'Not many people, Antinoes,' Parysatis said caressingly, 'have seen Parysatis in her bath and lived to tell the tale. Stand up and let me look at you.'

He did as he was told, pressing his hands to his thighs to stop them shaking. Parysatis opened her eyes and looked closely at the young warrior's face, while the eunuch continued his massage. Then, with a sudden gesture, she pushed him away and sat up, revealing her youthful breasts.

She clapped her hands. The girls hastened out of the pool and lined up next to her. The oldest was not yet fifteen, while some were still children. Their smiles concealed neither their embarrassment nor their fear.

'Parysatis' nieces,' the Queen said, her mouth smiling but her eyes still icy. 'You may choose. Antinoes – Parysatis' nephew. I'd like that.'

Antinoes said nothing. Parysatis grunted and clicked her fingers at the girls, who quickly got back in the pool.

'Since when have warriors talked about love, O hero of the King of Kings? You'll be the laughing-stock of the Apadana if this gets out.'

She stood up and ordered her handmaids to rub her body with scented oils. Antinoes lowered his eyes.

'You're a child, Antinoes. You have no idea what's serious and what isn't. Fortunately, this Jewish girl of yours has more brains than you do. She knows what it means to be sensible.'

The girls were laughing and splashing each other now. Parysatis frowned angrily and screamed to them to get out. Her command echoed against the vault of the bath-house. The armed eunuchs ran alongside the pool, driving back the Queen's nieces with the tips of their spears. With squeals of terror, the girls disappeared into a narrow tunnel at the other end of the room.

'I could feed your Lilah to my lions,' Parysatis said in a low voice, when calm had been restored. 'Then you would be released from your promise. But something strange has happened, Antinoes. I've started to like this Jewish girl. She pleases me. And she's sensible enough not to have any desire to keep her promise.'

Parysatis' cooing laughter mingled with the thick steam of the pool. She pushed away her handmaids, walked up to Antinoes, took hold of his chain and raised his head. 'Don't you want to know why?'

Antinoes held the Queen's gaze and said nothing.

'Place your lips on mine, hero of the King of Kings,' she ordered, 'that I may know what your Jewish girl tastes.'

Carefully, Sarah opened the door of Lilah's bedchamber. Axatria, who was changing the linen, jumped. 'You startled me, Mistress.'

'Isn't Lilah here?'

Axatria's face lit up. 'She ran to Antinoes' house,' she said, in a low, conspiratorial tone. 'She couldn't contain her impatience. They haven't seen each other for four days. She has many things to tell him.'

Excited, Sarah closed the door of the chamber behind her. 'Is that it? Has she spoken to Ezra?'

Axatria stuffed the dirty linen into a basket, and shook her head. 'She spoke to him, yes, but not in the way you think.'

'Don't be so mysterious!' Sarah said in annoyance. 'Tell me.'

'Lilah says Ezra must go to Jerusalem.'

'To Jerusalem?'

'Yes, with men from Susa and Babylon, to finish the work of the sage Nehemiah. She says he's the only one who can do it.'

'What are you talking about, girl?'

Axatria had to tell her the whole story: Lilah's visit to the lower town, the encounter with the man named Zachariah and, word for word, or as near as made no difference, what Lilah had said to Ezra.

Sarah had to sit on the bed to listen to the end without fainting. When Axatria finished, she remained still.

Axatria had no intention of allowing anything to spoil her joy. 'I always knew Ezra would become a great man,' she said proudly. 'Lilah says the God of heaven will convince the King to send Ezra to Jerusalem. She knows it. And I believe her.'

Sarah looked at Axatria sadly. But then words broke through the wave of desolation that had submerged her. 'You aren't even Jewish,' she said, with a sharp laugh, 'but you're going to teach me what Ezra is worth and what the Everlasting expects of him?' And with that she left the bedchamber.

When night fell, Mordechai sent for Axatria. She had been weeping, and her red-rimmed eyes showed that she was ready to pick a quarrel. But Mordechai was gentle with her, and she repeated what she had told Sarah.

He listened carefully. Now he, too, fell silent, puzzled by what he had heard. 'Are you sure of what you're saying?' he asked at last. 'Lilah said that, in spite of everything, she was going to marry Antinoes?'

With a sigh of exasperation, Axatria repeated Lilah's

words. '"I shall marry him, Axatria. I promise." That's what she said.'

'Lilah's mad. We're worried sick about her marriage, and all she can do is proclaim Ezra the saviour of Jerusalem.'

'If she says Ezra can do it, she's right!' Axatria protested, her voice trembling with resentment. 'She knows it better than you do.'

Mordechai raised his hand to demand silence. He was smiling. 'Our Lilah has more than one trick up her sleeve. She's thought this out carefully. When he's in Jerusalem, Ezra won't be too bothered about who she marries.'

Axatria and Sarah looked at each other pensively.

Sarah was not very convinced, but she nodded. 'May the Everlasting hear you,' she sighed.

Antinoes' mouth was sweet and warm. Lilah abandoned herself to it. As his hands swept her up in his caresses, the anxieties of the last few days fell away from her, like scales.

With kisses, she led him on the waves of desire. They breathed as one, although he was impatient while she lingered between their embraces, stretching the time as if it should never end.

At last they rolled apart, and lay side by side, catching their breath, hair tangled, hips still touching, lips bruised, hands incapable of ceasing their caresses.

Antinoes' bedchamber was heated by braziers, and lit by a single oil lamp. Lilah listened to the rain hammering on the leaves in the garden. She heard a door slam and, in the distance, fragments of conversation, a hand-maid's voice. She was not accustomed to the sounds of Antinoes' house.

'The other day, at your uncle's house,' he murmured, 'you didn't tell the truth. Parysatis is refusing to let us marry.'

A shudder went through Lilah, as if the cold air from outside had entered the room. It was over: the truth was out, as clear as daylight. She closed her eyes, as if that could protect her for a few moments more.

'She sent for me this morning,' Antinoes said. 'I was in her bath-house.' He could see Parysatis' mocking face behind his closed eyelids.

Lilah turned on to her side, kissed his lips, then placed her fingers over them. 'No,' she whispered, 'I didn't tell the truth. But how could I tell you? I still felt too ashamed. The way she looked at me! And not only that – she touched me too. I was wearing a tunic that left me almost naked before her. I had to listen to her telling me who I could and couldn't love. I was afraid of the lions, but there was at least a moment when I thought it would be better to be eaten by them than humiliated by Parysatis.'

Lilah stopped and smiled. Antinoes tried to speak, but again she pressed a finger on his lips to silence him.

'Then the idea came to me.' She sat up, leaning against Antinoes' hip. She stroked the back of his neck, his powerful shoulder muscles. She was still smiling, but without joy.

'There I was, before Parysatis. "What am I going to do with you?" she said. "What can I do with a Jewish girl?" She threatened me. "I could do anything I like with you. Make you my handmaid. Feed you to the lions. I could make you my slave. That's something we don't have in this palace: a beautiful Jewish girl who's a slave to our every whim. I could give you to my monkeys if I felt like it. There's only one person I wouldn't give you to, and that's the man you chose – that Antinoes you like so much."'

Lilah was still trying to smile through her tears. Antinoes held her close to stop her shaking. But she continued speaking, forcing out the words as if extracting them from stony ground.

'It wasn't only cruel. It was unjust. I wasn't listening to her. We can't listen to such things. Hatred closes our ears. We become deaf. What is this kingdom where a mad queen has the power of life and death? I thought. She soils the air we breathe. She soils the very thing that makes us man and woman. She besmirches the love between husband and wife. What is more unjust than the power of the strong when it's unchecked?'

She shivered, and clenched her teeth. Antinoes sat up, drew her to him and laid his head between her breasts. Through the beating of her heart, he heard the words throbbing in her chest.

Lilah took a deep breath and went on: 'It was then that I thought of Ezra. Not precisely of him, but of what he's been saying since he started living in the lower town: that the Everlasting has given us a Law so that His

151

people can live without oppression, so that the sons and daughters of Israel can hold their heads high and not have to submit to the insults and whims of the kings of Babylon and the pharaohs with their false gods. But we have stopped following Yahweh's decrees. We have broken our vow, broken the Covenant that protected us from the powerful and their idols. Because of that, we no longer have Yahweh's hand over us but Parysatis' hand.'

She stopped, almost breathless, and dug her nails into Antinoes' skin.

'Parysatis is mad,' he said softly, 'but she's the only one. The Jews are respected in Artaxerxes' kingdoms. You live among us like any other people. I'm a Persian and you're in my arms.'

She kissed him and caressed him. No, her words were not directed against him. There was no greater love than theirs. But he had to understand.

'Antinoes, Parysatis' power has no limits. It will corrupt everything. You saw her today – don't tell me, I don't want to hear it. I can imagine, and what I can't imagine I sensed earlier in the taste of your first kiss. You, the son of a lord of Susa, who tomorrow will be one of those before whom the peoples of Persia and all Artaxerxes' kingdoms will bow down, were humiliated by her just as I was. I know.'

Antinoes did not contradict her.

'As I was saying, the idea came to me,' Lilah went on. 'Ezra must go to Jerusalem while there is still time. He must complete Nehemiah's work, and give us back a land where no one will humiliate us. He must accomplish what he was born for. And we must help him. Nehemiah left with the support of Artaxerxes the First. Ezra must leave with the support of Artaxerxes the Second.'

'How?'

It was late, but they were still talking.

The clouds scurried beneath the moon. The rain had ceased, but a cold, strong wind had risen and was whistling between the wooden shutters. Antinoes had covered himself and Lilah with a huge bearskin from the Zagros mountains. They were whispering in the shadows as they had so often whispered during their childhood. But their words were no longer childish words.

'You think Ezra hates you,' Lilah was saying. 'He doesn't, he only hates the life we lead here while Yahweh is waiting for us over there. You alone can teach the cupbearers and eunuchs of the King's table Ezra's true worth, and that thousands will follow him when he sets off for Jerusalem.'

'It will be many days before the King lends an ear to my request,' Antinoes replied.

'What does that matter? We can wait.'

'Do you think Parysatis will wait?'

At that they fell silent, for those words were like ice in their bellies, and they did not yet dare to confront them.

To dismiss them, Antinoes resumed, in a lighter tone, like a true warrior and a hero of the King of Kings, 'Artaxerxes might be interested in the idea of bringing order to Jerusalem, rebuilding its walls and making it a fortified town. Jerusalem is the weakest point on our western borders. They say Pharaoh has his eyes on it. If Jerusalem fell to the Egyptians, the Greeks would rejoice. It would give them the coast and the ports of Tyre and Sidon. From there they could trade, and also send armies towards the Euphrates. Yes . . . I'm sure that's how I need to present things. Some of the generals will be happy to hear it. Tribazes will listen to me, I'm sure. And he'll be better able to persuade the King than I would.'

Lilah smiled in the shadows, searched for the warmth of her lover's body so that she could melt into it and inspire him with her strength.

But then Antinoes murmured, 'Parysatis wants me to marry one of her nieces. She won't budge, I know.' He hesitated. 'She claims you've already agreed to break our promise.'

Lilah gave a dry, contemptuous laugh. 'Parysatis knows nothing about real life. She knows only her own desires.'

'She'll kill you if you don't obey. She'll humiliate you more than she already has, then kill you in the cruellest way she can find.'

'Will she kill you, too?'

'Without hesitation. And no one in the Apadana will protest. Not even Tribazes, who wishes me nothing but good. Parysatis hates him more than the others, if that's possible, because he led the army that defeated Cyrus the Younger. Parysatis' hatred is stronger than Artaxerxes' trust. But I don't think she'll touch me. There'd be no point. She'll kill you and say, "Now, Antinoes, you no longer have a promise to keep."'

They listened to the wind. The red glow of the braziers danced on the walls.

'We no longer have a promise,' Antinoes whispered. 'We'll never be man and wife.'

Lilah rolled over and wrapped herself round him. She kissed his neck, chin and temples. She made him tremble with desire again, drew him out of the shadows where he left his thoughts and pride. She made their young bodies dance, skin to skin, as free and untroubled as they had ever been. And when he was again inside her, she whispered, 'I have only one word, my beloved. And I shall keep it. We will be man and wife.'

'Lilah!' Antinoes breathed, trying to restrain the surge of his hips.

'Who will know it? If you're brave enough, who will know it? Not even Ezra!'

Master Baruch's Smile

With Lilah's help, Antinoes wrote a tablet in his fine handwriting, asking for an audience with the King of Kings. Ezra's name was mentioned, as well as the reason for the request. The tablet spoke of Artaxerxes the First, Nehemiah, and peace and order on the western borders of the kingdoms, which were still threatened by the Egyptians and the mercenaries of the Upper Sea.

Antinoes, unfortunately, had spoken the truth. It would take a long time before the tablet, addressed to Tribazes, the head of the armies, was passed to the scribes of the Apadana. There, as custom demanded, it would have to be copied in duplicate, according to the rules of the Citadel, in the Persian language as well as that of ancient Assyria.

Then the tablets would be handed over to the cup-bearers of the Council of a Thousand, which, when it had time among all its many tasks, would judge their contents together with the chiliarch, the great lord

Tithraustes. The chiliarch himself would then take time for wise reflection, after which he would pass his judgement to the counsellors of the King's table. Under their supervision, a new, more appropriate request would be written on the huge royal scroll, without beginning or end, known as the Book of Days.

Finally, Artaxerxes the Second, King of Kings, would make his appearance to deal with the affairs of his kingdoms. The scribe of the Book of Days would read the request, Tithraustes would give his opinion, and the King would decide what should be written in response to the petition of Ezra, son of Serayah, an exiled son of Israel living in the lower town of Susa.

At this pace, the first snow had fallen before the King's answer had arrived, and everyone was on edge. More than anything, Antinoes feared Parysatis' spies. Realizing that their embraces were no longer enough to cheer them, Lilah decided it would be more sensible if they stayed away from each other until they knew the King's decision. Antinoes would also avoid Mordechai's house.

'It seems Parysatis has already succeeded in separating us,' Antinoes sighed as they said goodbye.

'Never!' Lilah said, kissing his lips one last time. 'She'll never separate us. Besides, you're nearer to me now than when you go off to war . . .'

Days passed, and still there was no news.

Ezra, whose resolve had been weakened for a time by Lilah's conviction, and to an extent by Master Baruch's words, was the first to mock. 'So, the Everlasting doesn't seem to be taking any notice of my sister's opinions,' he said sarcastically, as Lilah and Axatria came in, bearing their basket of fruit and barley. 'Artaxerxes hasn't sent for me. He has his god Ahura Mazda who, supposedly, supports him in everything. Why should he care about the Jews, or Jerusalem, or the Law of Moses? I was right not to listen to your daydreams, Sister. My studies with Master Baruch are sure to bring me closer to the will of Yahweh than your imagination.'

'You're not very patient,' Lilah replied, dismissing his jibes. 'Not very patient, not very trusting, and not very provident. You should be taking advantage of this time to gather those who will go with you. You should be telling people about your hopes for Jerusalem.'

'My hopes for Jerusalem?' He shook with laughter. 'Lilah, those who wish to go with me may sit in this courtyard for as long as they like, provided they respect my studies. Then their journey, like mine, will lead them to the Word of Yahweh and the Scriptures of Moses.'

Lilah had expected Master Baruch to support her, but the old man refused to intervene on one side or the other. He seemed to huddle behind his beard, overcome by age and fatigue, unable now to surprise or infuriate others with well-chosen words.

But when Lilah bent down to bid him goodbye, he took her face between his soft old palms and gave a big smile that made his eyes sparkle as if he were laughing. He said nothing, but held Lilah's face, as if he were freeing it from the weight of the earth.

She realized that he was encouraging her, and her anxieties slipped away.

When she next saw Ezra, he mocked her again, so harshly that she thought she detected a touch of jealousy. She decided not to go back to the lower town until she could take the King of Kings' answer with her.

Axatria was horrified. 'What if it doesn't come? What if there is no answer? What if—'

'There's no "what if", Axatria. There'll be an answer, and it'll be the one we're expecting. Ezra will appear before Artaxerxes.'

Axatria looked at her as if she had lost her reason.

The month of Tevet arrived and cold struck the Susa region. For three days, the sky was hazy with snow. Big flakes covered Mordechai's house, wrapping it in silence. Lilah seemed as cold and white as the snow, as if the wait were draining her of blood.

Slowly and silently dawn was breaking. The weavers and Mordechai's men were not yet at work. Lilah gazed out at the daylight, as she did each morning, trying to summon the strength to keep her impatience in check. Sarah's voice made her jump more than the hand on the back of her neck.

Before she could speak, her aunt hugged her. 'I had to be close to you for a moment. I've thought it over. You're right about Ezra – I told Mordechai: Lilah's right. I don't know if it'll happen, if the King will give him an audience and he'll set off for Jerusalem. We'll see. But you're right. Ezra is Ezra. Yahweh's hand is upon him. It's been obvious for a long time.'

They embraced with a laugh that sounded more like a moan.

'You aren't getting much sleep,' Sarah said gently, stroking her niece's cheek.

'No one has been getting much sleep lately,' Lilah replied. 'Neither you nor Uncle Mordechai. Oh, my poor aunt, Ezra and I have given you more worry than pleasure.'

Sarah held her a little tighter. 'Dreams, that's what you've given me, Lilah – dreams. And I haven't always been very clever.' She laughed again. This time, it was like a sob. 'Sarah – that's the right name for me. Sarah of the barren womb. Just like Abraham's Sarah. Except that the angels of the Everlasting won't be paying me a visit when I'm really old . . .'

'Aunt!'

Sarah placed her fingers on Lilah's mouth to silence her. Her eyes were shining feverishly, and her low voice was made hoarse by the harshness of the words that came from her lips. 'You can't imagine the shame! The shame of not having given Mordechai a child. The shame of being so happy when you and Ezra arrived in this house. It was terrible. Your father and mother had just died and because of that I was finally able to live like a woman. Children in my house! Oh, you can't imagine! Mordechai was transformed, too. I became a real mother – in my own eyes, at least. You always call me Aunt, but for so long I wanted to hear you call me Mother. Then you grew up, and another dream came true. You became a woman, a beautiful woman, the lover of a handsome man. One day your belly would swell as mine never would. I used to wake at night thinking I heard your sons and daughters crying. Yes, that was my greatest wish, to have grandchildren running and yelling in this house, to forget about the carpets, the weaving, the customers. For years I dreamed that Lilah's children would soon throw themselves into my arms. If I hadn't been a mother, I would at least be a grandmother.'

She fell silent, her whole body trembling. Lilah remained motionless, with a lump in her throat. Sarah took a deep breath, and her lips curved in an ironic smile. 'Sometimes I dreamed of the children Ezra might have . . . but that didn't last, I must admit.'

Lilah smiled, too. At last, tears welled in Sarah's eyes and rolled down her cheeks, and she said, very quickly, in one breath, as if fearing she would not be able to finish everything she had to say, 'Now I know I shan't see children running in this house or be woken by their cries. To the end of my days, I'll be Sarah of the barren womb. Do you understand?'

'Aunt . . .' Lilah murmured.

Sarah shook her head, stubbornly and bravely. 'No, don't say anything. There's no need. I know. That terrible mad Queen will never allow you to marry Antinoes. And I know you. You won't yield either. If you can't marry him, you won't marry anyone else. You won't be anyone else's lover. You'll be like me: a woman with a barren womb.'

Sarah was looking her niece straight in the eyes. In her voice, there had been perhaps a faint tinge of hope that she might be contradicted, but Lilah could not find anything to say in reply and lowered her eyes.

Sarah nodded. 'I suppose you're right,' she whispered. 'But you may change your mind later. We never know what the Everlasting expects of us. And you're so young – little more than a child.'

A door slammed in the courtyard, then silence returned. They separated, as if their bodies were suddenly turned in again on their sadness.

'Perhaps you could . . .' Sarah hesitated. What she had to say was difficult, and she no longer dared look at Lilah. 'I know that you take herbs,' she murmured, 'when you see Antinoes. You could be pregnant, then he'd have to—'

'But to what end?' Lilah interrupted, without raising her voice. 'To have a child and give it a life of shame? Antinoes could never make it his son or daughter without the wrath of Parysatis falling on the child. She wouldn't rest until she'd destroyed it.'

Sarah frowned, and said nothing. They were both silent.

There was more noise in the house now. Mordechai's voice rang out, then those of the handmaids in reply. Soon they would hear the clatter of the looms.

'It's so cruel,' Sarah muttered. 'If there's anyone who doesn't deserve this, it's you.'

'No one deserves to suffer Parysatis' madness.'

Sarah turned abruptly and gripped Lilah's hands. 'What I'd like to know is whether or not you're going to follow him.' Her eyes were intense, her mouth harder, as if she were getting ready to receive a blow. 'If you also leave for Jerusalem, Mordechai and I will be alone again. He'll never leave Susa.'

Lilah shook her head. 'Oh, Aunt Sarah, I don't know – I don't know.'

A few mornings later, Axatria returned from the lower town, her cheeks red. Alone, as before, she had taken clean clothes and food to Ezra and Master Baruch. She had found Sogdiam in a state of great excitement. For the past few days, Zachariah and some twenty members of his family, brothers, uncles and nephews, had been coming to listen to Ezra reading from the great scroll of the Law of Moses.

'Sogdiam says that each time the reading is over, this Zachariah and his family crowd round Ezra, asking, "When will you lead us to Jerusalem? Why are we wasting our time here?" Ezra has constantly to explain to them that they can set out for Jerusalem without him. "The road is there," he says. "You have only to take it!" He says that he isn't Nehemiah, that he can't go back to Jerusalem before his studies are over and without the agreement of the Citadel . . . But you know this.'

'And what does Master Baruch say?' Lilah asked.

'Ah, Master Baruch!' There was a gleam in Axatria's eyes. 'Master Baruch doesn't say a word while Zachariah's family are talking to Ezra. But look!' She drew a small papyrus scroll from her tunic. 'Just as I was about to leave, he asked me to arrange his bed. I'd already done it a little earlier, but you know Master Baruch's whims . . . While

I was plumping the pillows, he slipped this into the sleeve of my tunic. Ezra was reading in his corner, and didn't see a thing. "Give this to Lilah," Master Baruch whispered. "Only to Lilah."'

Lilah had unrolled the papyrus while Axatria was speaking. A few lines were written on it, the letters so fine and the ink so pale that she had to go out into the daylight to decipher them.

My dove. Be strong. Ezra loses his temper, but he listens to you as carefully as he listens to Yahweh. The hand of Yahweh is upon you. Have no doubts. Think of the sea that Yahweh opened before Moses. Have no fear, my dove. Go to the most powerful, make yourself heard, and all will be well.

'What did he write?' Axatria asked impatiently.

She had to repeat her question twice before Lilah read her Master Baruch's words.

Axatria was disappointed. 'That's not very helpful, is it?' she said. 'He may be going off his head a little. Sogdiam says he hardly ever gets out of bed. When he slipped me this scroll, his eyes were laughing, like a child's. That happens with the very old. They become like children again.'

Lilah did not reply.

What Master Baruch had not written, she could hear as clearly as if he were whispering in her ear.

★   ★   ★

This time it was not the third cupbearer who came to fetch Lilah, but a eunuch from Parysatis' guard. He had short hair and smooth cheeks, and wore a bearskin cloak and a large red turban.

Lilah was taken to the Queen wearing the same costume in which she'd left Mordechai's house. Over a tunic of yellow wool, drawn in at the waist by a blue belt, she had put on a big woollen veil woven with silver threads and embroidered with green and purple silk. Her hair was held in place by an ivory comb carved with five-pointed stars. Opalescent amber earrings hung from her ears, and she had wound a matching necklace twice round her throat.

She held herself erect as she walked, chin high, mouth full and firm. She was not only beautiful: one glance was enough to convince anyone of the strength of her will. Even the handmaids and eunuchs noticed it as they led her through the maze of corridors and halls.

She was not kept waiting long.

The Queen received her in a bedchamber as round as the inside of a tent. The walls and floor were covered with carpets and tapestries. In the middle of the room a fire was burning in a bronze hearth, the smoke passing out through the ceiling along a brass conduit.

Lying on a bed suspended from the beams and covered with animal skins, Parysatis was playing with some Egyptian kittens. They all had black fur and green eyes. She chuckled happily, tickling them and cursing whenever one of them scratched her wrist. Her thin white tunic, identical to the one Lilah had seen her wear during her previous visit, was spattered with tiny bloodstains. She did not seem to hear the announcement the eunuch made as Lilah walked in through the tapestry that served as a door.

Lilah advanced to within ten paces of Parysatis and bowed low, eyes closed.

When she straightened, Parysatis' eyes were on her. The Queen stared at her for what seemed an age, while the kittens, eager to play, sought her hands, clawed her tunic, scratched her thighs and stomach.

The handmaids and eunuchs moved about the room, stoking the fire and the perfume-burners, their steps muffled by the carpets. Then they vanished, all except two eunuchs who stood guarding the door. Lilah did not dare to move, even though she was starting to feel numb.

Parysatis was still staring at her, untroubled by the kittens, which had now snuggled between her thighs. Her eyes were so fixed, the pupils so enlarged, that Lilah wondered if she had taken a potion.

Without warning, Parysatis threw the kittens across the room and turned away from Lilah on to her side.

She pulled a leopardskin round her shoulders. 'Well,' she said flatly, 'I knew you didn't lack nerve. But to address a request to me – Parysatis? That's something I've never had inflicted on me before!'

'Thank you, my queen, for replying.'

'Who said I'm replying, you conceited girl?'

Lilah lowered her eyes. Beads of sweat formed on the back of her neck.

'No one asks anything of Parysatis.'

'No, my queen.'

'So why did you send me that tablet, fool? Are you so determined to make me angry?'

'No, my queen.'

Confident and determined as she was, and bolstered by Master Baruch's words, fear gripped Lilah's chest like a vice. She had to take a deep breath.

The most foolhardy of the kittens was climbing towards Parysatis' hand. She caught it by the tail, and it mewed. 'I'm waiting,' she muttered.

'My queen, I thought you were the only person who could help me.'

Parysatis gave a cry, which turned into a laugh. 'I? Help you? Are you mad? Why should I help you?'

The laugh ceased as suddenly as it had started. There was a silence.

Parysatis pressed the kitten between her breasts and stroked it. 'Help you in what?'

'My queen, my brother Ezra wants to ask the King of Kings for permission to take our people out of exile in Susa and Babylon and lead them to Jerusalem.'

With her index finger, Parysatis was forcing the kitten to open its mouth wide. It bit her. Parysatis chuckled, took it by the neck, and thrust it out of sight under the leopardskin, against her hip. She looked at Lilah, and raised an eyebrow.

'Why? Aren't they happy here?'

'Zion is the land marked out for our people by Yahweh, our God, my queen. Today Jerusalem, our city, is in ruins, for we are here instead of there. Chaos reigns there, decay is gathering pace. Nothing is respected, neither our laws nor those of our great king Artaxerxes. If the fall of Jerusalem is not good for us Jews, it is not good for the King of Kings either. Soon the Greeks and the Egyptians will be able to seize the city. That would weaken all of the western borders.'

Parysatis' eyes had become sharper as Lilah spoke. 'Politics! You appear before Parysatis, acting like a queen, and talk to her about politics! What business is it of yours? Such things are not for women – let alone girls like you.'

'My queen, that is why I would like my brother Ezra to appear before the King of Kings.'

Parysatis groaned and shook her head. 'So obstinate, and always ready with an answer. Why your brother and not someone else?'

'Because he alone can do it, my queen. He and no one else.'

'"He and no one else,"' Parysatis mocked, aping Lilah's voice. 'And, of course, you're the one who decides that! A Jew from the lower town, wallowing in dirt and poverty, listening to the stale whining of an old man who ought to have died long ago! And he's supposed to be the leader of the Jews?' Parysatis' laugh was as sharp as a rattle.

Lilah shuddered. She felt as though thousands of needles were piercing her lower back.

'Ah, you see! I surprise you. Parysatis knows more than you think. I know everything, Lilah, everything. Never forget that.'

A long silence followed. A distant look had come into

the Queen's eyes, as though she were thinking of something else. Lilah thought she could hear the kitten mewing beneath the leopardskin. The other kittens were playing soundlessly under the bed.

'You ask,' Parysatis said abruptly, 'but what are you offering in return?'

Lilah said nothing, and lowered her head.

'This is what you offer,' Parysatis muttered. 'Your brother leaves for Jerusalem, and you follow him.'

Lilah did not look up.

'I want your answer, girl!' Parysatis cried.

'Yes, my queen.'

'You go to Jerusalem and forget Antinoes.'

On Lilah's back, the needles had become fangs. 'Yes, my queen.'

'Forget promises, forget marriage. Forget Antinoes between your thighs. Do you understand?'

'Yes, my queen.'

Parysatis' cooing laugh burst out in the thick air, as sinuous as a snake. 'That's what you came to tell me, isn't it? That you're afraid of me and you're begging me to let you go a long way away from your great love. Farewell, promise! But you're too proud to admit it. Not brave, really, just proud. A proud little girl who plays at being a lady, that's what you are. Now you may thank me.'

Lilah looked up, ashamed that she could not prevent the tears streaming down her cheeks. 'Thank you, my queen,' she murmured.

Parysatis smiled and screwed up her eyes. Her upper

lip was curled over her small teeth, and the folds round her mouth had spread to her cheeks, making her look ten years older. She took her right hand out from beneath the leopardskin, still holding the kitten. She threw the little animal at Lilah's feet, where it rolled over and lay motionless. It was dead, its neck broken.

'If you want Parysatis' advice, Lilah, make sure I forget you.'

Her eyes were wide open in the darkness of the bed-chamber. Parysatis' words kept going through her head. The kitten's mews, its dead body, everything merged together, confused and terrifying.

What had the Queen said? What had she said herself? She could not remember. Was she to understand that Parysatis would help her, would talk to the King of Kings, advise him to send for Ezra? How could she know?

Had she humiliated herself in vain?

What had she agreed to?

Never to see Antinoes again.

Never to love Antinoes again. Never to kiss or caress him.

And perhaps she would get nothing in return.

Again and again the Queen's words, the whole scene, twisted through her thoughts, like an endlessly spinning top.

'Lilah . . .'

She was so absorbed in her thoughts that she did not hear the whisper.

'Lilah!'

She made out a shadowy figure. She was no longer alone in the room.

'Lilah . . .'

For a split second, she thought it was Antinoes, taking advantage of the darkness to join her in spite of Parysatis' spies.

But she could smell a woman's scent. At last she recognized the voice. 'Axatria!'

'Not so loud, there's no point in waking the whole house!'

'What's happening? Why have you come up here without a lamp?'

Axatria was thrusting a shawl into her hands. Lilah resisted, ready to protest.

'Sssh, don't make a noise . . . Sogdiam is downstairs.'

'Sogdiam? What's he doing here?'

'He'll tell you himself. Hurry up.'

Axatria was already pulling her towards the door and the shadowy corridors.

A few moments later, Lilah found Sogdiam in the kitchen, huddled in front of the last embers in the hearth. In spite of the blanket Axatria had put round him, his teeth were chattering, his hands held tight round a cup of steaming herb tea.

He tried to stand when they came in, but his deformed legs were numb with cold and could hardly carry him. Lilah and Axatria rushed to stop him falling.

'He's been wandering around the city since sunset,' Axatria said.

'I had to hide before I came here.' Sogdiam pulled the

blanket over his head. 'If not, the guards would have caught me. No chance of passing unnoticed with my legs.'

'Has something happened to Ezra?' Lilah asked.

'No, no. Ezra's fine. I've come because of Master Baruch. He's not well.'

'What's the matter?'

'Let him drink his herb tea and get warm or he'll be ill,' Axatria said. 'I'll go and find him a dry tunic. His own tunic is like a block of ice.'

'At first,' Sogdiam said, regaining his strength, 'I didn't notice anything. Master Baruch kept complimenting me on my cooking, and asking for a little more of this, a little more of that. And I was happy to give it. I thought, Master Baruch has a good appetite and really likes my dishes! I cooked him fish, millet balls, barley biscuits filled with stuffed pigeons, olives and dates . . . All good food. When I started I didn't know the recipes, but I learned quickly. One recipe leads to another, then another . . . Master Baruch ate everything, left nothing. And if Ezra didn't like what I'd made or wasn't hungry, he'd eat Ezra's portion, too. Of course I thought it strange, but you know how Master Baruch is. He's the strangest character I've ever met. One day he's laughing, another day he doesn't open his mouth or his eyes. One day he's grumpy, the next day he talks all day. Four nights ago, I woke up and heard him moaning. This time, he was really ill. I waited for Ezra to call me to help him tend to him, boil him herbs, as you taught me. But they didn't ask for anything. Master Baruch didn't want it. I stayed there in the dark like an idiot, listening to them argue. "You're making yourself ill, Master," Ezra was saying, "and I know why. You're flouting Yahweh's will." "Don't boast, my boy," Master Baruch answered, moaning. "You know nothing at all. Apart from your pride, you know nothing. I'm old, and the old die, that's all." "You can't make yourself ill like this, Master," Ezra said again. "The Law forbids it. Sogdiam will look after you." To which Master Baruch retorted, "Go back to your studies, then. You're wasting time, Ezra. You shouldn't be here, losing sleep over an old man. Only a fool would bother with such things!" Anyway . . . They argued like that for hours . . . In the morning, when I went to see Master Baruch, he was exhausted. To tell the truth, I thought he was dead. Ezra was quite shaken. He couldn't study. Zachariah and the others were out in the courtyard, as usual, but he sent them away. I made some herb tea for Master Baruch, but when I put the cup beside him, he refused to drink it. You'll never guess what he said.'

Sogdiam, eyes bright with excitement, looked from Lilah to Axatria, then back to Lilah. "'Sogdiam, my boy," he said, "if you want to be a good Jew, make me a nice loaf of barley bread filled with pigeon's eyes, fish sperm, offal from a lamb killed according to Yahweh's Law, onions, a lot of garlic and curdled milk." That's what he said – after a night like that!'

'And did you make it?' Axatria asked.

'It was impossible. Where could I find a lamb killed

according to the Law in the lower town? And, in any case, Ezra forbade it. He claims Master Baruch is trying to kill himself even though the Everlasting has not demanded it of him.'

'So?' Axatria prompted.

The excitement drained from Sogdiam's eyes. He rubbed his cracked lips and turned to Lilah. 'That's why I'm here. Master Baruch has decided he won't eat or drink until I've made his filled bread. What can I do? Where can I find the offal? I couldn't stay in the lower town, fretting, so I came to you. But with my legs, it's not easy to get about in the snow, especially at night. I lost my way. Ezra had told me where the house was, but how to find it in the dark, with all these streets and houses?'

Lilah was speechless. She drew Sogdiam to her, and kissed his temples.

'It's all right, my boy, it's all right,' Axatria said. 'As soon as it's light, we'll leave in the chariot. We'll hide you under a blanket. As for the offal, there must be some in the house, if Master Baruch really wants it. The one certain thing is that he mustn't die of starvation.'

By the time they reached Ezra's house, there were so many people in the street that Sogdiam had to reveal himself and speak before they were allowed through. How had the news that Master Baruch was dying spread through the lower city? Lilah had no idea. It was as if the air itself had spread the rumour.

They went through the gate. The courtyard, although

also overrun with people, was strangely silent. Lilah recognized Zachariah. She ran to the study.

Ezra, dark rings under his eyes from exhaustion and sadness, was sitting on his stool beside Master Baruch's bed. He stood up when she came in, and took her in his arms with a sigh of relief. 'He's still breathing,' he whispered, before she could ask.

Lilah knelt by the old man's bed. His eyes were closed and his face, surrounded by his beard and hair, was at peace. For a moment, she could not move for tenderness, fear and sadness. She gazed at the old man's lips and nostrils: pale, without a sign of life. Shyly, she touched his brow. It was barely warm, like his cheeks. It was too late, it seemed to her. Ezra was wrong: Master Baruch had stopped breathing.

Without her realizing it, a moan escaped her. She looked up at Ezra, who shook his head and knelt beside her. Delicately, he held a thin sheet of silver in front of Master Baruch's nose. It misted over.

Sogdiam and Axatria had been watching their every gesture from the doorway. 'Is he still breathing?' Sogdiam asked, in a barely audible voice.

Lilah nodded.

'In that case, we mustn't waste any more time,' Axatria said softly. 'Come to the kitchen.' She pulled the boy's sleeve.

'To do what?' he protested.

'To make his filled barley bread.'

'You're mad! He won't eat anything now, in the state he's in.'

'How do you know? He's alive, he asked for barley bread, that's all that matters. Come on, hurry up and light the oven.'

Axatria was right. She was speaking the very words that Master Baruch would have wanted to hear.

Lilah tried to smile, but did not have the strength. She sat down on the edge of the bed. Her shoulders began to heave under the wave of sobs that overwhelmed her. Ezra put his arm round her and drew her to him. She sought out his hands, intertwined her fingers with his. She bit her lip to stop herself shaking too much. For the first time in years, she saw tears glistening in Ezra's red-rimmed eyes.

She yielded to his embrace. Their heads touched. Through their clothes, Lilah could feel the warmth of her brother's body. She had almost forgotten that Ezra had a body as young as hers. It had been such a long time . . .

Brother and sister. Ezra and Lilah.

It had been such a long time!

It was just before dusk that Master Baruch awoke. His eyes opened suddenly and his gaze was bright and alive. He immediately recognized the faces of those bending over him, and smiled. 'My dove,' he whispered, 'I knew you would come.'

'Sogdiam came to fetch me, Master Baruch,' Lilah said.

'A good boy . . . a good boy.'

His eyes closed. Lilah thought he had fallen asleep

again. But the fingers of his right hand were moving. 'Both of you,' he whispered in an almost inaudible voice, without opening his eyes.

Lilah and Ezra did not understand immediately. His old fingers moved more nervously. Finally Ezra placed his hand on Master Baruch's right hand and Lilah took hold of the other. The old man smiled slightly.

They remained like this for a while.

The murmur of voices could be heard in the court-yard. From the kitchen, where Axatria and Sogdiam were performing a miracle, there came a delicious aroma.

Again Master Baruch's eyes opened wide. Clear and lucid, they came to rest on Lilah. 'It will come to pass,' he breathed. 'You did what you had to do, I know. Have no doubts. It is Yahweh's wish.'

Lilah's eyes misted over. For the first time since she had left Parysatis, the shame that had clung to her like an extra skin was dissolving. It was as if Master Baruch's simple words had purified her.

Now he was looking at Ezra. 'Everything has an end, Ezra,' he said.

'Master . . .'

'Listen to me. Everything has a beginning and an end.' He paused for breath, and to recover a little strength. 'Remember Isaiah's words. "At dawn, you will be born again, you will grow quickly, and justice will walk before you . . . and Yahweh will bring up the rear with all His weight."'

After this great effort he fell silent again. But his will remained strong – they could see it in his eyes.

'A time for study and a time to rebuild the walls of Jerusalem,' he murmured. 'A time for Baruch ben Neriah to thank Yahweh.'

Ezra was about to speak, but the old man's eyes closed again.

Lilah thought it was over. But after a moment of total silence, Master Baruch's fingers squeezed hers. 'I can smell barley bread, filled barley bread! What a delight . . .'

Lilah sought Ezra's eyes. He nodded. 'Sogdiam has just baked it for you, Master.'

Master Baruch's eyelids and lips quivered. 'Bring it in, bring it in.'

Ezra ran to find Sogdiam and Axatria. The bread was placed right in front of Master Baruch's face. Old as he was, the smile that lit up his features was as radiant and carefree as that of a young man greedy for life and brimming with hope.

A moment later, he stopped breathing.

All night long, candles burned in the house. Although no one person made the decision, tallow, wicks and oil were found. By the time the clouds had cleared to reveal the stars, the courtyard and the streets around Ezra's house were illuminated by hundreds of lamps.

Zachariah and his people sang, and Ezra read some words from the scroll of Isaiah, which Master Baruch had known by heart:

Rejoice with Jerusalem, be glad for her, all you who
    love her,

Rejoice with her, all you who have mourned for
  her,
You will drink your fill at her comforting breasts,
You will drink with delight at her overflowing
  breasts . . .

In the morning, the sky over Susa was filled with mist.
It made the sun white and the snowy ground dazzling.
When the white disc of the sun reached its zenith,
which, at this season, was lower than the Citadel, they
came. On foot, without a chariot, but armed. Ten
soldiers with felt helmets and fur capes, spears in their
hands. They cut through the silent crowd. When they
reached the gate, their officer asked for Ezra, son of
Serayah.

When Ezra appeared, the officer handed him a wax
tablet. 'By order of our king, Artaxerxes the Second,
king of the peoples from east to west by the will of
Ahura Mazda, the great god, you, Ezra, son of Serayah,
are ordered to appear by the statue of Darius the father,
at the foot of the southern steps to the Apadana, the day
after tomorrow. Present this tablet before midday and
you will be taken to him. That is the will of the great
King Artaxerxes.'

The soldiers turned back the way they had come, and
the crowd stood aside to let them pass.

The visitors were struck dumb with amazement.
They repeated the officer's words to themselves without
grasping their meaning.

Ezra held the tablet in his hands, incredulous, and as

nervous as if the wax concealed a magic spell or a poisonous insect.

Lilah's legs were shaking. If Axatria had not been behind her, she would have collapsed.

The King had summoned Ezra!

Parysatis had spoken!

Master Baruch had been right!

Zachariah was the first to cry, 'Praise be to God! Praise be to the Everlasting!'

His cry was echoed by the onlookers, and spread through the courtyard. The men raised their hands to heaven, applauding, then flung their hats, turbans and caps into the air. Tears of mourning became cries of celebration. The joy was so intense that the other inhabitants of the lower town were taken aback, even shocked.

By the time evening came, Sogdiam had had to explain a hundred times why there had been such laughter. This, he said, was perhaps the true miracle of Master Baruch's death, and the reason for the beautiful smile with which he had savoured the final moments of his earthly life.

But as they were about to place the old sage's body in the earth, Ezra stood up suddenly, and looked fixedly at Zachariah and Lilah. 'It's impossible,' he said.

He went to find the wax tablet from the Citadel, written with all the skill of the Apadana's scribes, and waved it above his head. 'It's impossible!' he said again. 'I can't appear before the King.'

All those who heard him froze. They repeated to

themselves what he had said, as earlier they had repeated the good news. This time, a curious silence spread from the courtyard to the surrounding streets.

'Why is it impossible?' Zachariah asked at last in a quavering voice.

'Whoever appears before the King must bow down. He must bend his knees and even blow a kiss to Artaxerxes.'

'Yes,' Zachariah said, with a frown. 'We know.'

'Whoever does not bow down,' Ezra went on, waving the tablet, 'is seized by the eunuchs, and the audience is cancelled.'

'May the Everlasting protect you!' Zachariah said. 'You'll bow down and everything will be fine.'

Ezra roared with anger, and started walking up and down in front of the astonished crowd. 'How can someone who must lead Yahweh's people to their land bow down?' he cried, looking at Lilah.

But it was again Zachariah who replied. He went up to Ezra and tried to calm him. 'Come on! What harm is there in bowing to the King of Kings? It's the rule. Even the lords of the Citadel, even the envoys of the Greeks, have done it. There's nothing shameful in it.'

'Zachariah!' In his anger, Ezra hurled the tablet from him. It flew between earth and sky, and the crowd cried out in horror. Sogdiam leaped towards it and caught it before it could hit the ground and break. He landed heavily on his back, but his grimace of pain was mingled with relief.

Ezra barely glanced at him. He pointed at Zachariah,

then at those around him. 'What is not shameful for the
Gentiles is shameful for us!' His voice swelled, and he
opened his arms wide: 'This is how it starts! You want
me to lead you to Jerusalem. You want to carry the
stones to rebuild the walls of the Temple. You want
to be the hands that will purify it, that will open its
doors, and you don't even know what it means to bow
down! Artaxerxes walks hand in hand with his god
Ahura Mazda as if he were the master of the universe.
He demands that we bow down before him as if he
were a god of heaven and earth!' Ezra's voice was less
furious now. It quivered more in sorrow than in anger.
'Zachariah! And all of you, sons of Levi, sons of Jacob,
sons of the *kohanim*, including the first of them, Moses'
brother Aaron! You who ought to carry them within
you as the blood carries your steps, have you forgotten
the words of Yahweh? "You shall not bow down before
any idol. You shall not bow down before any false god,
or before any man who claims to be a god."'

The quivering voice fell silent.

Heads bowed.

Lilah, who had bent to help Sogdiam, felt her body
grow cold. Had so much effort been in vain? For a
moment she hoped that Master Baruch would raise his
voice and suggest a solution to Ezra. But Master Baruch's
voice was silent now for ever.

'There is something you could do,' Axatria said unexpectedly.

All eyes turned to her.

She was looking at Ezra with a shy smile. 'If the King

isn't a god, he doesn't know how to separate true from false.'

Taken aback, Ezra frowned. 'What do you mean?'

'That you can look as if you're bowing to him without actually doing it. Watch.'

She stepped forward and bent her body gracefully. As she did so the thin bracelet she wore round her wrist slipped off. She bowed deeply to pick it up from the melting snow, and at last stood up, blowing on her frozen palm in what might have been a tender kiss.

There was a silence. Then Sogdiam burst into laughter, others too, and as Ezra blushed to the roots of his hair, the laughter spread through the courtyard.

Axatria, just as scarlet as Ezra but with a twinkle in her eyes, murmured, 'Yahweh will know you did nothing shameful. But Artaxerxes won't, because he's only a man.'

Lilah saw Ezra reach out his hand towards Axatria. Now he, too, was laughing heartily. She closed her eyes and thought she could see Master Baruch's smile.

The Book of Days

Before she opened the iron-clad door of the tower, Lilah paused and held her breath. There was nothing around her but the immense silence of the city. It was too cold, the night too dark, for Parysatis' spies to venture out. The street was empty. Not even a stray dog.

She closed the door behind her noiselessly, crossed the ground floor and slipped into the garden. She walked rapidly, hands in front of her for protection, brushing against tree-trunks and bushes. The darkness was so dense that she bumped into the wall of the house when she reached it, grazing her fingers on the icy edges of the bricks.

She had to go round the columns at the entrance. By the time she knocked softly on the shutter, she was soaked to the skin.

'Who is it?' he asked, almost immediately.

'Lilah.'

Those were the last words they spoke for a long time.

He undressed her close to the braziers. His breath burned her skin as he made love to her with almost painful slowness.

Later, when she was asleep, the fine hairs on her temples stuck to her skin with sweat, he began to caress her again. He took her with the gentleness of a dream. She barely woke, breathing in his kisses.

Outside, the night of Susa was still profoundly silent. The snow was falling again.

When Lilah rolled once more on to Antinoes' chest, the pleasure did not prevent her tears from flowing. Nevertheless, these tears were like a gentle, comforting rain for her eyes. Antinoes' caresses had washed her clean, calmed her.

She clung to his neck and he held her tightly against him. For a brief but indelible moment, they were as indestructible as the night and the stars.

Before morning, Antinoes woke her so that she could take advantage of the darkness to leave the house. He had made ready for her a fur cloak lined with silk.

She would have liked to tell him that nothing had changed, either in her heart or in her will, that he was already her husband for all eternity, that Parysatis' threats did not frighten her. But at that moment, Antinoes whispered, 'I'll be with Ezra in the Apadana.' He kissed her again. 'Have no fear. Everything will be all right.'

No, she had no fear now, not any more.

Ezra presented himself at the gate of Darius just before sunrise. He was dressed in a new purple and blue tunic that touched his feet. It had been given to him the day before by Zachariah and the men who had been occupying his courtyard. Their wives had coloured and woven the wool with such skill that it flowed and shone with the brilliance of Oriental silk. On his head he wore a stiff felt hat, on which they had embroidered, in blue wool run through with silver thread, the seven-branched candlestick described by Yahweh to Moses.

A cylindrical leather case hung on his chest from a solid strap round his neck. Inside, Ezra had slipped the precious scroll of Moses' Scriptures, which his father's fathers had handed down to him through the centuries.

Accompanied by Zachariah and a handful of associates, he climbed the long flight of steps. Rising from the royal city, it ran alongside the great wall of the Citadel for one *stadion* in length. Images of the battles of Darius, the first and greatest of the Kings of Kings, stood out in relief from the brightly coloured bricks. They had been drawn with such clarity that every one of the soldiers could be identified.

Above and below, to a height of fifty cubits, there were other images, of wild beasts, fabulous monsters, and the men of the peoples Darius had conquered, who now paid tribute to Artaxerxes the Second.

The gate of Darius was at the top of the steps. No one, not even the King, could reach the square of the Apadana, then the Citadel, without passing through it.

Its two leaves were so massive that it took four mules attached to a winch to move them. It was framed by the defensive wall and two towers, a hundred cubits high and just as wide, crenellated at the top. The bricks of the towers were light blue and yellow. Above them Ahura Mazda spread his gold and bronze protecting wings, over twenty-seven cubits wide. It was said that they reflected the sun so strongly that, at certain hours of the day, they could burn the eyes of those who gazed too long at them.

Two huge identical statues of Darius, five times life-size, faced each other on either side of the bronze and cedar leaves of the gate. Real hair, from thousands of heads, had been used to make their wigs and beards. The necklaces and bracelets, each the diameter of a chariot wheel, were of real gold, cast from the spoils of battles fought in Hyrcania and against the Parthians. The Egyptian sculptors who had made these colossal statues had set precious stones in the eye sockets. At dawn and dusk, when the sun's rays struck them, a blue and purple ray formed that forbade entry to all living creatures and purified the entrance to the Apadana.

Three times every morning, horns would sound, the gate would half open, and the courtiers of the royal city and the lords of the Citadel would crowd through it and bow down before the statues of Artaxerxes on the Apadana. Each would present to the guards a bronze and gold disc, as large as a man's palm, bearing the effigy of the King of Kings. The medals were handed down from father to son. If lost, they were not replaced. If an owner sinned, the medal was destroyed, and his family and descendants banished for ever from the Apadana.

Strangers from all parts of the world, some from the lands ruled by the King of Kings, some from barbarous and unknown nations, mingled with the crowd. All kinds of faces could be seen, all kinds of eye and skin colour, as well as the strangest clothes. The most disconcerting languages were spoken. But few of these people were allowed to walk between the breathtaking eyes of the immense statues of Darius.

To pass through the gate and enter beneath the shade cast by the towers, strangers had to present a wax tablet written by the scribes of the Apadana ordering them to appear.

When Ezra showed his, a guard inspected it carefully, then handed it to some scribes, who studied it in their turn. He was allowed to pass but, in spite of his protests, Zachariah and his companions were not. They had barely time to shout a few words of encouragement before they disappeared into the crowd held back by the guards' spears.

Ezra was directed towards a narrow gallery, where he was searched. With a care that was quite humiliating, the guards made sure that he was not concealing any weapons, vials or ointments. Then, despite his violent opposition, they pulled Moses' scroll from its leather case and unrolled it.

While Ezra watched angrily, two young eunuchs slid the tips of their index fingers over the scroll, then held them out to be licked by a puppy in a cage. They waited until it was clear that the animal had not been poisoned, and at last allowed Ezra to go through the gate of Darius.

Blinded by the daylight, he entered a world that few men had seen.

There, everything was so inordinately large, Ezra had the fleeting impression that he had been reduced in the flash of an eye to the size of a child. On the left, beyond the parapets, the Shaour, tiny from this distance, shimmered as it meandered through the snow-covered fields, like a thread in a carpet. On the right, the houses of the upper town were like a child's building blocks, the gardens dark strips where green peeped through beneath the snow. The sky was so pure and so close, it seemed you needed only to lift your hand to touch the clouds.

Before him lay the courtyard of the Apadana. The floor was of marble, each flagstone so tight to its neighbours that a fishbone could not have slid between them. It stretched to the palace walls, which were smooth, without an opening, like a perfect cliff of brick.

Everywhere there were statues: of Artaxerxes the Second, Ahura Mazda with his bearded head and eagle wings, granite lions, steel and silver snakes, sensual porphyry nudes of the goddess Anahita, the raging horses and bulls of the god Mithras, clad in leather and gilded furs. Offerings burned in bronze bowls, and many people bowed before them, singing praises. Some lay on the icy flagstones, others danced and bared their chests to the cold. Yet more stood motionless, bent double as if the frost had turned them to stone.

Several guards were strolling about in green and yellow tunics, the sleeves and necks embroidered with jewels and gold rings. Taller than most other men, they seemed taller still in the woollen hats that held their curly hair and were tied beneath their oiled beards. The ivory handles of curved daggers protruded from leather and silver baldrics, and they carried spears from which hung globes of silver or gold, according to their rank.

Two of them came straight up to Ezra and demanded to see his tablet. Then, without comment, they led him to the other side of the Apadana, where there was a roof supported by twelve columns covered with thick gold leaf and so huge that it had taken a thousand men to transport and raise them.

Pressing the leather case containing Moses' scroll to his stomach, Ezra hurried behind the guards to the area beneath the roof, which was alive with activity. Amid a crowd of scribes and aides, lords came and went. These were the men who ruled the kingdoms in the name of the King. The guards did not linger. They took Ezra to one of the many doors leading into the palace, then through the maze of corridors and courtyards.

They stopped on the threshold of a vast hall with a carpeted floor, and stepped aside to let him pass. The hall was divided into two by a veil. The visible half, where tables and cushions had been laid out, was brightly lit. Behind the veil, the light was dim.

A host of servants bustled between the low tables and the seats, on which sat, in all their finery, those to whom Artaxerxes had granted the glory of being present today.

Puzzled faces turned to Ezra as he entered, and the buzz of conversation diminished for a moment. A man stood up and signalled to him. It was Antinoes: Ezra recognized him despite his sumptuous costume and the round hat that covered his hair.

As he stood there frozen in surprise, Antinoes came up to him and held out his hand. 'Come and sit with me,' he said, by way of greeting. 'The King isn't here yet and the meal hasn't started.'

Ezra hesitated, then replied in a harsh voice, 'I haven't come here to eat.'

Antinoes smiled. 'I suppose not, but the King won't receive you before he's had his meal.'

He explained how audiences were held. The King ate alone, or in the company of the great chiliarch and a few concubines. Then he would send for whomever he wished to see among those whose names had been written by the scribes in the Book of Days.

Antinoes pointed to the veil. 'Until then, you won't see him. He stays on the other side of the veil. The light is arranged in such a way that he can see us but we can't see him or even be sure where he's sitting. He changes his position at every meal.'

'Are you telling me it's not even certain that Artaxerxes will receive me?' Ezra asked, his voice as harsh as before.

Antinoes indicated the dozens of courtiers around them. 'Almost every one of these people has received a tablet for the audience, like you. As you can see, there are almost a hundred of them. Not even ten will be called before the King.'

Ezra's eyes grew wide in astonishment, and his mouth quivered with anger.

Antinoes placed a calming hand on his wrist. 'Don't worry. You'll be received.'

'How can you be so sure?'

Antinoes gave a sad, affectionate smile that surprised Ezra as much as the hand on his wrist. 'Come on,' he said. 'There's no point in standing. When you enter this hall, the greatest virtue is patience.'

Reluctantly, Ezra allowed himself to be led to a table. As soon as they were seated, eunuchs placed food and drink on the great platter before them. Before they walked away, they casually tasted from each of the goblets in order to demonstrate that they contained no poison.

Once he had got over his surprise, Ezra asked again, 'How can you be so sure the King will receive me?'

'Because he must.'

Ezra frowned. 'Do you, a Persian, also think the hand of Yahweh is upon me?' he asked ironically.

'That may be so, since Lilah believes it. But what is certain is that Artaxerxes will give you an audience soon because, like your God, his mother Queen Parysatis wants it.'

'I don't understand,' Ezra said, his face hard.

Antinoes recounted how Lilah had decided to make her brother's true worth known to Artaxerxes, and how she had gone to Parysatis to plead her cause.

When he had finished, Ezra looked away, then asked after a moment, 'Would Parysatis dare to throw Lilah to the lions?'

'Without hesitation.'

Ezra was silent again before continuing. 'So you won't be able to marry her?'

Antinoes looked at him in silence.

'And what are you doing here?' Ezra asked.

'I was summoned because I'm the one who wrote to request an audience for you.'

For the first time since he had started speaking to Antinoes, Ezra's expression softened. 'You wrote the request?'

'We used to be brothers, Ezra,' Antinoes said, almost angrily. 'I haven't forgotten that, even if you claim not to remember. In your determination to respect your God's laws, you've become harder than a brick wall.'

Ezra avoided his eyes. His hands kneaded the leather case that contained Moses' scroll.

'Don't get me wrong,' Antinoes went on. 'You really owe your presence here today to Lilah. She's the one who believes that the hand of your God is upon you. She's the one who thinks you have a future that I don't understand. But I love Lilah as a man can love only one woman. And my love is not like yours. All it asks is her happiness.'

Ezra had turned pale. He sat stony-faced, indifferent to everything around him. 'No, it's to Yahweh that I owe my presence here.'

Antinoes nodded, and smiled sadly. 'I suppose that's how you see things. But I'd say that your God has placed His will in Lilah's hands. His will, added to your sister's courage. Because nothing is more dangerous in this city than to let Parysatis decide. There's always a price to pay.'

There was a slight movement at the other end of the room. The last courtiers still standing sat down. 'What do you mean?' Ezra asked, uneasily. 'What price has Lilah paid to get me this audience?'

Suddenly silence descended on the hall like a wave.

'The King has sat down behind the curtain,' Antinoes murmured, without moving his lips. 'You mustn't speak now until you're ordered to. Eat, or if you don't want to eat, keep still. Remember, he can see you – and you can be sure he'll be looking at you.'

As Antinoes had predicted, patience was the greatest virtue anyone waiting for an audience could possess. The King's meal was interminable, and the silence that hung over the hall made it seem even longer.

From time to time, the courtiers would hear murmurs from the semi-darkness beyond the curtain, female voices, a short burst of laughter. They themselves ate in silence. The only sounds came from the dishes and the bowls of lemon water that the servants brought for them to rinse their fingers. They all ate slowly, heads bowed over the brass platters. But no one took a morsel until the eunuchs had first tasted each dish as it was placed before them.

Ezra sat stiffly on his cushion. In spite of Antinoes' warning, he could barely conceal his irritation at the long wait. Like the others, he felt the silence weigh on him, and was uneasy at the thought that the King could see them but that there was no way of knowing exactly who he was looking at. Clearly Artaxerxes liked to be thought a deity. To the courtiers, he probably was. Ezra's mood darkened.

Nervously, he fidgeted with the ring Axatria had given him, which he wore on his forefinger. It was a red stone, set in silver, that Sarah had filched from Mordechai's chest. His uncle's fingers were broader than his own. All he had to do was part the index finger from the middle finger and the ring would slip off. He hoped he would soon have a chance to do so, but was starting to doubt it. Beside him, Antinoes had applied himself conscientiously to his food, which showed that he was not really hungry and took little pleasure in the meal.

Suddenly, harps, flutes and drum struck up a melody behind the veil, and a youthful but powerful voice – Ezra guessed it belonged to a eunuch – started to sing. The words glorified the manliness and warlike power of Artaxerxes and his ancestors. Then, as suddenly as it had begun, the music stopped and the veil was flung back.

The crowd of courtiers stood up. Antinoes pulled at Ezra to follow the others' movements.

Hardly had they got to their feet than two guards came up to them.

'Ezra, son of Serayah,' one of them said. 'Artaxerxes, master of nations, King of Kings, wants to see you.'

While the eunuchs and servants wore sumptuous clothes, and the tunic of the chiliarch Tithraustes glittered with gold and precious stones, Artaxerxes was dressed in a simple white tunic. His long beard was threaded with gold braid and over his wig he wore a tall hat woven with gold and stones. The wig itself was so voluminous, it made his face seem unusually long and thin. Ointments had been applied to his eyelids to blacken them, and his grey eyes given colour with a touch of kohl. Between the shadows of his beard, his lips had been painted to emphasize their voluptuous shape. He was sitting on a huge chair decorated with stars made from emeralds and pearls, and his feet rested on a stool of gold and ivory – it was said that he carried it himself as he moved about the palace, and even when he rode in a chariot.

On his right stood the chiliarch, and behind, the three scribes of the Book of Days, helped by some twenty young eunuchs, crouching quietly until they were needed. To his left, the musicians waited for a gesture from the King. All around, fifty guards, among the tallest ever seen, formed a circle.

As he reached the boundary marked previously by the veil, Antinoes bowed. He went no further, but Ezra continued walking straight towards the King.

A murmur went through the courtiers.

The King's face remained impassive.

Ezra took a few more steps, put his head down and made a little bow, right hand dangling towards the floor. The ring slipped from his fingers, and he bent as if following it in its fall. He stayed down for a brief moment, then straightened, and blew on his palm as Axatria had done.

Unfortunately, he lacked her grace: the movement he had made was so unlike a bow that the chiliarch Tithraustes signalled to the guards. Artaxerxes raised his hand from the armrest of his seat and smiled with amusement.

Taken aback, Tithraustes glanced uncertainly at his master, before doing his duty. 'Ezra, son of Serayah, Jew of Zion,' he announced. 'My king, he has come to ask you for help and support in leading to Jerusalem those of his people who have been living among us, in the Susa region and in Babylon, since their fathers' exile. That goes back, my king, to the days when Darius was not yet King of Kings.'

Like all the people in the hall, Ezra remained still until the King, who was no longer smiling, spoke. 'Your greeting, Ezra, is not that of a man who loves me, yet you have come to ask my help.'

Antinoes saw Ezra's shoulders and neck stiffen. Then he heard his clear voice: 'Do not see it as an offence on my part, my king. I give you all the respect I owe you. But it is true, my love goes to Yahweh, my God. As for bowing down, I obey the Law that Yahweh gave my people.'

The answer was so unexpected that the scribes and the chiliarch turned to Artaxerxes, waiting for him to explode. Instead, the King gazed hard at Ezra. 'That is not a pleasing answer,' he said, 'unless you can explain it to me.'

'My king, as the chiliarch said, my people are the people of Jerusalem and Judaea, the land that Yahweh, master of the universe, apportioned to us at the birth of time – provided that we follow His laws and decrees. Your father, your father's father and the great Cyrus, King of Kings, recognized the justice of Yahweh's laws. They considered them good and useful. That's why the great Cyrus, having conquered Babylon, made a decree in Ectabana, giving us the right to live according to these laws and to establish them in Jerusalem and throughout Judaea.'

Artaxerxes appeared to reflect for a moment, then turned to the scribes. 'Is this true?' he asked. 'Is it written in the Book of Days?'

There then began a strange ballet. The scribes and their aides rummaged through the chests with which they were surrounded. From these, they took out hundreds of papyrus scrolls, checking their contents on the wooden handles. They performed this task swiftly, indifferent to the eyes watching them. At last, after what seemed quite a short time, given the scale of the work, one of them unrolled a scroll some five or six cubits long. With an expert eye, he looked through it, then smiled, stood up and bowed.

'Yes, my king,' he said. 'Cyrus the Great spoke in favour of the Jews of Jerusalem.'

Artaxerxes, who seemed now to be enjoying this battle of wits, turned to Ezra. 'And you, do you know the words he spoke?'

'Yes, my king,' Ezra replied, without flinching. 'Cyrus, King of Persia, declared, "Yahweh, God of heaven, gave me all the kingdoms of the earth and entrusted me with the task of building him a temple in Jerusalem, in Judaea. Whoever among you is of his people, may his God be with him! May he go up to Jerusalem and build the Temple of the God of Israel, the God who is in Jerusalem."'

There was a moment of stunned silence, followed by murmuring among the onlookers. Artaxerxes pursed his lips, and ran his fingers through his golden beard. 'Are you claiming that Cyrus knew your God but knew nothing of Ahura Mazda, Anahita and Mithras?'

'Those were the words he spoke, my king.'

Artaxerxes grunted, and pointed at the scribes. 'What does the Book of Days say?'

This time, the answer came quickly. 'O my king, what Ezra has just said is written word for word.'

There were more murmurs. Artaxerxes looked thoughtfully at Ezra. 'These laws of your God of heaven,' he asked, 'who knows them?'

'I do, my king.'

'All of them?'

'All of them.'

'How can this be?'

'Because I've studied them every day for many years.'

'Where?'

Ezra raised the leather case and took out Moses' scroll. 'They are written here, my king.'

'And who wrote them?'

Ezra recounted how Moses had led Yahweh's people out of Pharaoh's Egypt to the mountain of Horeb where Yahweh had dictated his Commandments to him, laws and rules that concerned all things and all occasions in life, so that then, through the children of his brother Aaron, they could be transmitted from generation to generation.

'And you claim to know each and every one of them?' Artaxerxes asked.

'Yes,' Ezra replied.

Artaxerxes smiled and pointed to Ezra's hat. 'If everything proceeds from a law, why did you have that candlestick embroidered on your hat?'

'Because Yahweh commanded Moses, "You will make a candlestick of pure gold. Its base and its shaft will be of hammered gold. Its flowers, buds and branches will form one piece with it. Six branches will extend from its sides . . ."'

When he fell silent, Artaxerxes made a sign. A guard came up to Ezra, took the scroll from his hands, and handed it to the scribes, who proceeded to search in it for the commandment Ezra had just quoted.

'My king,' they said at last, 'what Ezra has said is written here word for word.'

Now there was only astonishment and silence. Ezra's audience lasted so long that no one else was received that day. Artaxerxes asked a thousand more questions and each time had the answers checked in the Book of Days. Then he asked Ezra what help he expected from him.

Ezra explained what Nehemiah's task had been and why it had remained unfinished. He recalled how King Darius had instituted a search of his archives and cellars for the objects stolen by Nebuchadnezzar during the sack of Jerusalem, as well as the measurements of the Temple that had to be rebuilt. That, too, Artaxerxes commanded to be checked in the Book of Days. Once again, Ezra was found to have told the truth, word for word.

'Ask me for what you want,' he said at last, 'and you shall have it.'

'It can only be to your advantage for law and order to prevail in Jerusalem, my king,' Ezra declared. 'Today the walls of Jerusalem are again cracked and broken. Disorder enters in like the wind and profits your enemies. Day after day, Jerusalem becomes a more and more open breach in the frontier of your kingdoms. And through this breach the chaos of war, the chaos of nations without laws, can reach even you. Give me the power to leave Susa with those of my people who wish to follow me. Give me what I need to rebuild the Temple and make it worthy of Yahweh, and I will give you calm, peace and stability. Jerusalem, made strong again by the Law of Yahweh, will protect you from the Egyptians and the Greeks.'

'May Ezra's words be written in the Book of Days,' Artaxerxes replied. 'May it also be written that I, Artaxerxes, King of Kings, grant him what he asks.'

'Ezra came back to the lower town a hero,' Lilah said. 'It was already dark. Zachariah and his family escorted him with candles and torches from the royal city to his house. They sang and danced all night long, and then, as soon as dawn rose, they ran to the Jewish houses to spread the good news. By now, there isn't a single child of Israel in the upper town who doesn't know that Ezra, son of Serayah, is going to leave for Jerusalem, with the agreement of Artaxerxes, in order to rebuild the Temple.'

There was a touch of mockery in Lilah's voice, but mostly it was calm and gentle.

They were in Antinoes' bedchamber. The shutters had

been carefully lined with blankets so that no light could be seen from outside. 'It's when you think Parysatis' spies are dozing that they're most alert,' Antinoes had said.

'Ezra is the only one who doesn't seem happy,' Lilah continued. 'As soon as anyone congratulates him for impressing Artaxerxes with his answers during the audience, he cries, "I know very little. You think it's a lot because you're ignorant." Or else, "Until I have a letter from Artaxerxes in my hand, it's pointless for you to sing my praises. It isn't yet certain that Yahweh's hand is upon me. I'm carrying on with my studies." Zachariah protests, of course. Then Ezra loses his temper: "Where are the Levites who are supposed to be going with me? You promised me hundreds. But when I count you, I can't even see ten who are capable of reading Moses' scroll. There are thousands of exiles in Susa, yet I don't see them crowding into the lower town, ready to set off for Jerusalem. They say they're impatient to leave, but where are they?"'

Antinoes laughed at her imitation of her brother's voice. Lilah rolled on to her back, stretched out on the bed and gazed up at the dark ceiling.

'Uncle Mordechai is impressed too,' she went on. 'He won't go to Jerusalem – his workshop and my aunt's mean too much to him. But he feels guilty. He's going to give my brother some chariots so that he can travel comfortably. When I told Ezra, he replied, "They're all like our uncle, my sister. All those fat children of Israel are ready to give me their gold as long as they're not obliged to get up from their cushions. They have no desire to see Jerusalem again. They're content here, in the arms of Artaxerxes. Do they imagine Yahweh isn't judging them?"'

Antinoes had stopped laughing. They were both silent. The silence weighed on them, but the words that remained to be said weighed even heavier on their hearts.

Antinoes' face crumpled. 'But you're not like your uncle,' he whispered. 'You're Ezra's sister, and you'll go with him to Jerusalem . . .'

Lilah did not reply at once. She closed her eyes. Antinoes looked closely at her mouth, her chest swelling as her breath came faster.

'Yesterday,' she said at last, 'Ezra asked me, "And what of you, my sister? Will you follow me or will you stay with your Persian?" That made me angry. I replied that my Persian had a name. And that I shan't give him an answer until he has spoken it.'

She fell silent, her eyes still closed. Antinoes did not dare move – he hardly dared to breathe. He had no doubt about Lilah's decision. But his hands shook as if he expected something different to emerge as if by a miracle from her beloved mouth.

'I went to the lower town,' Lilah resumed, softly. 'He greeted me more tenderly than he has for a long time. "Antinoes told me," he said. "He told me you went to see Queen Parysatis for me."'

Lilah's voice broke. She bit her lip, and tears formed beneath her closed eyelids.

'He said, "I know it was Antinoes, your lover, who

wrote the letter in my name seeking an audience with Artaxerxes. I've been unfair and harsh towards him. I can speak well of Antinoes now. But that changes nothing. You must understand that all I'm doing is following the Law of Yahweh. I have no other choice. How could my sister live her whole life with a man who's not a child of Israel? At the foot of the mountain of the Commandments, Yahweh said to Moses and Aaron, 'How dare you let the women who have lain with Midianites live? They are unclean. The bitter water of my curse will flow over them.'"'"

Antinoes had seized Lilah's hand. She clung to him, holding him so tightly that she seemed suspended in the air. 'He keeps saying he needs his sister,' she said. 'And it's true. I know it. I've always known it. Just as I know that what he's doing is great.'

'I know it, too,' Antinoes replied at last. 'And so does Parysatis. There's no miracle. You must go with Ezra to Jerusalem.'

Lilah opened her eyes, and her tears flowed. She gazed into Antinoes' face. 'I could hide. Only go as far as Babylon. Wait there until Parysatis forgets me. We can meet again in a year – yes, in a year Parysatis will have forgotten me. She might even be dead.'

'Parysatis will never forget you. Wherever you are, if you're with me, her cruelty will reach you. And don't count on her death. Demons live on for a long time. In any case, Ezra will never leave you in Babylon either.'

Lilah raised Antinoes' hand to her lips. 'Will you forget me, then?'

'No. I'll carry you within me all the days of my life.'

Gently, he made her stand, then took off her tunic. He held a candle in each hand, the better to see her naked body, and walked round her.

'Every inch of you will be stamped on my eyes,' he promised. 'I will see your face, kiss your breasts and your belly in my dreams. I will be inside you, night after night, and in the morning I will have the scent of your kisses on my lips. In the morning, my penis will grow hard at the memory of your hips.'

Lilah realized that Antinoes was weeping too. She smiled. 'You came back to Susa to make me your wife . . .' she said softly.

'There are too many people who don't want our marriage.'

'I made a promise, I must keep it.' She took the sheet from their bed and held it above her, like a canopy. Then she began to move round Antinoes, with a light, dancing step. 'I am Lilah, daughter of Serayah,' she whispered. 'I choose my husband according to my heart and before the Everlasting, Yahweh, my God.' A radiant smile lit her face, while she danced the wedding dance and her arms moved the sheet so that it was over her lover's head. 'I choose Antinoes, he who chose me on the first day of love.'

Antinoes started to laugh and raised his arms to hold up the sheet. They both turned and turned, looking into each other's eyes, hips swaying.

'I am Lilah, daughter of Serayah. As long as Yahweh gives me breath, I will have no other husband.'

'I am Antinoes, lord of the Citadel of Susa. May Ahura Mazda and Anahita protect my love for Lilah.'

They laughed, tears glistening on their cheeks, their joy as intense as their despair.

'I am Lilah, daughter of Serayah, and before the Everlasting I keep my promise. I am Lilah, wife of Antinoes. That is written in the Book of Days to the end of time.'

'I am Antinoes, husband of Lilah. May Ahura Mazda bring me Lilah's kisses to the end of time.'

Part Two

The Rejected Women

Antinoes, my husband,

Almost a year has passed since we turned beneath the wedding canopy. A year since your lips last touched mine, and your hands last caressed my breasts and hips.

A year that has been so long, I no longer have any yardstick by which to measure it.

Not a day or night has passed that I have not whispered your name, that the desire to hear your voice and feel your breath on the back of my neck has not wrenched my heart and crushed the few joys that are left to me.

Yet I have been patient.

On our wedding night, I promised that one day we would meet again, in Susa or in Babylon, perhaps in Jerusalem, perhaps somewhere else in the world. I promised that Yahweh would not keep us apart for the rest of our lives. I promised that a day will come when Lilah, your wife, will be at your side, will bear your

211

children and watch them grow. Antinoes and Lilah will be a real husband and wife, not just ghosts and memories.

Today, however, I fear I cannot keep that promise.

It is not of my own free will that I say this. Not at all!

But something so terrible has happened that I no longer know what tomorrow will bring. I no longer know what I can and cannot do.

I am writing to you because I am afraid, because I no longer know what is just and what is unjust.

It is like being swept away by a swollen river, struggling in the current while the banks recede.

And yet, as I write, I tell myself it is madness to blacken this papyrus with words. For I know nothing about your present life. I know nothing about you, my beloved husband. In truth, I am not even sure you are still alive. But I cannot think about your death. That is impossible, Antinoes, my love.

Have you been in many hard battles? Have you sustained wounds, known victory?

Sometimes, during the hours of despair, when solitude becomes as cold and clinging as winter mud, when the colour has gone from the trees and the sky, and the beating of my own heart frightens me, I think that another woman may have taken the place I left empty and become your wife.

Then I reproach myself. I punish myself by dreaming about the things I chose to reject: going away with you, far from Parysatis, far from Ezra, far from Susa; being at your side, seeing your eyes and mouth, watching your nostrils quiver with each dawn, each twilight.

I know that a man as handsome and strong as Antinoes my husband cannot remain alone. How could he live with only memories of a woman's love and caresses – memories that by now may be no more than smoke scattered on the wind?

For that is our truth, my husband. We are no more to each other now than the ghosts of memory.

These thoughts torture me endlessly.

But they torture me less if I talk to you like this, putting words down on the yellow fibres of the papyrus.

I am writing this letter to you, but I have nowhere to send it. No country, no city, no camp, no house. This is just my madness, my dream of keeping you alive and by my side.

Antinoes, my beloved, my husband before the Everlasting, the only man who has placed his lips on me.

To make you understand – if that is possible – the madness around me today, I must begin with our departure from Susa.

The order that separated us came the day after our wedding night. That very day, you had to leave Susa for Karkemish in the Upper Euphrates. Parysatis had done her work: she was separating us with an expert hand.

You and I were both paying the price for the letter with the seal of Artaxerxes, which guards from the Citadel placed in Ezra's hands.

Zachariah climbed on to a strong basket that Sogdiam brought him, and read the scroll aloud so that even those in the street outside the house could hear.

Since then, I have heard them repeated so often that today I can write them without thinking.

Artaxerxes, King of Kings, to Ezra, scribe of the Law of the God of heaven:

I give this order to those in my kingdom who belong to the people of Israel, the priests and the Levites, and who have volunteered to leave with you for Jerusalem. May they go there, for you are sent by the King and his seven counsellors to bring order to Judaea and Jerusalem according to the Law of your God . . .

Everyone listened, open-mouthed, their hearts warmed in spite of the cold.

I, Artaxerxes, order all the treasurers beyond the river to do as Ezra asks, to give him a hundred talents of silver, a hundred *kors* of grain, a hundred pack-saddles of wine, a hundred pack-saddles of oil, and salt without limit . . .

When the letter had been read in its entirety, there was no explosion of joy such as there had been after Ezra's audience in the Apadana. There was no singing or dancing. The faces around me were solemn.

Artaxerxes' letter was not only an order, not only an expression of power: it bore witness that the hand of God was now upon Ezra. I had known it for months, and so had Master Baruch, but now everyone knew.

It took several days to prepare for our departure. Now that it was certain, volunteers arrived in their hundreds and thousands. Many came from the villages around Susa. Soon, the lower town was overrun, and the inhabitants started complaining. Zachariah was granted permission to use an area of wasteground on the banks of the Shaour, near the lower town, and pitched his tents there.

But in spite of the large number of people who had chosen to follow him, Ezra was not content. 'Yahweh demanded the return of all our people to Jerusalem,' he stormed, 'not just a few!'

He sent enthusiastic young men to every Jewish house. In response, my uncle Mordechai and others came to visit him. They explained that not every family could leave Susa and abandon the work of a lifetime: the factories, the workshops, even the posts in the Citadel which had often been obtained in the first years of exile.

'The exile is over,' Ezra replied, without listening to their complaints. 'You have no good reason to remain among the Persians, except for your gold and your comfortable cushions.'

And so, for five days and five nights, the Jewish houses of Susa were full of as much weeping as joy. There were some who were leaving and others who were staying. Fathers sent their sons, sons refused to follow their fathers. Lovers, wives, sisters were separated, or torn as I was.

Contrary to what I had feared, Aunt Sarah did not beg me to stay. She locked herself in her bedchamber, her eyes red with tears, indifferent for the first time in her life to what was happening in the workshop.

In truth, it was those who were staying behind who had to bear all the sadness. The sadness of separation and the sadness of shame, for Ezra's harsh words had struck home.

To assuage his anger – perhaps Yahweh's, too – those who chose to remain offered all the wealth they could. We were given wagons, food, clothes, carpets and tents, livestock of all kinds and hundreds of mules. Some even offered slaves and servants.

Those were strange days.

And the way I lived through them was even stranger.

To tell the truth, I felt no joy, and reproached myself for it. Hadn't I wanted what was happening more than anything? But, however much I reproached myself, nothing brought me peace or satisfaction.

I had already started to miss you, Antinoes. I had imagined that I had hugged you in my arms tightly enough to keep the imprint on me of what I had lost, but the burden was heavier to bear than I had imagined it would be. I began to doubt that I was equal to it. I was no longer the confident woman who had mustered the courage to confront Parysatis.

I was only a young woman of twenty-two and a wife of a few days. I was terrified. My whole life stretched before me, a life I could not even imagine.

Fortunately, Ezra guessed nothing of my doubts, for I did not see him before the departure, or even during our journey to Babylon. Zachariah and his family were always around him now, as well as a band of young zealots who had come from all parts of the Susa region.

They drank in his words and his rages like morning milk.

It was not that anything disagreeable had occurred. No one had spoken a harsh word or made an unpleasant gesture. But it soon became clear to me that I was no longer welcome near my brother while serious decisions were being made concerning our departure. They were men's decisions, things only men knew about!

I was not hurt by this. I had my own preparations to make, and many tears to wipe away. Axatria was as nervous as a she-cat who has lost her kittens. She lived in dread of not being able to come with us, because of the rumours that were circulating: Ezra's young zealots were saying that my brother wanted only Jews with him. Only the children of Israel could take to the road and return to Jerusalem, they claimed. The servants, and even Gentile wives and husbands, could not join the travellers.

Eventually this rumour died down. Instead, it was announced that Ezra had ordered a two-day fast on the banks of the Shaour before our departure.

Oh, Antinoes, my beloved, if only I could lay my head on your shoulder! I had to interrupt this letter to bury a child. At the moment, that is the most terrible of my tasks, though not the least frequent. It is difficult for me to take up my stylus again without my hands shaking.

I am sure you can imagine our departure from Susa, so I will not waste words on it. Uncle Mordechai had made a chariot for Axatria and me, and Aunt Sarah had decorated the seats with the most beautiful rugs from her workshop. Beautiful and strong: I still sit on them, although the chariot itself has been pressed into other uses.

There were at least ten thousand of us. In the evening, when the front of the column reached the place where we were to make camp, the rear was still far out of sight. Ezra was at the head, of course, followed by Zachariah and his family, and the young zealots. There were no women at the head of the column. Then came the families, in order of tribe, according to the lists Moses and Aaron had drawn up beneath the mountain of the Commandments.

On the morning of the first day, we found Sogdiam standing at the side of the road, with his weight on one hip. As we helped him into our chariot I felt happy for the first time in a long while. We laughed as he told us how he had tried every means to stay at the front with Ezra. It was hopeless: he was still a long way, he moaned, from being a good enough Jew to have that right.

He had also not greatly appreciated the previous two days of fasting, and devoured the meal we gave him with a tiger's appetite.

We were lucky to have him with us during that long journey. I am lucky to still have him with me today. He has performed a thousand miracles, and not only in cooking soup and filled bread loaves.

That day, it was through him that we learned our first destination. We were moving towards the banks of the Euphrates and Babylon.

'Ezra is very unhappy,' Sogdiam told us. 'According to

him, there are too few of us. He thinks the Jews of Babylon will be more receptive to him than those of Susa.'

It took us nearly a moon to reach Babylon. We had to go as far as Larsa before we found a bridge across the river, which was then in full spate.

Each day was hotter than the last, but slightly less oppressive. We grew accustomed to raising the tents and taking them down again, to walking long distances, to our backs growing stiff on wagons and chariots. For many it was difficult to sleep surrounded by the noises of the night – the cries of wild animals, the rustling of insects and snakes.

The light of the stars, the play of the moon and the clouds brought back to me our nights in the tower of your house. Those memories made the next day easier. After a while, I became inured to the thousand discomforts of the journey.

Ezra had sent Zachariah ahead. When we reached Babylon, we were greeted with songs and flowers and some land had been prepared for us to pitch camp. It was so far from the city that the great ziggurat, with its gardens, looked more like a mountain than a building.

The next day I saw Ezra. Axatria and I had just made our beds in the tent when he lifted the flap.

I barely recognized him. His tunic was grey with dust, his hair long. He told me later that he had lost the ivory ring I had given him, which usually held it in place. He was thin, and his grim expression was frightening to behold. His eyes shone with fever. He held the leather case containing Moses' scroll so tightly that the bones could be seen through the skin of his fingers. It never left him, day or night. Clearly, he had fasted longer than anyone else.

Axatria was unable to hide her distress, and reproached him for his pitiful appearance. He silenced her and ordered her to leave us alone. She obeyed, without showing the least anger.

A little later, Sogdiam brought him some herb tea and looked at him sadly. Ezra barely noticed him.

'Why is your tent so far from mine?' he asked me. 'Why haven't I seen you since we left Susa? I wasn't even sure you were in the caravan.'

I replied that there was no reason for him to be unsure that I was there, since we had agreed that I would be. 'And this is my place,' I added. 'You chose those you wanted around you, and I didn't feel welcome among them. It doesn't seem to be a woman's place . . .'

He avoided my eyes. Then, Antinoes, you would have recognized the young Ezra, whom you sometimes mocked – as handsome and delicate as a gazelle, full of fire, yet lost somehow.

I was about to smile when he said, 'I miss Master Baruch. Not a day goes by that I don't miss his counsels. And I miss you, too. There's no reason for you to be so far from me.'

I asked him what he was finding so difficult. Everything, he replied bitterly. Nothing was going as he had foreseen. He was trying to follow the Law of Moses in everything he did, but as soon as he took a step forward, a thousand obstacles arose before him.

'It's ignorance more than anything else!' he cried passionately. 'You have no idea how ignorant these people are, Lilah. There are no Levites I can trust to care for the sacred objects of the Temple, and yet, according to the Law, it is they who must do so until we reach Jerusalem and place them in the Temple. God of heaven, how is this possible? It seems there's no longer a single priest in all Babylonia descended from the families inscribed in King David's register! And the few who remember their duties can't perform them.'

'Why not?' I asked in surprise.

'Because they have no thumbs!'

It was true. It had been a tradition among the Levites to cut off their thumbs since the early days of the exile. Following King David's instructions, the priests were excellent musicians: they played the ten-stringed lyre as part of their sacred duties. When Nebuchadnezzar had decided they would play for him they had cut off their thumbs so that they could not be humiliated in this way. Succeeding generations had followed suit.

'Ezra,' I asked, 'why do you let yourself become so discouraged? You are not alone.' I calmly repeated what I had said to him so often before his audience with Artaxerxes: 'Trust in Yahweh. If He wants you to go to Jerusalem, if it is His will that you rebuild the Temple, His desire that the Law so dear to you be respected, why would he put obstacles in your way?'

'Because we're so unclean, so imperfect, that we're unable to please Him.'

'Isn't that why we're going to Jerusalem? To improve

ourselves? To learn to live according to the Law? To return to the path of justice and the Covenant?'

'We're a long way from it, Lilah. Such a long way!'

I laughed. 'Yes! We've only come as far as Babylon. We haven't yet crossed the desert. But it may be that Yahweh is less impatient than you are. Fortunately for us.'

We continued the discussion until Ezra said, 'Take down your tent, and pitch it close to mine this evening.'

I agreed, a little reluctantly, on two conditions: that Sogdiam and Axatria could remain with me, and that the wives, sisters and daughters of those with whom he had surrounded himself at the head of the column could do the same. He granted my requests.

The next day, I succeeded, to Sogdiam's great relief, in convincing Ezra not to order another fast of purification. Many of us were already weakened by the journey and needed strength, not hunger. Ezra accepted reluctantly. His young zealots, however, had not looked kindly on my arrival with the other women, and that I should convince Ezra to put off a fast was even less to their liking. From that moment, they regarded me with mistrust – a mistrust that has grown ever since.

That day Ezra had an altar erected and, instead of the fast, for three days he made offerings. More than a thousand rams were sacrificed, and almost as many lambs, with ten bulls and several goats. Smoke hung over the camp, and the smell clung to the tents for a whole moon.

That was how long it took Zachariah to return with a

hundred young Levites, who all had their thumbs but knew little of their duties.

We spent four Sabbaths in Babylon, where Ezra recovered his strength and confidence. Finally, from among the descendants of the princes appointed by David, two great families, he named the twelve priests who would be in charge of the Temple: Sherevyah, Hashabaya and their brothers.

It was an opportunity for an evening of feasting and chanting, an opportunity for everyone to be carefree. Once again, it was clear to everyone that the hand of Yahweh was upon Ezra.

Not that this prevented petty squabbles: as soon as they were named, those responsible for the sacred articles of the Temple started worrying about the journey ahead. 'Ezra, we have two or three months of wandering before us. We're going to cross the desert, and we know it's swarming with Amalekites and all kinds of brigands. Our wealth will attract them like flies.'

There were a great many of us now, Ezra replied. We were a whole city on the move; anyone would think twice before they attacked us.

'That's what you think, Ezra! May the Everlasting bless you, but you've spent your life studying – you're not accustomed to these things. Crossing the desert is quite another matter. Many – too many to count – have disappeared or been robbed. Many wives, mothers, sisters and daughters have been raped . . .'

Finally the true reason for the uproar emerged from the lips of one of them: 'Why didn't you ask Artaxerxes for an armed escort? He would have granted you one. Why don't you ask the satrap of Babylon? Artaxerxes' letter entitles you to one.'

Annoyed, Ezra replied that Abraham and Moses had not needed an armed escort when they had crossed the desert.

Sherevyah and one of his brothers, Gershom, had already proved their knowledge of the Scriptures. Now they stated that Moses had had an army, and that Joshua was a great soldier, as was Aaron's son, their ancestor as well as Ezra's.

That night, Ezra came to see me, trembling with rage. Since that business with the fast, he had not sought my counsel. Neither did he ask it now. All he wanted, though he did not realize it, was for me to caress him with my words – perhaps even with my hands, because his neck was tense with anger. I asked him to share my meal, but he refused to eat.

'There is nothing new in this,' I said to him, with a smile, trying to calm him. 'You must simply keep telling them how things are, until they start to trust you. How many times did Zipporah ask her husband Moses to return to Egypt and take on Pharaoh before he agreed? He was afraid. He did not feel capable of doing it. Yet he was Moses.'

Ezra understood what I meant. Lit by torches, he climbed on to a wagon. His voice was so loud, most of the vast camp could hear him.

'I know what you're all afraid of: that we'll be cut to pieces during our journey. You want to know why I didn't ask Artaxerxes for an escort to protect us. My answer is simple: I would have felt such shame, for myself as well as for you. Is it to the King of Kings, the master of the Persians, that you will turn when you are afraid? If that is so, I say to you clearly: you can stay here and I'll go on alone. An armed escort when we are marching towards the Lord Yahweh? When we are marching towards His Temple and wish to live according to His Law? Who are you? Where are the children of Israel? Where are those to whom Yahweh once said, "I am making a Covenant with you"? Tomorrow we will fold our tents and move forward with our wagons and chariots filled with food and gold for the Temple, with our women, children and cattle, and we will go to Judaea under the protection of Yahweh. What you must tell yourself before anything else, what you must take into your hearts, is that the hand of our God protects us, while the full force of His anger falls on those who abandon Him. If you must fear something, fear the Everlasting! For one thing is sure: you are not yet worthy of His justice.'

And so, when the next day dawned, our noisy company of twenty thousand set off again, leaving behind the ramparts of Babylon. Strangely, the further we drew from them, the more the city walls seemed to glitter. In the milky light before the sun had fully risen, the staircases and gardens of the ziggurat appeared to rise so high that they melted into the clouds.

Then the city disappeared behind a hill of grey dust.

And because everything reminds me of you, Antinoes,

seeing Babylon vanish like that, so simply and so utterly, was like losing you all over again.

Antinoes, my beloved.

I had never imagined that murmuring those words would help me to get from one day to the next.

I murmured them as I'm sure Ezra would have liked me to murmur the laws he taught us sometimes in one of our temporary camps, whenever he granted us a few hours' rest.

It was at about this time, too, that a curious dream came to me, several nights in a row, a dream that would have amused you. I saw myself in our caravan, exactly as it really was. It was evening, and Sogdiam came to see me, with a mysterious expression on his face. He took me aside from the column, and led me to a place from which there was nothing to be seen but the immensity of the desert, its gorges and ridges of sand.

Suddenly, Sogdiam disappeared. I looked around, turning and turning, and at first there was only desert, only stones and sand. Then, far in the distance, some figures appeared. Within a moment, they were climbing the nearby dunes. I couldn't make out their faces, but I could see clearly the horses, the camels, the weapons hanging from the saddles. I was afraid that these were the bandits we dreaded so much. I ran back to the caravan and took shelter in my tent. To my surprise, I warned no one of the danger, especially not Ezra. I fell asleep, just as I usually fell asleep in reality, murmuring the name of Antinoes.

After a short time, I was woken by a hand on my

mouth. I was not afraid: I had immediately recognized my husband's skin, and his smell.

You carried me to your horse. At dizzying speed, we rode towards Jerusalem. We were surprised to find it a peaceful city, with none of the horrors that had been described to us. We settled there, and threw a great wedding banquet, at which you gave me gifts. In public we were man and wife, which was exactly right for the city as it was, a city pleased with the love that lived within its walls. When Ezra arrived, he simply had to resume his studies.

I woke from this dream torn between its happiness and the bitterness around me. But the dream came back over many nights, and one day, at dusk, I decided to leave the column. Just as I had in the dream, I walked until I could see nothing but desert. And there I waited, stupidly, until late at night for you to appear.

Sogdiam and Axatria made a great fuss when I returned. They had assumed I was lost and could not find my way back to the caravan. Not a likely occurrence: it would have been hard to miss the thousand fires glowing in the dark. The following night, my dream did not come and I have not had it since.

The more we advanced, though, the more I began to feel at peace again. I even felt a certain pleasure in our undertaking. It has to be said that we were a prodigious sight. My Antinoes, you who have seen great armies, you may be able to imagine our river of men and women.

The wheels raised clouds of dust as they turned, and made an almighty din. There was never a moment's silence. There was always shouting, weeping, the braying of mules, the groaning of camels. Even at night. At night, in fact, the camp, with all the hearths lit, was like a river of fire. Occasionally I was reminded of the river of stars that crosses the sky, which since ancient times the people of Susa have called the way of Gilgamesh.

Some claimed that to walk from the front to the rear of our column while it was resting would take from dusk to dawn.

And, of course, it was alive with incidents, both comic and tragic. Dozens of wagons overturned, and hundreds of men and animals were injured. There were disputes, love affairs – some open, some secret – births, marriages and deaths. There were even two murders, and a few thefts, on which Ezra, like Moses, had to pass judgement.

One night, Sogdiam saved my life by surprising a snake slithering silently two paces from my bed. Although he is not the nimblest of men, he killed it with his kitchen chopper. These snakes were the thing we feared most: small but extremely poisonous, constantly thirsting for the milk in our pitchers, they killed more than a hundred women and children during the two months of our journey.

My most beautiful memory is of what I learned during those days. I acquired the most wonderful of skills: that of helping women in childbirth. I learned to support a woman during delivery, to control the rhythm of her labour, to welcome the baby's head and sometimes its limbs, to draw it out into the light so that it can take its first breath, to make sure that first breath is sweet.

Yes, that was the beauty of those days.

Then, one afternoon, we crossed the Jordan, and the next day we saw the hills of white stones surrounding Jerusalem.

I had to interrupt this letter because night fell. We don't have enough candles or lamp oil, and there's no point in my wasting them on writing a letter in the dark – to someone whose address I don't even know.

The night was quieter than many others, with no attacks, no screaming, no injuries. We were all able to get a little rest, and are starting the day with renewed strength. It is a strange thing to be surprised every morning by the rising of the sun and to wonder if we will live long enough to see dusk.

It is all over for the beautiful, elegant Lilah. My tunic is no more than a long strip of cloth I've worn and washed too many times. The one garment I still have left that is at all becoming is my shawl, although the colours are so faded now, they can barely be told apart. My hands have carried so many sacks, so many stones, so much firewood and have been torn on so many thorns, they look like those of the workers in my uncle Mordechai's workshop.

And my face! We have no mirrors, but whenever I happen to glimpse my reflection in a pail of water I scare myself. Almost nothing remains of the beauty that stoked

Parysatis' jealousy. Now, the Queen would not even look at me.

I don't suppose you would either.

My skin is dry and weatherbeaten. Every day there are longer, deeper lines in my brow. There are fine lines at the corners of my eyes and lips, like cracks in glazed pottery that has been roughly handled. My face seems to have aged ten years.

Blazing sun, wind, rain, scorching heat, hail and frost, these are the ointments that have produced such fine results – that, and the fact that I grimace more than I smile.

The soles of my feet are covered with calluses from the rope sandals I wear. But I'm happy to wear them. Without them, I would have to walk barefoot, as many do, over the hot, sharp stones.

A week ago, for the first time, I lost a tooth. I'm still able to hide the gap because it's at the back of my mouth. But I can write it here, because there is little chance that you will read this letter.

Last night I thought about that for a long time, as I waited for sleep. There are so few ways for me to get this letter to you. Perhaps I could persuade Sogdiam to leave me and go back to Susa. But, brave as he is, it would be a long and dangerous journey for someone whose legs are not strong. Although it is hardly less dangerous for us to stay here and ruin our bodies and hearts.

Yes, our hearts. For among all the injustices that punctuate our days, nothing could be more unjust than the fact that our bodies and minds are becoming ugly in this beautiful country, this land of milk and honey that the Everlasting granted to Abraham and Jacob, Moses and Joshua, Sarah and Leah, Rachel and Hannah, and all those who preceded us.

I can assure you, Antinoes, that when I first set eyes on Jerusalem, I really saw the land of milk and honey, the good, vast land, inexhaustible in its sweetness and riches, which had so often held our imagination spellbound as children in Babylon, Jewish children exiled and far from home.

It was the end of spring, and the earth had come back to life. The fruit trees – cherry, peach, plum – were in blossom. Olive trees swayed, grey and silky, on the hillsides. Cliffs of pale rock rose on the ridges like languid hands. Great cedars and ageless oaks lent their shade to the flocks. Lambs leaped between bushes of sage, thyme and myrtle, arousing the smell of the earth like a lover drawing fragrance from the body of a woman. And where ploughshares had passed over it, the earth was almost as red as blood, like real flesh.

And there amid the hills, like a jewel in its casket, Jerusalem lay waiting. The walls, built from the smooth, pale stone of the cliffs, gleamed white. There are no bricks here: everything is of stone, as if those who built Jerusalem had imitated the Everlasting making mountains.

Everything was calm and peaceful. As we approached we made out more clearly the cracks in the outer walls. But there was nothing disturbing in that. Swarms of swallows sang above the ruins, where they had built their nests. Stones that had once been the base of defence towers were held entwined by opulent shrubs with little yellow flowers. Agave, tamarisk and even olive trees had long been growing between the cracked blocks, from which the mortar had oozed like sap.

Water gushed from invisible springs beneath the walls and we discovered pools so pure and blue that they did not seem real.

No, there was nothing threatening about any of this. It seemed as if the city, with an almost maternal gentleness, welcomed the fields and hills in a perfect, unbroken dialogue.

Alas, our sense of serenity stemmed merely from our joy in finding what we had so long desired. It was a fantasy, a lingering dream that would soon fade. I know now how hard those stones are, and that the ruins represented violence and hate. I have learned that the calm was nothing more than the aftermath of defeat and destruction.

Now, when I close my eyes and dream of beauty, of the milk and honey I thought I saw when we arrived, I cannot help weeping. Why is it that the most magnificent flowers conceal the deadliest poison?

Although Ezra had sent Zachariah and some of the young zealots ahead to inform the inhabitants of our arrival, we were not greeted with much enthusiasm. After all, Nehemiah had left behind him the memory of a huge effort that had ended in terrible failure. In addition, the city is not large, and in our caravan there were nearly as many people as those already living there.

You can imagine, Antinoes, what it must have been like for the inhabitants of Jerusalem to discover this multitude on the hills. Twenty thousand men and women, ten thousand wagons raising dust and scattering the flocks, a whole noisy nation on the march. And now this impatient, disorganized rabble was coming to a halt outside their walls.

We sang and sounded horns to proclaim our joy and relief at having arrived. We spent a whole night dancing, the most joyful I was ever to know. Our hearts relaxed, like a bow after the arrow has flown. Without drinking a single cup of wine or beer, we were intoxicated because we had at last seen our Jerusalem.

When the next day dawned, it was raining. We were exhausted, although our minds were still dizzy with joy. But we had only to go through the Water Gate, as it was called, to grasp the scale of the task awaiting us.

Inside, Jerusalem was as ruined as its outer walls. Half of the houses were unoccupied. Many were roofless, half burnt, the walls torn apart. A terrible stench rose from disused wells. Occasionally, one house had collapsed on top of another. Entire streets were filled with rubble.

When the old men of the city led Ezra to the Temple he howled with distress. Nehemiah had completed it but already it was devastated. Where once there had been doors, there were now fragments of charred wood. The altar for burnt offerings had long since been profaned –

its cracked basin had become home to ten cats as wild as tigers and a playground to their offspring. A tamarisk had overrun the great staircase at the entrance. In the open hall, more tamarisks and a medlar tree rose higher than the walls, whose crenellations had collapsed. In places, there were signs of fighting. Carved stones and columns had been broken with heavy mallets. Thick grass grew between the marble flagstones, pushing loose the sanctuary steps. The right-hand wall gaped open, as if a monster had walked through it. As for the great courtyard outside, the inner walls were no more than remnants, and the flagstones were piled high with refuse.

The following night, there was no singing or dancing. The darkness was filled with the cries of Ezra, the Levites and the young zealots. They tore their tunics, covered their heads with ashes and prayed until dawn.

And so here we were, as distraught and helpless as Jerusalem's inhabitants. A few old men gathered round Ezra and joined their lamentations to his.

But after the tears, the rage and the despair, decisions had to be made. Ezra wanted to proceed immediately with the purification of the Temple. Many of the priests and the Levites, Sherevyah, Hashabaya and their brothers, supported him.

It was then that Yahezya spoke for the first time. He had always lived in Jerusalem. Thin and gentle in face and body, he had welcomed us with unreserved kindness. As Ezra and his people debated, he spoke up in his polite manner: 'I understand your impatience, Ezra. You came here to rebuild the Temple. You find it in this terrible condition and no task seems more urgent. But look around you. Thousands of you are at the gates of Jerusalem. You don't know where to pitch your tents. I dare say a great many will have to settle in the valley that leads to Hebron. Unfortunately, the land there is disputed. Do you think the Moabites and Horonites, Gershem, Toviyyah and all the other kings and chiefs around the city are simply going to accept you? Don't forget, Ezra, it was their brute force, their wickedness, that reduced Jerusalem to the ruin that so distresses you. Every time we raise a stone, they tear it down. Nehemiah suffered because of them. He confronted them. Nehemiah is dead. They are still here – or their sons are. Do you think they'll leave you in peace when it would be so easy for them to make you suffer?'

Yahezya's grey-green eyes looked at us calmly. In spite of the gravity of his words, his voice was gentle.

'It might be more sensible to build solid roofs,' he went on. 'With so many of you, it won't take long to rebuild those houses that are not so badly ruined. You have wives, mothers and children to shelter. The Temple is unclean, but it's been unclean for a long time. The only thing Yahweh is impatient for is your success, Ezra. If Toviyyah brings war and bloodshed to your tents, you will only be slowed down even more.'

One of Ezra's young zealots laughed sharply. 'Obviously you've been living in Jerusalem for a long time, Yahezya. Listening to you, it's clear why the Temple of Yahweh is in such an unspeakable state. Who are you to say what the Everlasting is impatient for? He led us here, holding His hand firmly over Ezra. What are you afraid of? It's this Toviyyah of yours who should be afraid of us, because we're here through the power and will of Yahweh.'

Many nodded.

I knew that Yahezya had spoken the truth, but I did not protest. Wasn't it largely my doing that our people thought like this? Hadn't I said endlessly that we must fear nothing and trust to Yahweh's protection in all things?

I kept silent. Not that Ezra would have listened to me anyway: he had not cared about my opinion for a long time, since well before we arrived in Jerusalem. He simply wanted me near him. Doing the sensible thing no longer mattered to him, nor to those who crowded round him, their mouths full of praises.

The meeting went on for some time, but the final decision came as no surprise. Ezra declared that our most urgent duty was to proceed with the purification of the Temple.

As Yahezya had predicted, we had to pitch our tents as far away as the valley of Hebron. Then Ezra asked the Levites, priests and others who would be working in the Temple to fast for two days, living on nothing but prayers, in order to be in a state of purity to undertake the task awaiting them.

But the way things came to pass was, alas, quite different . . .

★   ★   ★

Axatria and I were washing linen when Sogdiam came to find us, all excited, and urged us to go with him to the Water Gate.

Ezra had been there since morning, leading the fast with the help of the priests who would be involved in the purification. The most fervent of the men in our caravan were there too, praying with the priests and the Levites, packed together so tightly that it was impossible for us to get through. The women had climbed the little hill opposite the entrance to the city on the other side of the pools. By the time we joined them, rumours of an unusual event had already spread.

From our vantage-point, we could see the white she-camels, the white mules and the magnificent costumes that had emerged as if by magic from the city. A murmur swept through the crowd like a wave. Awed and fearful, someone whispered, 'It's Toviyyah, the great servant of Ammon!'

I recognized the name – Yahezya had mentioned it. Some around us thought that the white mules and camels had appeared overnight by a miracle, but Sogdiam explained kindly that he had seen them come an hour earlier by the north road. They had entered Jerusalem through the Jericho gate.

Toviyyah is fat, not unlike one of Parysatis' eunuchs. I suppose he is younger than his corpulent frame and air of dissatisfaction suggest. He is a child of Israel but his family have refused to recognize Yahweh as their God and submit to His will. On the contrary, they took advantage of the abandoned state of Jerusalem after the exile to pillage what wealth remained, suck out its strength and turn it to their advantage. And it was that wealth that he displayed proudly before us that morning.

But while it was easy enough to dazzle those who had always lived amid the poverty and decay of Jerusalem, we were unimpressed: we had come from Susa and Babylon, the treasure-house of the world.

We might have eaten dust on our journey and might look like beggars, but we recalled vividly the palaces of Babylon and the Citadel of Susa.

A silver ladder was brought to help Toviyyah down from his she-camel. He asked to see Ezra, his sharp voice echoing between the pools.

Ezra stepped forward, hair covered with ashes, tunic open, the precious leather case containing Moses' scroll swinging against his bare chest. 'Do you want me?' he asked, surprising us with his composure.

Toviyyah's lower lip curled. He circled round Ezra, and regarded the priests, Levites and zealots disdainfully. They were dressed as shabbily as Ezra, a strange species that seemed half man, half animal and dwelt among the ruins. They moved close to Ezra, forcing Toviyyah and his guards to step back.

'It seems you have a letter from the King of Kings in Chaldea!' he whined. 'You entered the city of Jerusalem brandishing this letter and proclaimed it your home! You're saying the Temple belongs to you and your priests, and everyone here must submit to you and your throng because you have that papyrus scroll in your possession!'

Angry voices were raised in protest. But Ezra put up his thin hand and demanded silence. He pulled Artaxerxes' letter from the case where he kept it, along with the scroll of the Law, and waved it under Toviyyah's nose, although he took care not to let him touch it.

'You're right about one thing,' he said. 'This is indeed a letter from Artaxerxes, King of Kings, master of the kingdom of Judaea. But you're wrong about the rest. Jerusalem isn't mine, any more than it's yours, and the Temple doesn't belong to the priests. But this city was set aside for the children of Israel by Yahweh. This is the Temple, and this the altar, where the people of the Covenant present burnt offerings to their God. This is the land of Canaan where the Law and the justice Yahweh taught to Moses must hold sway. And I am Ezra, son of Serayah, son of the sons of Aaron. The reason I'm here to bring this about is because the hand of Yahweh is upon me and upon those who follow me.'

This long speech seemed to glide off Toviyyah, like water from a bird's feathers. He looked at the huge crowd and smiled. 'And just because you're supported by Yahweh,' he mocked, 'you think that all you have to do is come here with a letter from the Persian king and your dreams will come true?'

Ezra said nothing.

Toviyyah's smile grew wider. 'You're a young hot-head. This letter you hold is worthless. I, Toviyyah the Ammonite, rule here, and I decide what's good and what's bad. And don't count on the armies of the Persian to support you – they haven't been here for many moons.'

His words were greeted with an icy silence. Pleased with this reaction, Toviyyah flung open his arms and addressed us all in his shrill voice, which was even shriller when he spoke loudly. 'Look at you, all of you! You arrive in a country your fathers' fathers left because they couldn't defend it. Your God abandoned them, as He abandoned Jerusalem. Your fathers' fathers went off to the rich fields of Babylon and forgot all about Jerusalem and their God. And now you've come back, singing, but knowing nothing about the land of Judaea. You've come back, proclaiming, "This is my home, it belongs to me, I should burn incense in the Temple!" But I say, "No!"'

The priests and zealots around Ezra muttered angrily, but my brother again ordered them to be silent.

Toviyyah's fat cheeks shook with rage. He pointed at the men covered with ashes. 'It's Toviyyah who decides whether or not the walls of Jerusalem can heal. It's Toviyyah, the great servant of Ammon, who decides what's good and what's bad for the Temple of Jerusalem. And it's Toviyyah who receives taxes.'

Again, his words met with an icy silence. We were all too stunned to protest. What he had said was worse than anything we had expected. His words had clothed truth in lies and trampled on our most cherished hopes.

But Toviyyah was enjoying himself. 'Ammon bids you all welcome,' he said, smiling contemptuously. 'He'll be happy to receive his share when you start working in the fields. For the fields beneath your feet, where you've pitched your tents, don't belong to you and never will. Here, the Persians are of no importance – the soldiers of Egypt and Greece chased them away long ago. The only person who can protect you is me! I have two thousand armed men for that.'

At that moment, a stone struck his thigh.

Ezra had thrown it.

The gathering was plunged into disarray. Toviyyah's guards moved to seize Ezra, but the young zealots rushed forward, yelling, and pushed them back. The guards seemed ready to fight, but a gesture from Toviyyah stopped them in their tracks. He knew it was pointless: there were ten of them and twenty thousand of us. But he knew that he had other means with which to strike at us.

In their anger, the young zealots jostled Toviyyah, then lifted him on to his she-camel, which bellowed with fear and stood up so abruptly that he almost fell off. He clung to the saddle, waving his arms and squealing like a frightened bird, until finally he regained his balance . . . only to find that he was facing his camel's hind-quarters. The crowd exploded with laughter.

Imagine, Antinoes, my love, twenty thousand people laughing! The sound must have echoed as far as the Jordan.

Only when the laughter had died down did Ezra speak.

'You're wrong again, Toviyyah. Since the day Nebuchadnezzar entered Jerusalem, your father and your father's father have been wrong and have passed on their error to you. Now, a man may deceive himself, but a child of Israel cannot deceive Yahweh. You think the letter that brought me here was written by Artaxerxes – but no! It was the will of Yahweh, His desire to return to His Temple, that dictated this letter. And you're wrong if you think we fear you – all we need is the help and strength of Yahweh. But you did right in coming here today. As you see, we've torn our tunics and covered our hair with ashes. It is the day of purification. Today we're preparing to wash the soil of Judaea clean of the refuse that covers it. And you are part of that refuse.'

Deathly pale now, Toviyyah, with his guards' help, turned in his saddle. Then he looked once again over the vast crowd. All at once, he burst out laughing. He whipped the neck of the she-camel and disappeared into the city. A little later, we saw him trotting along the road to Jericho.

We had mocked him, but as we watched him riding away, his laughter seemed more threatening than all of his poisonous words.

And not without reason.

That night, the fourth or fifth after we had arrived, the war began.

The tents furthest from the walls of Jerusalem were laid waste. Blood flowed, and screams tore the air. Men, women and children were cut down without pity. Wagons burned, lighting the darkness so that it appeared to be broad daylight and we could see clearly that the worst was yet to come.

★   ★   ★

It feels strange to be describing these events. They took place only ten months ago, but to me they already seem very distant.

Perhaps it is because I have seen so many dismembered bodies since then, so many women running through the night, clutching their dead children to their breasts or screaming in pain.

Not that I've become hardened – don't think that, Antinoes, please don't think that! But there comes a moment when you become like a grave that has been filled to the brim and cannot take any more bodies.

And I, who have only ever really learned one skill, that of helping women to give birth, must support those who open their legs so that the blood of life can flow once more, while my memory is still red with the blood of death.

I had to stop writing, because I was sent for.

Sometimes, the absurdity of what I am writing paralyses my wrist, and I cannot move my stylus across the papyrus. If only I could be like a gourd or a jar from which the contents pour out until at last it is empty. I am speaking to you, Antinoes, my husband, yet all the things I have told you remain inside me.

Perhaps that is one of the ways in which Yahweh is taking His revenge.

You try to remember, to force the words out of your mind to stop it exploding with pain. But then you suffer all over again because you remember . . .

But who knows? Perhaps you will read these words, my distant husband, and they will rekindle in you your love for Lilah.

That first disaster lent weight to Yahezya's words and gave him the courage to go back to Ezra and the priests, and put forward his ideas again. Still as calm and gentle as ever, he explained that our attackers had not been Toviyyah's men. 'However wicked he is, and however much he may hate us, Toviyyah wouldn't strike us. He claims he knows nothing about Yahweh, but he fears Him. Yesterday Toviyyah tried to obtain your submission in return for his protection. You refused both. So, he spread the word that your wealth was for the taking, like ripe fruit on a tree, and that he wouldn't defend you.'

'Who attacked us, then?' people demanded.

'Either the Moabites, or Gershem's men. From the arrows and the other traces we found, I'd say it was Gershem's men. Gershem's kingdom adjoins the territory of Judaea along the Jordan. In the last few years, he's attacked Jerusalem many times, just as he did during the time of Nehemiah. Not lately, though – Jerusalem was too poor and empty for him.'

'How can we be at war with these people? We don't even know them.'

'You *are* at war,' Yahezya assured us sadly. 'Here you are, defenceless, unarmed, with thousands of women and children. You have wagons filled with clothes, furniture, carpets – even gold. Pardon my frankness, Ezra, but your weakness is as obvious as your wealth. A godsend for those whose only law is plunder and war.'

These words left everyone dumbfounded. I am quite sure Ezra had never thought about this. To be honest, neither had any of us, including me.

Zachariah was the first to object that no one had come to Jerusalem to make war, and that Yahweh could not have been waiting for us on the soil of Judaea merely to see it soaked with our blood.

'That may be so,' Yahezya replied. 'But you don't know how things used to be here in Jerusalem. Nehemiah rebuilt the walls, and he never hesitated to fight. "We're rebuilding Jerusalem," he used to say, "with a trowel in one hand and a sword in the other."'

There were cries of protest, but Ezra agreed with Yahezya. 'He's right. Master Baruch, who taught me everything I know, showed me letters that Nehemiah wrote to Babylon and the King of Kings. Those were indeed his words: "With a trowel in one hand and a sword in the other".' And he declared that from this day on, those words would be ours too.

So began our new life in Jerusalem.

The purification of the Temple was postponed. Some set to work building permanent houses inside the city while others repaired the holes in the outer walls.

Yahezya led Zachariah and his people to a place near Jericho, where the blacksmiths worked, to buy swords and spears. It was a risky undertaking: Toviyyah's soldiers might have slaughtered them on the road before they had even acquired weapons to defend themselves. In fact, they did not encounter the slightest difficulty. Yahezya was almost certainly right: Tovviyah refused to recognize the power of Yahweh but he feared it all the same.

As soon as they returned, groups of men were formed and trained to defend us.

And so, before the great heat of summer made the work harder still, the city was repopulated, the streets cleared, the fields ploughed and sown. It was also a time when bonds of true friendship formed. The work varied a great deal from one house to another. Ezra and I were given a narrow building near the Temple. It only required about ten days of work, because the roof had not fallen in, but other houses took much longer. We all helped each other unhesitatingly, as the need arose.

Meanwhile Sogdiam had transformed a lean-to into a kitchen for all. It proved a great blessing for the many who had only the poorest of hearths. Every morning and evening old women, who had grown fond of Sogdiam, came to help him bake hundreds of loaves. He told them stories, making them weep with laughter – I had had no idea he knew so many. Day after day, they supplied food for a starving people, a people exhausted from cutting stone and wood, mixing and carrying mortar.

Those who went to the hills to fell the trees we needed or to pull blocks of stone from cliffs known to the old men of the city were accompanied by armed men. But, apart from a few fights with thieves, there were no more attacks.

In a short time, the city had come back to life.

Children ran in the streets. Gardens sprang up. Work-shops opened. Those who had had trades in Susa practised them again. People smiled at each other. Couples came to see the priests, and sometimes even Ezra, to ask for their marriages to be blessed. Children were born. When the building work ended, I went back to working with the midwives who had taught me the skills of childbirth. Every day, I had the great joy of welcoming one or two new lives into the world.

To everyone's surprise, even Yahezya's, Toviyyah did not reappear. He made no attempt to approach Jerusalem and check on the progress of the rebuilding.

Merchants came to buy and sell. They told us that the neighbouring peoples were talking about us, with respect and a degree of fear.

We concluded that our determination intimidated them. The priests sang Ezra's praises, for Yahweh's hand was still upon him.

Thus, for a brief time, one moon perhaps, we were carefree again, intoxicated with the joy of our mission.

Then, one morning, we awoke to the sound of lamentation. Sogdiam told me that the time had come, and that Ezra was beginning the fast for the purification of the Temple.

The priests, the Levites and all those who answered his call gathered before the ruins of the sacrificial altar. There, with much wailing, they again tore their garments and covered themselves with ashes. After another day of prayer, Ezra gave the order to clear the refuse from the Temple courtyard.

For nine days, from dawn to dusk, they lifted the soiled stones one by one – a colossal task – carried them outside the city, and dumped them in an unclean place that the old priests had designated for the purpose.

They demolished the sacrificial altar and built a new one, according to the Law, with raw stones from the hills.

Then the old men who had been there in Nehemiah's time came to see Ezra. 'We need the *nephta* fire!'

They led Ezra to a well no one had noticed, hidden beneath a heap of irreparable ruins. Once the rubble had been cleared, they lifted the undamaged lid of the well. At the bottom, instead of water, lay a stinking black substance, like pitch. The old men explained to Ezra that he had to coat the floor of the Temple with it before the rest could be rebuilt.

'But how can I rebuild cleanly once this stuff is everywhere?' Ezra objected.

The old men laughed. 'Let Yahweh do His work,' they said. 'Let the sun do its work!'

So they spread bucketfuls of the foul-smelling pitch on what remained of the old wood and the loose marble flagstones.

The air stank for leagues around the Temple, and many of us worried that soon we would not be able to breathe it. But when the sun struck the Temple in the morning, the pitch melted, smoked a little, and finally turned as glossy as black gold. For a moment, everything shone. Then, with a deafening whoosh, a blue flame sprang up.

'*Nephta!*' the old men yelled, dancing about. '*Nephta,* the cry of Yahweh!'

A moment later, the fire had gone out, leaving the flagstones dry and no hotter than if the sun alone had touched them.

It had been such a wonderful and surprising spectacle that for days children ran in the streets of the city imitating the cry of Yahweh.

Ezra and his people resumed their toil. They made new sacred objects to replace those they had not brought. The Levites put the seven-branched candlestick in the holy of holies, set up a new table on which they burned incense, and made new lamps to light the Temple. The carpenters, working under their orders, finished the doors, the porticoes, the gilded coronas and the escutcheons that decorated the front of the building. At last, one day in the month of Av, Ezra declared the Temple clean and ready to welcome our chants. For three days and three nights, we sang at the tops of our voices, tears streaming down the most hardened cheeks. The streets rang with the sound of lyres, citharas and cymbals.

There was a huge offering, like the one that had preceded our departure from Babylon. The smoke rose and covered the newly built roofs of Jerusalem.

That night the fire still glowed so brightly that, when other cries and other flames sprang up on the other side of the city, we did not immediately realize what was happening.

Outside the walls, a troop of Gershem's men were galloping towards the city, screaming at the tops of their voices, five or six hundred of them, a snake of fire in the fields and hills. All at once, they launched a rain of burning arrows into the sky.

At first, it was strangely beautiful, as if the sky were full of shooting stars. But their orbit brought them down on to our thatched roofs.

New flames rose. New cries and screams rang out.

By the morning, more than half of the restored houses were in ashes.

Yahezya had been right. Blood, fire, tears: that, for us, was Jerusalem.

Ezra wet my tunic with his tears. He could not show them in public so he came running to me like a lost child.

I was astonished by the body I held in my arms. Ezra had become so frail, I could have lifted him. Did he think that his mind and his passionate love for Yahweh were enough to keep him alive?

Perhaps.

But he was angry too, even – although he would not have dared admit it – with Yahweh. He struck his brow with the leather case containing Moses' scroll and asked, 'Why is Yahweh inflicting this on us, Lilah? Where is our sin? Hasn't the Temple been purified? Don't we respect every Law? Why has He left us so defenceless? Lilah, what is our sin?'

How was I to answer? The whole city was weeping, as he was, but no one understood. Some put out the fires, others tended the wounded. Everywhere, the dead were mourned.

I was in no mood to look for an explanation.

While everyone wondered what sin we had committed, I was beginning to fear that I had made a mistake in urging Ezra to come to Judaea. It seemed to me that, of the two of us, I was the one who had to bear the responsibility for what had happened.

But it was a terrible thought, so I dismissed it.

Like everyone there, anger made me defiant. I still hoped to find in Ezra the strength and justice we lacked, so that Yahweh might finally reward us.

All I could do now was support my brother to the best of my ability.

He was exhausted by constant fasting. His hands were scarred from pulling and carrying stones. His skin was infected, due to a combination of wood splinters and the ash with which he had covered himself during the fast. There were purulent swellings on his shoulders, and his feet were torn and bloody.

But the wounds on his body were nothing compared with the agitation in his mind: he had been under enormous pressure during the purification of the Temple. The new priests, those who had come with us, the Levites and the zealots were all trying to win him over and influence his decisions. They all had strong but divergent opinions, and could argue from dusk to dawn, tangling you in a labyrinth of words until you no longer had any idea what they were talking about.

They all considered themselves scholars, and cleverer than other people. They constantly cited the lessons of the patriarchs and prophets. Some time before the purification of the Temple, the old priests who had stayed in Jerusalem after the death of Nehemiah had reluctantly but proudly revealed a hidden cellar on the other side of the city. There, in spite of all the pillaging, they had preserved hundreds of papyrus scrolls and even a few tablets from long ago. According to them, no decision could be taken without consulting the wise men of the past . . . So the exhausting debates began again, more convoluted than ever.

No one person was any longer in a position to impose decisions that could guide and regulate our lives. On that day of mourning, I was sure of only one thing: that we had come to Jerusalem looking for light, and now we were groping in darkness. And the darkness would only increase unless Ezra recovered the power of his mind and was once again in a state to decide things undisturbed.

I ordered Axatria and Sogdiam to bolt the door of our house, and to prepare herb tea and food.

It took a great deal of persuasion before Ezra agreed to eat. Axatria's herb teas worked miracles. He fell asleep, and did not wake for two days.

While he slept, I had to defend myself against the zealots and the priests. They were angry that I had taken Ezra away from them. They screamed and shouted, rousing anyone who would listen to them.

The priests wanted to pray continuously in the purified Temple, and for some reason they felt they could not do so without Ezra. The Levites wanted my brother to give them specific tasks and appoint them to particular positions and ranks, according to the Law and the writings of David. Our house was surrounded but, fortunately, Ezra did not wake.

Since I would not yield, they concluded that I was plotting against them. I let them talk. But their anger had reached fever pitch, and the fear that Gershem's warriors would return merely increased it. 'Just wait until tomorrow,' I said to them. 'Let him rest! You're killing him with work. Do you want to march behind his coffin? Can't you understand how patient Yahweh is?'

My words aroused protests, as the wind raises sparks from a fire.

'What business is it of yours, woman?' they replied. 'Ezra should be in the Temple assuaging the wrath of Yahweh, and you stand in our way! Who has given you that right? It isn't our demands that exhaust Ezra, it's the stupidity of those like you who cannot hear the wrath of Yahweh. Don't you realize you're playing Toviyyah's game, and Gershem's? You're paving the way for all those who hate Israel! You're going to kill Ezra, and us with him!'

The stronger their words, the more aggressive they became. Sogdiam was powerless to protect me. Those he had fed devotedly for weeks now jostled him and called him a cripple, a good for nothing, a *nokhri* – a stranger. It was not until Yahezya and his friends came and stood in front of my door, armed, that we were left in peace for another night.

At last, after a good meal, after Axatria had rubbed his pitiful body with ointments and oils and massaged his tired shoulders, Ezra seemed in better condition. But when I told him, laughing, how we had had to defend his sleep, and had been insulted for our pains, he was not amused. At first, he wanted to rush out, as if he were at fault, but I held him back: that could wait awhile. I begged him to reflect before he was caught up again in the clash of incompatible demands and desires.

He yielded with a sigh. 'They're right to be angry, Lilah. Something is wrong with the way I handle things. We've only just purified the Temple and already our houses are destroyed. We've not long arrived in Jerusalem, and already the troubles are starting – just as they did in the time of Nehemiah. Tomorrow we'll rebuild the houses destroyed yesterday, but the following night Gershem or the Horonites will attack the Temple, smash the ramparts, destroy our crops in the fields . . . They'll attack anything, as long as it is ours, and they'll keep on doing it, endlessly, because Yahweh is not with us. I thought He was, but He isn't. The Covenant is still broken and these are the consequences.'

As he spoke, he fingered the leather case that hung round his neck. His eyes sought mine for consolation, which I was incapable of giving him. His heart was heavy, and I was powerless to lift it. The words he had spoken expressed exactly what I was thinking.

'Lilah, my beloved sister,' he said, with tears in his eyes, 'what must I do that Yahweh will judge us pure and good enough to grant us His strength?'

I could find nothing to say.

He froze.

He grimaced strangely and stared at me, unseeing. The muscles of his neck tensed. I expected him to run from one room to the next, as he did when he was angry or excited. Violently he tore the leather case from round his neck and pressed it to my breast. 'Everything we need to know is in this scroll!' he roared, shaking like a tree in the wind. 'What good are these walls? Yahweh doesn't care about walls! We're wasting time building houses that disappear in fires or fall down on our heads! Yahweh is mocking us. He doesn't expect us to become masons! He's testing us, and he'll go on testing us until we hear His Word. We must obey His Law, that is His will. And we go around asking, "Why? Why?" It's a question I answered in Susa, and my answer is still the same: because we're not living according to the Law!'

I smiled. I understood.

I took hold of his wrists and said calmly, 'Master Baruch used to say, "The word of Yahweh is in the Word of Yahweh. Nowhere else." He loved to repeat Isaiah's words. "Hear the Word of Yahweh! What is the point of offering rams and fatted calves? I want no more of the blood of bulls and goats. Stop bringing me these hollow offerings." You're right. Building the walls was Nehemiah's task. Establishing justice, teaching the Word of Yahweh, is Ezra's.'

He smiled. His frail body shook with joy as it had shaken with fever not long before. 'Yes, yes! What is the point of these walls of gold, this incense, if the Word of Yahweh falls on deaf ears and blind eyes?'

I tied the leather case back round his neck. 'Teach

everyone what is written in the scroll,' I said. 'You alone can do it. If Ezra commands it, everyone will agree.'

His dark mood returned as quickly as it had previously vanished. 'How can I? More than half of those who've come with us from Susa and Babylon can't even read or write. As for those who were living in Jerusalem before we arrived, they're worse still.'

'Anyone can learn to read and write.'

'Don't dream, Lilah,' he said, in a harsh, mocking tone. 'In Jerusalem, dreams lead to bloodshed.'

'I'm not dreaming. Let all who can read and write teach the others. Let them each copy part of Moses' scroll. They'll learn the Word of Yahweh by writing it.'

For a while, he said nothing. Then he closed his eyes, with a radiant smile that I could not remember having seen for many moons.

'The Temple of the Word of Yahweh will enter their hearts,' he said at last. 'No one will be able to set fire to it or reduce it to ruins. The joy of Yahweh will be a fortress for His people. And the people of Yahweh will be the people of the Book until the end of time.'

And that is how things were done.

It was not easy, and there was a great deal of reluctance.

Many of the priests considered it unclean for Moses' scroll to be copied by hands not designated for the task in King David's tablets. The Levites, too, greeted the idea with horror. How could Ezra think of abandoning the Temple, even if only for a short time?

The idea soon gained ground that this was proof of my

malevolent influence. This was why I had taken advantage of Ezra's weakness and kept him away from the Temple. And when Ezra quoted Isaiah, they quoted Jeremiah: 'Now the days are coming when I will make the cry of battle to be heard among the sons of Ammon. His cities and his daughters will be burned, and Israel will inherit the land from his heirs.' According to them, we had to make war on Toviyyah. Such was the will of Yahweh.

But Ezra held firm. 'Let us get to work,' he said. 'On the first day of the seventh month, the whole city, men and women, husbands and wives, will gather at the Water Gate. And everyone will read with one voice the Law that Yahweh taught Moses.'

Sometimes, after you have had one calamity, and you are sure that another is coming, happiness appears unexpectedly, at least for a time. It came now to Jerusalem, moving from alley to alley, from house to house, where people bowed their heads over letters and words. A song of joy rippled through the city, as hands guided other hands to move a stylus over a scroll. A song of joy throbbed in the houses, when, after learning the alphabet, fathers and mothers amused themselves reciting it at night to their children so that it might feed their dreams.

There was no longer any distinction between the great and the small, the learned and the untutored. All that remained was the will of a whole people to be strong in its knowledge and its words, including the great Word the Everlasting had given it, a nation that had the whisper of memory always on its lips, as a lover has his beloved's name.

Oh, Antinoes, my husband, you would have liked that time!

A time of milk and honey, a time of abundance in the land of Judaea! We were together, united in a single cause. All of us, men and women, young and old, were deciphering the same letters, uttering the same words, each and every one of us with the same desire for justice.

There were no more complaints, no more quarrels.

And perhaps the hand of Yahweh was upon us, for we no longer heard anything of Toviyyah, Gershem and the Horonites, or the harm they wished to do us.

I started to hope again. My doubts vanished. We had been right to urge Ezra to leave for Jerusalem. Our separation, Antinoes, was a good price to pay for his reward. In my heart, this was compensation for my humiliation at the hands of Parysatis.

For the first time since my arrival in Jerusalem, I felt at peace. I gloried in this madness called happiness and hope.

Yes, I thought, I could keep my promise after all. Soon, everyone would know Yahweh's Law, everyone would live according to His justice. Soon the Everlasting would renew His Covenant with His people, and the houses of Jerusalem would ring with peace and joy as now they hummed with thousands of voices reading.

Then my duty would be done, and I could set off for Susa, Karkemish or the other side of the world to rejoin you.

*   *   *

According to Ezra's wishes, on the first day of the seventh month of the year, rams' horns blew on the square in front of the Temple. Others echoed across the land, from Galilee to the Negev. Thirty or forty thousand people gathered by the Water Gate. There were so many of us, so tightly packed together, that the earth looked like a carpet of human flowers.

Ezra and the priests climbed the steps to the ramparts. The sun was not yet high and the air was cool. Swallows sang as they gorged themselves on insects.

And then there was silence. True silence. Over Jerusalem, and all Judaea. Those who were there will swear it to the end of time. A silence such as belongs only to the Everlasting fell on His nation at that moment.

Ezra took Moses' scroll from its container. In the silence, everyone heard the rustle of the papyrus against the leather. He spread the scroll, put one end between the fingers of an old priest, then unrolled it in its entirety. It stretched for perhaps five or six cubits.

Again in the silence, the forty thousand heard the crackle of the papyrus, which had once been touched by the finger of Aaron, heard Ezra's sandals scrape against the stones of the rampart.

The swallows were gone. There was only the blue sky, and the white stones of Jerusalem the beautiful.

Ezra placed his finger on the papyrus.

My throat was dry. Doubt took my breath from me.

What if this was madness?

What if Ezra's desire to turn a whole nation's heart

into the heart of a word was again nothing but a mad dream?

Was it possible that these thousands of people could become the nation of the Book, the nation that made the Word of Yahweh its Temple?

Then Ezra looked at us. His mouth opened, but no sound emerged. In its place, a single voice, made up of thousands of women's voices, thousands of men's voices, old and young, launched the first words into the sky.

> *In the beginning,*
> *Yahweh created the heavens and the earth.*
> *The earth was empty and formless,*
> *Darkness was above the deep.*
> *The spirit of Yahweh*
> *Moved over the seas.*

The voices trembled. Perhaps the blue sky trembled, too, and the white stones, and Ezra's finger.

Then his hand glided over the papyrus, and pointed to the following words: 'Yahweh named the light.' And the forty thousand, with one voice, continued the reading.

All Jerusalem trembled. All Judaea trembled.

The reading became a chant. Until the middle of the day, until we were sitting in our own shadows, we read. And everyone knew the words of the text.

At the end, our joy overflowed. We danced and laughed and wept, all at the same time.

'Today is the day of Yahweh, our God,' Ezra cried, 'not a day of tears! Go! Eat your fill, drink sweet wine and eat meat, for today is Yahweh's day! The joy of Yahweh is now on your fortress and no one can drive you from it! Open your eyes, open the scrolls of the teaching, and there you will find your Temple, for ever. Your Temple will be the Word and the teaching of the Everlasting: the Book. Tomorrow, go to the hills and gather branches. Tomorrow, build tabernacles in your houses, and in the public squares. Build them everywhere. Sit in your tabernacles and read the teaching of Yahweh. You will see that there is no need of walls to read the Law of our Covenant with the Everlasting. In the Book, you will be safer than anywhere else. And no one will drive you away. The Word of Yahweh is a fortress.'

And, like my forty thousand companions, I laughed and danced. In the evening, I danced in the arms of Yahezya, in the arms of Baruch, Gershom and Jonathan, Ackaz, Manasseh and Amos . . . There were so many names, so many arms in which a young girl, a young wife, a young widow named Lilah could dance.

We were no longer alone. We drank wine, ate meat, swayed our hips and swelled our chests, we, the thousands of wives.

We had read like the men, all united. Daughters of Israel, wives of the sons of Israel. All united, without distinction. All wives and mothers.

That was the last time.

Ezra was right: the joy of Yahweh is a fortress.

★ ★ ★

This is how it happened, three days after the reading and the celebration that ensued. Everyone was laughing, building their tabernacles and sitting in them to read.

The priests and Levites, those who call themselves the princes of the Temple, appeared before Ezra. 'You proclaim that Yahweh is happy with us. You are wrong. We say to you that Yahweh is angry. We warn you that soon those who hate us will strike harder than ever. They are already here. They are in Jerusalem, they are in your tabernacles.'

'What are you talking about?' my brother asked in surprise.

'How can you teach the Law if the Word of Yahweh is not respected? How can the children of Israel appease the wrath of Yahweh if the first of His rules is not respected? Open your eyes, Ezra. Look at the faces, listen to the words. The peoples who surround us and live in abomination have married their daughters to our sons! That is the truth of it.'

'Ezra, beneath the roofs of Jerusalem,' others cried, 'the unclean mix indiscriminately with the children of Israel. The unclean are among us. Worse still, they multiply like clouds. The Jebusites, the Ammonites, the Moabites, and so many others around Jerusalem, have given their daughters to the men of Jerusalem. Their babies have been filling our beds since Nehemiah left. And this rabble walk the streets of Jerusalem as if they were the children of Israel! Soon they, too, will be of an age to mix their unclean stock with that of the people of Yahweh. Our destruction is inevitable. And you, Ezra, would like Yahweh to renew His Covenant with us? To place His hand upon you?'

I was not present at the scene. A child was being born not far from our house and I had been sent for. But I was later told all the details of what had happened.

Hearing these words, Ezra rushed on to the steps of the Temple. There, he tore his clothes to shreds. He ripped his tunic and his cloak, as if twenty hands had grabbed hold of him. He demanded a knife. Before the eyes of the priests, the Levites and the zealots, he shaved his head and his beard. Now he was bare-headed and bare-cheeked, and as pale as a leper.

After that, he sat on the steps of the Temple and would not budge. He remained like that, mouth closed, eyes vacant, hands motionless.

The priests and Levites roused the crowd. People came from everywhere to see Ezra, and cried out at the sight of his head. They begged him to speak, to utter a word. But he remained silent. Instead, it was the priests who cried, 'Ezra is naked before the Word of Yahweh! Ezra fears Yahweh! Ezra bears all the infidelity of the exiles on his shoulders!'

It was then that I joined the crowd.

I saw him with my own eyes, huddled on the steps, his face haggard, his eyes hardened by sadness. His mouth was like a line cut by a sword.

He no longer saw anything, no longer looked at anything. Or perhaps he was thinking of old times, old promises from the days of our childhood, which he was now preparing to break. Yes, that was my first thought.

My other thought was that I no longer recognized him: he was not the man who had wept in my arms only a few days earlier.

My brother had disappeared, and his beautiful mouth, his eyes full of hope had disappeared, too.

Or was it the pallor of his skull and cheeks that made me think that?

At the evening offering, he stood up suddenly. The crowd around the Temple fell silent.

A terrifying silence.

As I write this, I am afraid again. My hand is heavy with the words it is about to lay down on the papyrus.

Ezra approaches the altar. He walks up to the beautiful new basin, only recently purified. We hold our breath. Even the priests and the zealots are silent. They, too, are overcome with fear. You can see it in their eyes, the way they clench their fists in front of their mouths.

Ezra falls to his knees. He reaches out his hands to Yahweh, palms upward. Sounds come from him, not words at first, only moans. Then he cries, 'My God, I am ashamed as I lift my head to you, for our sins are endless, our offences can be heard even in the vaults of heaven! We have been guilty since the days of our fathers, and we are still guilty. It is because of our sins that we have been delivered into the hands of foreign kings, have suffered violence and captivity, are humiliated, even now. We have abandoned your Commandments, as decreed by your servants and your prophets. "The land you are inheriting is unclean," they said, "soiled by the surrounding nations and the horrors with which they nourished it. Your daughters must not be given to their sons. Their daughters must not be married to your sons." Those were your rules. After all that has happened to us because of our misconduct, are we still going to disobey your orders, Yahweh? Are we going to ally ourselves with these nations and their abominations? How could you not be angry – so angry that you would destroy what is left of us? Yahweh, God of Israel, here we are before you, in sin. And we will not be able to stand upright until that sin has been atoned for. Oh, Yahweh, we cannot stand upright before you until the clean have been separated from the unclean.'

That day, that night and the following day, the zealots ran through the streets knocking on the doors of the houses.

You are clean, you are unclean.

You are a daughter of Israel. You are not.

Your children are unclean. Leave this house – leave Jerusalem! Go, you are no longer this man's wife.

Separate, separate!

Pack your bags and go! You have soiled our streets and our land for too long!

They pushed and shoved. They took the little ones and threw them into the streets. Even babies in their cradles they put into the streets. The big ones they pulled by their hair. Go, go, we don't want to see you any more!

The women cried that they were loving wives. Why chase me away? We have loved each other for years. I have always lived in Jerusalem! I read with the others before Ezra at the Water Gate! What is my sin?

They wept that they had travelled all the way from Susa with Ezra – I led the fast, I rebuilt the walls of the houses of Jerusalem, with my own hands I built a tabernacle in my garden to read the teachings of Yahweh. What is my sin?

The mothers cried out, and tore their babies from the hands of the zealots. My child, my child, what will become of you without a father?

The boys and girls sobbed in terror.

'Look at us!' their mothers implored. 'We have no other house, no other roof, no other family. Where shall we go without a husband, without a father? Why chase us away as if we were evil incarnate?' they asked. 'We have loved a son of Israel, we have cherished and caressed him. Where is the evil? Is our love evil? Why trample on us?'

The husbands and fathers were silent. Almost all bowed their heads in shame and hid their faces in their hands. They ran to the Temple, bowed down and begged forgiveness.

It was a late-summer's day, the kind of hot day when the swallows only fly as dusk approaches, and yet an icy wind was blowing through the streets of Jerusalem.

And those husbands and fathers who wanted to defend those they loved were beaten until they fell silent and their shame grew as their blood flowed.

The wives, the betrothed, the widows, the sons and daughters were driven towards the outer walls. They were driven with sticks, street by street.

For two days.

There were endless cries, which eventually gave way to resignation. Some took one direction, others the opposite direction. No one knew where to go. They worried over their meagre bundles, the children clinging to their tunics, the older ones carrying the babies.

At the Water Gate where, a few days earlier, we had formed a carpet of human flowers, the blood ran black, stinking of shame.

And we, the sons and daughters of Israel, stood on the walls, watching them move away. We stood there, terrified and incredulous.

We did not feel the pain yet. Only astonishment.

Would Yahweh be pleased, now that we had cast out the unclean?

Towards the evening of the second day, some boys and girls came running back along the Jericho road, towards Jerusalem, calling their fathers' names. Children of eight, ten or twelve. Some older. A hundred children, girls and boys. Running towards the gates of the city on a road white with dust.

Then, on the walls of Jerusalem, hands gathered stones. Hands lifted these stones and threw them.

Yes. I write the truth. They stoned the children until they fell or turned and ran. Until their mothers seized them and dragged them away, far from us.

Then I knew I could not stay.

It was all over for Lilah, sister of Ezra.

★   ★   ★

'How can you order such horrors?' I asked my brother. 'Don't you see the women and children on the roads? Don't you hear them?'

He replied that he had ordered nothing, it was Yahweh who decided everything. 'It is Yahweh who wants this, my sister, not Ezra. It was not I who received His Law and His instructions. All I did was read and learn. Who knows that better than you, my sister? You, who urged me to cross the desert to Jerusalem when all I wanted was to pursue my studies. It was you who begged Parysatis. It was you who lay with the Persian so that he would deliver my request to Artaxerxes. It was you who said to Ezra, "Go! Your place is in Jerusalem, your destiny is in Jerusalem, that is the will of Yahweh. His hand is upon you." Those were your words, Lilah.'

Yes.

Those were my words.

Yet Master Baruch had taught us the goodness of Yahweh. He had chanted Isaiah's words: 'You will succour the oppressed, you will plead for the widow.'

Ezra laughed. 'Isaiah said all kinds of things, sister. Was it not also Isaiah who said, "Put an end to mankind. It is a mere breath, of no importance"?'

The expression on my brother's face was terrible to behold.

I could not recognize him without his hair, his beard. A savage face, I thought, that reminded me of Parysatis' beasts. I was angry with myself for thinking such a thing, but that was what filled my heart.

I asked him, 'Where is Yahweh's justice?'

'Here, my sister,' he replied. 'In Jerusalem. His justice will protect us if we follow every one of his Laws.'

'I don't see any justice in forcing thousands of women and children out into open country, without fire, a roof or food. That isn't why we came to Jerusalem.'

He laughed. 'But it is, Lilah, it is! We came so that the Law of Yahweh would live among our people. We are making it live. Only what is written on Moses' scroll. That and nothing else!'

'I can't do it,' I said, to the man who had been my beloved brother. 'I can't be with those who throw stones at women and children. I can't separate the clean and the unclean by separating a wife from her husband, and children from their father. That is beyond my strength. It is beyond my love for Ezra, beyond my respect for our God. If I must choose, then I shall leave with them – with the rejected women, the strangers. That is the only place for me. Did not Moses, our master, say, "Welcome the stranger in your house as one of your own. Love him as yourself, for you, too, were strangers in the land of Egypt"?'

We looked at each other, our hearts closed, the light of our shattered love in our eyes.

'If you leave this house, my sister,' Ezra replied at last, 'if you leave Jerusalem, we shall never see each other again. I shall forget you. I will no longer have a sister. I will never have had a sister.'

I nodded, but said nothing.

I was sick of words. A stench hung about them, like the stench of the burnt offerings of rams and oxen that were spreading their funereal smoke once more over the roofs of Jerusalem the beautiful.

Sogdiam put his hand in mine. 'Don't cry,' he said gently. 'I won't leave you. I'm not from here either. I'm only from anywhere you go.'

I tried to dissuade him. Where I was going there would be no house, no comfort, little joy and much tragedy. And certainly no kitchen.

'I'll build one. Wherever we are, we'll need a kitchen, or we'll die of starvation.' He was laughing already.

'Will you come with me?' I asked Axatria.

She arched her back and lifted her chin. 'I won't abandon Ezra!' she hissed, like a snake.

'I'm not abandoning him, Axatria. Ezra is with his God, his priests and his zealots. He hasn't been with me for a long time. How can I abandon a man who's already turned his back on me?'

'Sometimes he needs you.'

'Not any more. After the things he's ordered, he doesn't need his sister.'

'You see? You don't love him! I've long suspected it. In the desert you didn't love him. When we arrived in Jerusalem, you didn't love him. The greater he's become, the more you've hated him.'

What was the point in protesting? 'Do you want to abandon those women and children outside the walls, who have nowhere to find shelter except in their sorrow?'

'Ezra has said it many times: it is the Law.'

'But not your law, Axatria! You're a daughter of the Zagros mountains. You're as much a stranger as they are.'

'Oh, you love to remind me of that, don't you? That just shows how much you despise me. You always have. The Law of Yahweh may not be my people's law, but Ezra is my law.'

'You don't know what you're saying, Axatria. Can't you see that Ezra has never looked at you with affection, let alone love? That you're only his handmaid and will never be anything else? Don't you know that? Don't you understand that by staying in Jerusalem with Ezra, you're trampling on your own life and dignity? You'll serve Ezra until he rejects you, because a time will come when he won't even allow strangers to be handmaids. Don't you understand that, if you stay in Jerusalem with Ezra, you'll never know love, never have a husband and children?'

She slapped me, then pushed me out of the house, screaming that I was only saying these things because I was jealous.

With the rage of someone in whom vengeance, sorrow and self-disgust have been brewing too long, she threw my few belongings out of the house that had been mine.

Now I am a rejected woman, like the others.

But I did not leave Jerusalem like the others.

While I was arguing with Axatria, Sogdiam had been telling everyone in the houses still friendly towards me that I was leaving.

With his limping gait he had run from one house to another.

'Lilah is going to join the women and children outside, and I'm going with her.'

It was like oil waiting for a flame. The sadness and shame that had been simmering in people's hearts since the day of the stoning now boiled over.

In less time than it takes to say it, twenty wagons were filled and mules harnessed to them. The former husbands gave tents, sheets, tent pegs . . . They wept as they gave, and if they could have, they would have offered their tears, too, as sweet wine.

The Jewish wives gave and gave.

The children gave their clothes and their toys to those who had been their playmates.

Two men gave even more: themselves. May their names be written here, and may Yahweh, if He so wishes, bless them. They were Yahezya and Jonathan.

When the wagons were lined up outside Jerusalem, it was quite obvious that I would find it hard to drive them with only Sogdiam to help me. 'I'll go with you,' Yahezya said. 'I couldn't stay in Jerusalem and work in my carpenter's shop, knowing that all you women were out there alone.'

'My wife is out there, I don't know where,' Jonathan added, his eyes filled with tears. 'She is three moons gone with child. I must see her and know if my child is a boy or a girl. I'm following you, Lilah.' He turned to the dozens of others who were like him, and cried, 'You too, follow us!'

They lowered their heads and wept.

But during the days that followed, many went out into the countryside, taking food and kisses to their former wives and their children.

Then Ezra decreed that this was forbidden. No clothes, no food, no wagons. Everything in Jerusalem was the fruit of the people of Yahweh, and this fruit could not be given to strangers.

First, we had to gather together the women and children, who were scattered throughout the land of Judaea. Some had already knocked at the doors of their fathers' and brothers' houses. Now they were weeping over their fate, cursing Jerusalem, themselves and their offspring: because they had married Jews, their own fathers considered them unclean.

Until the first rains of autumn came, we scoured the countryside in search of women hiding in bushes and holes, protecting their young like gazelles.

We travelled south, where Jonathan knew of some land that was vast and dry enough to set up camp. It took a lot of work: pitching tents, bandaging wounds, collecting herbs to cure the children's illnesses, tending women in labour, feeding the hungry . . . And already there were quarrels, jealousy and despair . . .

Then, one overcast day, Gershem's men came galloping towards us.

What a godsend for them! So many unprotected women!

They did not hold back. They took what they wanted.

They forced open thighs, never mind if the girls were virgins.

They raped. They took it in turns to rape.

They killed those who resisted.

The old women who pulled at their hair while the men raped the girls were disembowelled.

The children who tried to defend their mothers had their throats cut.

So did Jonathan, who fought to protect his pregnant wife. His wife was disembowelled and her bloody off-spring held up.

'The rejected women of Jerusalem!' The men of Gershem laughed. 'What a feast!'

They put the youngest and prettiest in chains, shackled them like a herd of she-camels and dragged them off to the desert where they lived.

It was bound to happen.

Not a day or a night had passed without our dreading it would happen. In Jerusalem, they had known it would happen. When they had expelled the women, they had known it.

And Yahweh, my God, had known too.

Last night, just before dawn, Sogdiam died.

They say his cart overturned and he was crushed beneath the wheels. They say he didn't suffer.

Sogdiam, my Sogdiam, is dead.

So are many others, of course.

They say Sogdiam was bringing back a wagon full of grain. He had been coming at night from Jerusalem more and more frequently. Some men there still try to give us a little food – grain or vegetables – so that their former wives and children will not starve to death. But at night the Bethany road is dangerous, furrowed by the autumn rains. Or perhaps it wasn't the rain, but Gershem's men, or Toviyyah's. Neither miss an opportunity to strip us bare or murder us.

I did not think to ask if the grain had been stolen, which would have meant that Sogdiam had died for nothing.

My Sogdiam is dead!

I would like to weep but I can't. My hands are cold, my feet are icy. Perhaps my heart has frozen too.

I am gripping my stylus and writing.

I must seem confused to you now, Antinoes, my husband. I mix past and present. It is because of Sogdiam's death. But it is true, too, that everything is confused in my mind, my heart, my body.

Yesterday, towards evening, Sogdiam sat beside me for a long time. 'You write and write!' he said reproachfully. 'You spend your time writing like a scribe. Who will read your secrets?'

'You,' I replied.

He looked at me as if we were dancing under the wedding sheet. I felt his warmth next to me. His mis-shapen body. I had only to look at him once a day and I could breathe more easily. When he slept, his eyes smiled.

Oh, my Sogdiam, who fed me like a mother! A boy of barely sixteen. A child who'd become a man. A child I'd swept up in the whirlwind of my confusion when I'd urged Ezra to leave for Jerusalem.

Sogdiam, my beloved child!

It isn't true that I am writing this letter for Antinoes. I know that now, and it would be a lie to maintain otherwise. Antinoes, my husband, will never read it. Sogdiam, my handsome, crippled child, will never take him this papyrus scroll in a leather container hanging from his neck.

Antinoes is far away. He is no more than a thought that wrenches my heart every time I write his name.

He is far away, as far as the life I did not want, did not choose, did not accept. He has forgotten me. He is clasping a woman in his arms at this moment, as the ink slips from the stylus and enters the skin of the papyrus.

That is the truth.

I have no husband now. I have no Sogdiam.

That is the truth.

I write this letter as I wrote, one night a long time ago, in my bedchamber in Susa, to Yahweh: 'O Yahweh, why must we stop being children?'

O Yahweh, why couldn't Sogdiam stay a child? Why did he have to die? Why must I become cold? Why must I be no more than a hand that writes so that you may hear another voice, different from those raised today in Jerusalem?

Why so many painful questions?

★　　★　　★

Man is humiliated,
man is brought low, do not lift him,
hide in the stone,
take shelter in the dust,
terrified as you are by Yahweh,
by his dazzling greatness.
Now at last the arrogant eye of man is brought low,
man's pride will bend.
Yahweh alone will be held on high that day.

These words also are Isaiah's. They come often to my lips, though I don't know if they are good for us or not. They come to me like the angry clouds that race above our heads, chased by the whistling north wind.

They are the words I sang over the grave of Sogdiam, my child.

All the women who were there repeated the words after me. It was not as beautiful as our chanting at the Water Gate, but it rang out in the desolate air around us.

We are tired, though, of chanting for those we bury.

Just as my fingers are worn and calloused by the stylus.

Among the older women, there is a great desire to lie down anywhere on the ground and go to sleep at last, seeking the eternal oblivion that will come to us all soon. I could see it in their eyes as the earth covered Sogdiam. And I was surprised to feel the same desire, I who am only twenty-five.

From time to time, I lift the back of my hand to my lips. It was there that Sogdiam touched me for the last time. But my skin no longer bears the memory.

★   ★   ★

Yahezya has been wounded in the stomach, but he can still speak, can still lead us. He asked me to gather together those who are still alive. He told us we should go to the sea of Araba where there are caves, which are easier to defend than an open field. He knew the way. He led us there, struggling to keep breathing until the cliffs of Qumran and the caves were within sight.

That is where we are now, with no land to cultivate, but protected by the walls we have built in front of the caves.

That is where we are now, gone to earth like desert rabbits.

Sogdiam used to bring us grain from Jerusalem. But Sogdiam died beneath his cart.

From time to time, former husbands came at night to see their children and weep in their arms. But many no longer had wives. They were either dead or in the arms of Gershem's men.

Sometimes, the former husbands came to see their rejected wives, caressing them in a way that recalled the time of their love. Then they left.

In the minds and bodies of the women, these caresses, this love disappeared, just as the memory of Antinoes has disappeared from the mind and body of Lilah.

For us, the rejected wives, I say and I write, 'Time is dead.'

Yahweh pushed us outside, and time, for us, is dead.

That is the truth as spoken by Lilah, daughter of Serayah.

What I, Lilah, am writing, no one will read. My words belong neither to the sages, nor the prophets, nor Ezra. They will vanish in the sand of the caves of Qumran.

But I write because this must be said: these women, these wives, were innocent.

Their children were innocent.

This I write: the injustice of it will lie heavy on men until the end of time.

Epilogue

Just over a year after the foreign wives were expelled from Jerusalem, a man came looking for Ezra outside the Temple after the evening offering. 'I have learned that your sister Lilah died yesterday,' he said.

Ezra stiffened, as if the only way he could grasp the man's words was to revive a memory he had long since dismissed from his mind.

Then he asked where she had died, and after he had been told, he thanked the messenger and returned to his tasks. He had much to do at that time, for he was establishing the names and responsibilities of the priests, the Levites, the Temple porters, the blowers of horns and others, as laid down since the reigns of David and Solomon.

But next morning, before dawn, he woke two of the young zealots. 'Come with me. My sister has died near the sea of Araba. She was no longer a woman of Jerusalem, but she was my sister. It is my duty to see that she is buried according to the Law. If I do not go, who will?'

They took mules and crossed the silent city. Trotting to gain time, so that they would be back before evening, they took the Bethany road and sped towards the plateau of red ash, salt and stones that overlooks the vast, desolate valley surrounding the sea of Araba.

As they approached the edge of the plateau, Ezra became aware of a strange buzzing. It was as if thousands of bees were moving over a field of flowers.

He frowned, thinking perhaps that Yahweh was about to show him something unusual.

What he saw when he started on the path that descended towards the plain made him open his eyes and mouth wide. It was a brightly coloured carpet of human flowers, like that which he had seen, one day long ago, in front of the Water Gate in Jerusalem.

They were there in their thousands. Not only the rejected wives and their children, but the men of the city. They were all there, chanting in unison as they buried his sister Lilah in the dust.

A vast multitude of men and women, children and old people, chanting in unison, without waiting for Ezra's permission, the words of Isaiah so beloved of Lilah:

Now I shall give her,
like a river of peace,
like a river in full spate,
all the wealth of nations.

Surprised at the sight, Ezra's companions came to a halt.

He continued alone along the path, his face impassive. Then he, too, stopped.

His hands shook. From the assembled crowd, the throb of the chant of Isaiah rose towards him. For a moment, it seemed to him as if his cheeks, hardened by fasting and the sun and wind of the desert, were being struck by the words. His eyes faltered as they swept over the throng.

In the chanting, so powerful that it made the stones of the cliff behind him vibrate, he thought he could hear Lilah's voice, her laughter, her anger.

He saw her place her palms on his as she used to do in the old days in Susa, a long, long time ago, when the three of them were together: Antinoes, Ezra and Lilah.

He heard a voice whisper in his ear, 'You are Ezra, my beloved brother. Go, lead your people back to Jerusalem! Rebuild the walls of the Temple!'

And he caught himself replying, 'Lilah! Are you trying to teach me wisdom?'

Tears he had never before wept ran down his cheeks. His tired body collapsed with shame. Without realizing it, he began running towards the crowd. Like the thousands assembled there, like the women expelled from Jerusalem, he chanted Isaiah's promise:

You will be like a child,
Suckled at its mother's breast,

Lilah

Carried in her arms,
Dandled on her knees.
As a mother comforts her child,
So I will comfort you . . .

But no one paid him any heed.